5/06

DATE DUE   MAR 04

OCT 23 '04			
DEC 08 '04			
MAR 01 '05			
MAR 01 '05			
JUN 23 '05			
DEC 1 '09			
2-29-205			
GAYLORD			PRINTED IN U.S.A

Referred Pain

Also by Lynne Sharon Schwartz

Fiction

In the Family Way
Disturbances in the Field
The Fatigue Artist
Leaving Brooklyn
Balancing Acts
The Melting Pot
Acquainted with the Night
Rough Strife

Non-Fiction

Ruined by Reading
Face to Face
A Lynne Sharon Schwartz Reader
We Are Talking About Homes

Poems

In Solitary

Children's Books

The Four Questions

Translations

Smoke over Birkenau, by Liana Millù
A Place to Live: Selected Essays of Natalia Ginzburg

Referred Pain

and Other Stories

Lynne Sharon Schwartz

COUNTERPOINT
A MEMBER OF THE PERSEUS BOOKS GROUP
NEW YORK

Copyright © 2004 by Lynne Sharon Schwartz
Published by Counterpoint
A Member of the Perseus Books Group
All rights reserved. Printed in the United States of America. No part of this book
may be reproduced in any manner whatsoever without written permission except in
the case of brief quotations embodied in critical articles and reviews. For information,
address Counterpoint, 387 Park Avenue South, New York, NY 10016
Counterpoint books are available at special discounts for bulk purchases in the United
States by corporations, institutions, and other organizations. For more information,
please contact the Special Markets Department at the Perseus Books Group, 11
Cambridge Center, Cambridge MA 02142, or call (617) 252-5298, (800) 255-1514
or e-mail specialmarkets@perseusbooks.com.

Designed by Reginald R. Thompson
Set in 10.5 Centaur by the Perseus Books Group

Library of Congress Cataloging-in-Publication Data
Schwartz, Lynne Sharon.
Referred pain : and other stories / Lynne Sharon Schwartz
p. cm.
ISBN 1-58243-301-1 (alk. paper)
I. Title.
PS3569.C567R44 2003
813'.54—dc22
                                             2003015678

04 05 06 / 10 9 8 7 6 5 4 3 2 1

Contents

The following stories have appeared in these publications: "Heat," in *The Ontario Review*; "Twisted Tales," in *The Denver Quarterly*; "The Stone Master," in *Tri-Quarterly*; "The Trip to Halawa Valley," in *Shenandoah*; "The Word," in *The Threepenny Review*; parts of "Intrusions" (under the title "Full Disclosure"), in *Fourth Genre*; "Sightings of Loretta," in *Agni*; "Deadly Nightshade," in *Artful Dodge*; "Francesca," in *American Short Fiction*.

Referred Pain

Heat

When I was a young woman I had a secret passion. At first I didn't quite grasp that it was a genuine passion. I was married and thought I already had what I wanted. This other thing, I thought, was just fascination and fondness. Also he was too old and a little ugly. But as time passed I recognized it for what it was.

It was his size, first of all. Very large. Imposing. When he got up out of a chair I could see the air shifting deferentially to make room for him, as if the very air at his proximity undulated in its yielding, like fabric or flesh. He was infused with gravity, like a rooted tree or a large piece of machinery, and walked with deliberation, as if he drew strength from the ground and was reluctant to lose touch with it. And his darkness. His skin was leathery, his hair so black and smooth it looked like metal. And his voice. Deep, as if it snaked up from someplace near his groin. Deep and a trifle harsh, almost with a sneering edge. Yet full of kindness. A kindly sneer, if such a thing is possible. And courteous, safe, gray eyes.

He came to our house, sometimes with his wife. He sat in the big armchair, a golden drink in his hand, his feet rooted to the floor, his arms resting on the armrests like Lincoln in his stone chair in his monument. He spoke in his deep, pebbly, sneering, warm voice and smoked cigarettes, wrinkling his brow with each puff, holding the end facing inward so I wondered how his palm didn't get burned. He befriended my young, boyish husband, took him under his wing in their shared line of work. He was kind. And I wanted to be near him and hear his voice.

He felt it too. He looked at me with appreciation and desire, the kind of desire that is civilized and tamed when it would be out of the question to let it run free. The kind of desire that in a man of his age grows wry and ironic and mellow, yet doesn't shrivel or seep away. He made gallant, civilized remarks of the kind that older men are—or were—permitted to make to younger women, meant only half-seriously, tinged with rue, the erotic seasoning of his aging. I wanted to let him know that I did take them seriously, that I felt the same even though he was so much older. I didn't think of him as fatherly. No. I wanted to make him happy. I wanted to see how pleasure would make him look. I wanted precisely the wry, rueful, and, I imagined, heated gratitude he would offer in return. I wanted to whisper in his ear that I wanted him, and to see his melancholy surprise—for he was melancholic, he had had disappointments—and then to take off his clothes and make love to him as if he were a stony monument I was bringing to life with my hands.

But I never did this. It was out of the question. Even so, I nursed the secret feeling that the two of us might one day do the things commonly considered to be out of the question, however the question might be termed. My married life continued, and meanwhile I wanted to stroke the steely hair and take the leathery face in my hands and feel the texture of the skin, which I imagined would be coarse to my touch, and kiss the lips from which the smoke emerged and feel the large body quicken under my hands. I wanted to astonish him with the offer of myself, whisper to him that he was the sexiest man I had ever seen and watch his shy, surprised demurral and then see him emerge masterful and confident as he realized I was telling the truth.

But I never did. I was brave only in thought, not in deed. I went on with my life, with him remaining an unattainable pleasure, out of the question, and meanwhile he grew old, still looking at me with desirous, courteous gray eyes, till finally he got so old that he got sick, and sicker, and began to waste away, and I saw the wonderful sexy ugliness of him grow thin and wasted with disease.

One day his wife called and asked if I knew of anyone who could come over and cut his hair, for he was too weak to go out to the barber. I said as a matter of fact I knew how to cut hair quite well, which I did: I cut my own hair and, in the days when we couldn't afford haircuts, had cut my young husband's hair as well. I went with my two pairs of scissors, large and small, and an electric razor for the hairs at the back of the neck.

He was wearing a plaid bathrobe and slippers, reclining on the couch, propped up on pillows. He still looked at me with appreciation, but the lustful or desirous nuance had all but left his gray eyes, as if to say that now it was truly out of the question, while before it had been only morally or socially so because of convention or timidity or consideration for the others involved. His skin was no longer dark but yellowish like a bruise, as if the rich maroon of the blood beneath no longer flowed with vigor. I could see the bones beneath his face, especially the sharp cheekbones. No more golden drink in his hand, no more cigarette facing inward, to his palm. His ankles were white and, without socks, bereft. His neck was wrinkled. He needed a shave and the bristles were coming in white. I thought of offering to shave him too, but I had no experience with shaves and didn't trust myself to touch his throat with a razor in my hand, which might tremble or do something unexpected out of wild regret.

No one would call him sexy now but to me he still was: I remembered what he had been and could see it was all there in his mind. I also knew I could never make love to him now, even in thought; he would break under my touch, however gentle; he was brittle. I think I had always lived with the notion that as I grew older I would gradually shed my diffidence and one day amass enough nerve to do what had appeared out of the question. But it was taking me too long. He was too much older to wait for as long as it was taking me.

His wife had moved a large chair near the window and placed a sheet under it to catch the falling hair. She helped him up from the couch and over to the chair. It was a warm day, and he shuffled the shuffle of the aged in heat; he no longer drew strength from the ground but sank into it, preparing the way, digging the grooves of his grave.

He sat down carefully in the chair as if his bones, so close to the surface, might shatter from too hard an impact. I arranged a towel around his neck like a true barber and prepared to cut his hair. First I combed it, smoothing the strands down with my hand in the wake of the comb. He had a side part and the hair was straight, still plentiful and starkly black, though the sideburns and the hairs at the back of the neck were growing in white. I combed his hair gently and smoothed it down. The hair was not metallic as it appeared but soft, and very clean. His wife must have washed it that morning. All silky and springy to the touch. His body smelled very fresh too, even though the day was so warm. I began to cut. First in front, clipping bits from the locks that fell across his forehead. Then the top and the sides. I stood above him, looking down on his head. He sat docilely like a boy in the barber's chair, but unlike a boy he emitted a heavy immanence like that of a man receiving skilled ministrations, while I circled around him, clipping here and there, combing down and smoothing. Clip, comb, smooth. Then I worked on the sideburns with the small scissors, holding them very close to the skin but careful not to nick him. I tilted his head sideways with the pressure of my hand to have easy access to the sideburns; at that, his eyes closed for an instant, then slowly opened. I did one side then walked around him and did the other. As I walked I glanced out the window; there was the park where he would probably never go again. He followed my gaze: the greenery, the blazing blue sky. His wife sat nearby and watched, and she and I kept up some idle talk though I couldn't say much; I was concentrating on the haircut. He said nothing, as though the effort would be too great. Or perhaps he was too absorbed in this, our first intimacy, my body circling close around him at eye level—he would be breathing me in—and didn't want to interrupt his concentration by words.

After the sideburns I straightened his head with my hands—he was so willing and responsive under my hands—

then went behind him and clipped in back. When I tilted his head forward with the pressure of my hand, he let out a little groan—I had pushed too hard. I apologized. I patted his head in apology as you do a child's. I lightened my touch. I plugged in the electric razor and started on the back of his neck. I must have nicked him because his body gave a little start and his lips parted, then closed again. I saw his wife wince in sympathy. She was worried, I could tell, that this was taking too long, it was too hard for him to sit upright for so long, so I tried to work faster, and yet I didn't want the haircut to be over. I shaved the back of his neck clean, turned off the razor, and circled around him examining my work and clipping stray hairs here and there. A few fell on his lap. I glanced down, hesitating, and he brushed them off with a faint smile. Though he looked wearied, even asking to be released by now, I didn't want to release him, I loved so much the feeling of his head under my hands, of standing so close, closer than I had ever stood except for a brief greeting or farewell, and of touching him under his wife's anxious eyes. I wished I could touch his face and neck and shoulders too, to give him some small bit of what I had once dreamed of giving in abundance, but here, now, that was truly out of the question. Maybe if his wife had left the room for just a moment I might have leaned down and whispered in his ear, I've always had a passion for you, I've wanted you all along. But probably I wouldn't. Now, although not out of the question—why is it that death always changes the question?—that would be in poor taste; it would be mocking his weakness, now that he could do nothing more but prepare to die clean and neatly shorn.

Finally, reluctantly, I released him, and my hold on him.

Two weeks later he was in the hospital. I went to see him. As soon as I reached the doorway I knew I shouldn't have come. It was an intrusion. It was past the point for visitors. There was a nurse bending over his face, maybe removing a thermometer from his mouth. His wife was asking her about a "procedure" that had just been done. He was propped up in bed, framed by the two women bending anxiously over him, like a Christ figure in a Renaissance painting, a deposition, with the Marys drooping on either side. He was gaunt. The bristles of his beard had grown in white. The skin of his face was so fine and translucent that I could see the contours of the skull beneath. But his hair was neatly combed; it was, I saw with satisfaction, a good haircut. A little grown in but structurally excellent.

He caught sight of me standing tentatively in the doorway. His gray eyes flickered with surprise and reflexive appreciation but no civilized lust whatsoever. That was all gone. Instead he showed a pained, almost irritated look— not simply the pain of his illness but an irritation at me, as if the eyes were asking, Why didn't you ever, then ...? Why bother me now?

I lowered my eyes in shame at my mistake and he took pity on me. He was so much older and more worldly. He still had resources. He raised a hand and beckoned me in. I stepped forward soundlessly. While his wife and the nurse continued to talk, unaware of me, he murmured in a voice hoarse and strained, past rue but not past kindness, hot with fever, "My barber!"

Later I tried holding a cigarette the way he had. I held it with the lit end facing inward, to see what he had felt. A strong heat penetrated the center of my palm and radiated out to the tips of my fingers. I held it there till it burned down.

Hostages to Fortune

The Willards were a handsome pair; everyone in the neighborhood thought so. He was large and fair-haired, a man of few words who appeared firm but just, the kind who years ago might have run a small business where probity was essential, or maybe been a veterinarian. She was pretty in an almost too intense way, daintily built, dark, impelled by a nervous energy that suggested bursts of chatter. Yet with her neighbors she was the opposite of chatty. Never rude, she simply had the unsettling air of needing to rush off somewhere else. The Willards' well-tended good looks made it hard to judge their ages. They certainly seemed young to have grown children—away at graduate school or working, no one knew exactly; no one had ever seen them. The couple had moved from Boston to this civilized old suburb—sidewalks and trees and backyards—just three years ago. That was a bit curious, for people usually moved to the suburbs when the kids were small, then returned to town later if they missed city life. The Willards had done it the other way round.

Each morning they set off in their separate cars, his a newish Plymouth sedan, hers an old but hardy Volvo. He did something corporate, organizing seminars or conferences; again, no one knew for sure. She worked in arts management; she could be seen downtown at the symphony, flitting about, looking tense and competent. They kept up their property and were decent neighbors. Nick Willard had quite a nice flower garden out back, where he was often glimpsed on weekends. Not much else was known about them, and no one had ever been inside their house. Few visitors turned up. The Willards were unobjectionable, yet based on no evidence except their polite aloofness, their neighbors found them a trifle mysterious. Very wrapped up in each other, some murmured. Very wrapped up in their work, said others. There were no signs of secret vices or untoward habits; still, the Willards gave the impression of being very wrapped up in something.

Nick and Julia Willard would have been surprised to know that they appeared anything other than ordinary. They hardly considered themselves special; that distinction they reserved for their children, even if by now they had stopped using that word, "special." Because of these special children—Kevin, for the moment, but soon Joanne would be implicated—the air in the Willards' house on this balmy Friday evening in June felt constricted and congealed. The air seemed turned to glass. Certain forbidden words could shatter it.

Nick Willard blamed his wife for the frangible texture of the air. He had come home exhausted and rattled: Friday evening traffic from Boston the usual misery, faxes at work gone astray, and reservations for the next conference muddled, confirming his belief that it was risky to delegate even the smallest detail. Julia chose that moment to tell him about Kevin's phone call.

"It's a great opportunity. Paris, an international research team, so young?" She was practically flouncing around the kitchen. "Others would kill for the chance."

"First of all," he countered, "it's an ocean away. When would we ever see them? We hardly see them as it is. And what about Martha? She just hooked up with that gallery in Georgetown."

Kevin had married last year, soon after he moved to Washington. The Willards still reminisced over the perfect garden-party wedding under a dazzling blue sky: Kevin so grand in his tuxedo, Joanne, in her lilac bridesmaid's dress, lovably gamine—always too thin but luckily never anorexic. They were lucky in their daughter-in-law too, they agreed. Martha was just the kind of bright, warm-hearted girl they had dreamed of for Kevin. And a talented painter besides.

"Martha can set up a studio anywhere," Julia said. "What artist wouldn't want to go to Paris? I thought you'd be pleased."

"You thought I'd …?" She couldn't be serious. "I'll call them tomorrow. Martha's reasonable. Two years? What if they don't like it?"

"I wouldn't do that. It's interfering."

"Interfering? It's being a sensible parent. But you probably wouldn't appreciate that."

"Oh, come on, Nick. Not again! You can't say I haven't been a good mother."

No, he couldn't honestly say that. Better to say nothing at all. Scowling, he took a fresh drink up to the den and shut the door. When darkness fell he was still there, standing at the window, staring down into his garden. Or where the garden should be. The outdoors had become a black expanse in the moonless night. Gradually the two willows near the edge of the lawn took shape in the blackness, insubstantial and eerie, a darker blotch against the night. Everything he had lovingly planted around them was there too, though unseen—the roses, the violets and clematis and hyacinth, the apples he'd trained to grow on vines, medieval style, along a trellised wall. He would see it all again in the morning, and that gave him comfort.

Kevin's going to Paris was a galling prospect. And Julia shouldn't pretend so shamelessly: she knew how much he longed to have the children nearby. Yet ever since Kevin and Joanne started school, she'd been going on about how it was natural and necessary to let children go, give them independence. If he protested, she said he was obsessed, he took everything too far. He was trying to colonize her mind with the children, she would say, spoiling what had started out as their very special adventure. Special maybe, but no dizzy adventure, he had to remind her firmly. Raising children was a serious matter.

That was indisputable, but in fact the Willards' children had been remarkably easy to raise, as children go, and easy to manage: nothing more dramatic than the usual mishaps and illnesses, the vagaries of adolescence—comic in retrospect—the dithering about colleges and careers. And so this new struggle was all the more painful. Never before had there been intractable or drawn-out conflicts about the children. Only brief skirmishes, vehement, once or twice even violent (that would be Julia Willard; Nick, wisely, knew his own strength). Always, in the past, one of the two would give in before the situation, delicate and titillating as a house of cards, could collapse into ugliness. For the children, so cherished, so carefully nurtured, should never be used as a pretext for quarreling or bargaining or anything so base as blackmail. Both Nick and Julia grasped that perfectly.

Saturday morning, when Julia Willard returned from the gym, flushed and bouncy, Nick was waiting at the kitchen table. "I called," he told her. "It seems Martha isn't all that keen on Paris after all. Her father hasn't been well. He just had an angioplasty, and she'd rather not be so far away. There's a team in Pittsburgh working on the same project. They've asked for him too."

"Pittsburgh? It's not exactly a thrilling alternative. Why on earth go to Pittsburgh when you can be in Paris? It's not right to try to stop them, Nick."

"If her father's sick, she can get home more easily." He cocked his head in the brash way she remembered from high-school. "Martha said it, not me." He looked unpleasantly snide and, yes, boyish—a boy who'd easily disposed of a negligible threat.

That boyish swagger, so distasteful in a man his age, had been appealing long ago. For the Willards were lapsed high-school sweethearts; their meeting years later was a fluke, they both agreed. "Kismet," Nick Willard liked to joke. "I never even went to the symphony in those days." He won the tickets in an office raffle, had nothing better to do and no one he cared to invite. During the intermission he paced the lobby, solitary, drink in hand, looking in need of rescue. Who should turn up but Julia, rushing past with a clipboard and a rolled-up extension cord. They fell into each other's arms, then stayed up half the night in her

Back Bay apartment, in her bed, where between bouts of avid sex, they told their stories—both more successful at work than at love. "At the office I'm the boss, and I run a tight ship," he told her, grinning, holding her down with his elbows and knees. Julia remembered to this day how he demonstrated wrestling holds he'd learned on the high-school team, how she pleaded for mercy in mock alarm, his sly laughter as he promised to release her, but only if she would submit to his every command.... Who would have dreamed it—solid, steady Nick Willard, reappearing out of the blue? After sixteen years? Seventeen? Blond and hulking, still blessed with a wrestler's taut body, he was a haven after the fly-by-night men she'd spent more than a decade fretting over.

What Nick remembered was studying her body, softer-edged and more willing now than at seventeen—how readily it went from eager to languid and back again. She'd kept the supple frame and moody energy that had roused him in adolescence; her hazel eyes had the same glint; she still seemed electrically charged, poised to leap at life. His first marriage had ended soon after his son, nine years old, was killed on his bike by a hit-and-run driver. He thought he would go mad with grief. Even now, two years later ... He choked up when he told her about it, and Julia, listening, was near tears as well. Maybe it wasn't too late to try again.

It certainly wasn't too late for passion. The first year or so they made love with the voracity of the bruised but undefeated, outwitting fate. Then they would lie twined in the dark, conjuring up the family they might have raised had they not been sidetracked. The children, a boy and a girl, ideally, would be at the awkward age, bewildered by sprout-ing breasts and a breaking voice, struggling with geometry, tempted by drugs, entranced by the latest hip-hop idols. They talked and talked—or rather, Nick talked while Julia lay by his side happily sated, feeding his fantasies with an indulgent word now and then.

After the seemingly endless years of turbulent love affairs, Julia no longer expected to have children, and she had made her peace with that. She'd never really pined for babies anyhow. It was love she pined for. She loved everything about love—the desire, the ever-startling bliss, and the lush, dank lassitude after. Still, Nick was so keen on a family. Why not try to gratify him if she could? Especially when trying simply meant letting herself be loved, practically assailed by love, insistent and tenacious as his grief. And so they tried. And tried. If only desire and urgency could make a baby, she thought, and she pitied him even as she luxuriated in his assaults. Until, just when it seemed impossible, miraculously Kevin came to them. Willed into being, as it were, by the force of Nick's longing.

At first, Julia Willard was bemused, dubious. But at his urging she warmed to the idea. Right after Kevin arrived she made a blunder, though. "Come to think of it, I was sort of hankering for a girl," she said, ever so lightly.

Nick's face hardened. "Well, it's not as if we can send him back, can we?"

They were in bed, entwined. A passionate pair, still. Sex was panoramic, engulfing. Julia leaned back to give him a wry look. "No?"

He detached from her. "Julia! How can you say that?"

"Why? Is it against the rules or something? Maybe you should spell out the rules of the game before we go too far."

This he ignored. "Anyway," he said, "you knew. From when you had the amnio."

"The amnio? Oh, right, the amnio," she grunted.

"He's a beautiful baby, Julia. Besides, we can always try again."

"Oh, I get it. Sure, we can try again." Her voice was husky. She turned away and curled her body into a ball.

It wasn't long before he was pressing for another.

"So soon, Nick?"

"Why wait? You wanted a girl, didn't you?"

What was the old saying? she thought. In for a penny, in for a pound. So there, and far more easily this time, was Joanne—a dusky beauty of an infant with hair the same shade as her mother's, yet so much finer. Julia's heart melted whenever she thought of her, whenever they whispered about her in bed. She became nearly as absorbed as Nick was. How could she resist? Both children were turning out to be irresistible—beautiful, clever, everything parents could wish for. Their antics, their little triumphs at school, their enthusiasms staved off creeping middle age. And fortunately there was no need to consider leaving work to stay home. Even Nick wouldn't go so far as to expect it. Julia loved her job, relished dreaming up events and making them happen. Her cunning diplomacy was a legend in the field. "You'd better talk to him, Julia," the director would say about some famously willful musician. "No one else can get him to budge." Plenty of mothers managed a high-powered job, she told Nick. She could too. She was used to juggling acts.

Saturday afternoon, to avoid Nick, Julia Willard drove to meet a friend in town, where she found distraction but no real relief. The Willards had never been given to nattering on about their kids, boring others to tears. Their pleasure in Kevin and Joanne was too lusciously private. Like sex, Julia thought. Or like sex had been, before. For as their delight in the special children blossomed and unfurled, their love was scaled down, becalmed. Maybe that happened to most couples. But to them? Soon passion was little more than a prelude to the inevitable remembering. Remember when Joanne hid the stray cat in her room and in the middle of the night we heard kittens whining? Right, and Kevin couldn't stop sneezing so we had to give them all away. The time he got appendicitis at camp and we raced to that hospital in Worcester? Remember you were teaching Joanne to drive, and while you dashed into the drugstore she took a spin around the block alone? Right, I was about to call the police when she rounded the corner. Just missed the newsstand.

It was all inscribed in memory, forming an ongoing saga, like a chronicle they were compiling together. But it was time for the story to change. The children were on their own now, and Julia Willard wanted something more solid than memories. She wanted back what they had had those first two years, when Nick gazed at her as if he were about to forage for hidden treasure. She wanted the games they used to play in bed, games of threat and resistance and more threat and finally submission. It was all only words, harmless words, but bewitching. Their very own secret games. Was it so foolish to crave that again? They were hardly old, after all.

When she came home she found Nick on his knees in the garden, in the fading light.

"I called Kevin from the car," she greeted him. "It's not quite settled. Martha's father's doing better, and he didn't want them giving up Paris for his sake." Nick didn't answer, just bent lower and dug more fiercely. "Not all parents are so selfish," she said, striding off. She had to be back downtown soon to oversee a chamber music recital. It was a relief to get away, and a relief to find Nick asleep in the darkened house when she returned.

Being out, doing what she did best, gave perspective. Nick was right; she hadn't been quite honest, pretending he would enjoy Kevin's news about Paris. She knew all too well how relieved he'd been when Joanne chose a college close to home, how melancholy when Kevin, with her encouragement, accepted the scholarship to Stanford. "The Boston area has more good schools than anywhere in the country," Nick grumbled. "The world, maybe. Why California, of all places?"

But she'd brought him around, just as she had on the matter of vacations. She loved to travel and he didn't; he said the trips his work demanded were more than enough. Crowded airports, dim hotel rooms, packing and unpacking. Still, she simply must get away, she told him one winter early on.

"How can we?" he said. "School. Little League. The whole production."

She flung the blanket off in exasperation. "The children. Always the children. Enough is enough, Nick. This is going too far. They'll survive without us for a week or two."

"It's just ... I don't see how we can manage it."

"Nick!" she shrieked. "They don't have to take up every waking moment. Other parents go away." Then, seeing his face turn grim, she changed her strategy. "I know. There's Mrs. O'Malley."

"Who the hell is Mrs. O'Malley?"

"A very nice woman from across the street." They lived in town then, in the Back Bay. "I talk to her when I take the kids to the park. She baby-sits for people in the neighborhood. A chubby widow with time on her hands, and she can use the money. Let me arrange everything. Trust me, it'll work out fine."

Thanks to Mrs. O'Malley, they went to Trinidad, and the following year to Mexico. Julia Willard considered Mrs. O'Malley one of her most brilliant strokes. Later, when the kids were old enough to have plans of their own, gentle coaxing sufficed. Yes, she would agree in a murmur, it was all whizzing by too fast; it seemed barely any time had elapsed between wandering through toy stores and worrying over SATs. All only yesterday. But it couldn't be helped, could it? It was in the nature of things for children to break away, even in close families, even special children. He mustn't give them a hard time. No wonder they always told her their plans first. They were afraid he'd fuss, she explained. Though up to now he'd never gone beyond any fussing she could handle.

Late Sunday morning, having slept past ten, Nick Willard padded into the kitchen on bare feet. "Look, don't get alarmed, sweetie." Julia spun around and almost dropped the coffeepot.

"Sorry, I didn't mean to scare you. But I just called Joanne and she may have a little problem."

"What kind of problem?" Julia went pale and gripped the handle of the pot tighter. Joanne was in graduate school in Ann Arbor; on the phone, she mostly gave colorful accounts of the latest ventures of the theater arts program.

"She's been having tingling sensations in her legs and went to the health service. They'll run some tests. It could be nothing at all, or then again it could be something."

"Something? Like what?"

"Something neurological, I suppose."

Neither one mentioned the fainting spells Joanne had had when she was around twelve—Nick discovered that first too, nearly scaring Julia out of her wits. It was around the time she was urging him to let Kevin go on the wilderness program. The memory hung between them, unspoken. The doctors hadn't found anything wrong, and after a while the spells stopped as unaccountably as they'd begun. What with all the upset, though, Kevin ended up staying home that summer.

"I'll call her right away," Julia said as she slumped against the refrigerator.

"Don't bother. This was an hour ago, and she was leaving to meet friends. Going to some lake or other. They won't be back till tomorrow night. Is there any coffee left?"

When he reached for the pot her fingers whitened and resisted; he stepped back as if she might hurl it at him. She had thrown one of his clay flowerpots once, when he objected to Joanne's first boyfriend, a newly arrived Korean boy who spoke hardly any English. "What can she possibly see in him? They can't even have a conversation. What do you suppose they do when they're alone?" "He plays the violin like an angel," Julia said. "He's so good I'm going to recommend him for the teen apprentice program at the symphony." "Hah! And you say *I* go too far," he sneered. She threw the pot then, aiming not at him but across the room. When he saw that it meant so much to her, he backed down. Joanne was only fifteen; it would pass soon enough.

This time Julia didn't throw anything. She loosened her grip and simply sat. "It must be serious, if she went to a doctor." Joanne's penchant for alternative medicine was an old story; they'd always suspected it was a reaction to her brother's unqualified faith in medical science. The contrast had amused them in the past, but not today. "On the other hand, how sick can she be if she's going away for two days?"

"She may not be sick at all. She wasn't even planning to mention it if I hadn't called."

"She'd love the idea of Kevin and Martha living in Paris. She loved that summer program in Grenoble in high school. You didn't even want her doing that."

"That was long ago. Look, Julia, how about we give it a rest for a while? Let's get out. Let's drive to the shore."

She agreed listlessly. What did it matter where they went, with Joanne's health at stake? Early June was too cool to swim, but they walked along the beach, watching the surfers in wet suits skim and swoop on the waves. They made her think of sex, and again she wished they could return to an earlier chapter of their story, before it veered off on this unexpected path. She watched him, facing into the wind, hands in his jacket pockets, but he wouldn't catch her gaze. Even out of doors the air was stiff. At last he asked about the choral group she hoped to book for next winter, and then Julia asked his advice about a new transmission for her Volvo. He mentioned the gruesome spate of violence in the high schools. Luckily such incidents were almost unknown when their kids were in school, he said. Julia only nodded. Talking about the children was no fun anymore, a game gone stale. Worse, it was skirting danger. He knew how she felt about Joanne. It was wrong to have favorites, especially when there were only two, yet she couldn't help feeling closer to her daughter—dark and fine-boned, high-strung, a reminder of herself as a girl. Nick had wanted a daughter just like that, and he generally got what he wanted.

On Monday Nick Willard came home early. When he heard Julia pull into the driveway he was prepared. He waited patiently in the bedroom, watching her change into shorts and a shirt, empty her purse, pin up her hair. He still liked looking at her, though without the same urgency. She didn't speak, but she was often quiet when she first got home—she needed space, she said, after the daily frenzy of arrangements, schedules, phone calls. Finally she sank down beside him on the bed and took a deep breath. "A long day. How about you? Did you straighten everything out for the conference?"

"I did. I set them straight at the office too. They won't pull anything like that again. By the way, Kevin called." He let the words hang teasingly while she sat, legs crossed, expectant. "He had some interesting news."

"Really? What?"

He put an arm around her. "Guess."

"Come on, Nick, I'm not in the mood for games."

"Martha's pregnant."

Her part was to show the joy befitting the occasion, but she was taken unawares; he watched her features shift into a querulous confusion. "Pregnant? That's ... Well, it's wonderful. But ... I'm kind of surprised. I didn't quite count on being a grandmother. Yet, I mean."

It was true, they had never discussed grandchildren. But that didn't mean he hadn't imagined them. "I was surprised too. But it's what young couples do, isn't it? It doesn't make us any older."

"I suppose not." She sounded doubtful. Then she rallied, producing her eager look, head tilted, eyes wide. "So! A baby. When's it due?"

"Not till January, thereabouts. It's very early. She did one of those home tests. Maybe it'll look like Kevin."

He fell into reminiscing about Kevin as an infant, the golden-haired, ruddy baby of dreams, plump and succulent. He was lean now and his hair had darkened, but he was still striking. In college someone had once approached him about being a fashion model. That had caused a slight skirmish too: Julia found it amusing but Nick Willard was horrified. In the end, to his relief, Kevin had laughed it off, intent on pursuing his degree in microbiology. A good thing too, Nick said later; otherwise there'd be no plummy job at the National Institutes of Health.

"Well," Julia sighed, "it's nice news. But it doesn't change the Paris issue. People have babies in Paris every day." She paused. "It would have dual citizenship."

"It's better to have them at home. And then we could see it right away."

"We could fly over and visit."

That caught him off guard. He should have anticipated it. She was always ready to take off, ever since the days of the propitious Mrs. O'Malley. Now that they were freer, he obliged her every year or so—a walking tour in the Lake District, Greece, the Grand Canyon—though his own tastes ran more to a cottage on Cape Cod. The notion of visiting the kids in Paris did hold some intriguing possibilities, though, he had to admit … seeing the sights with the baby in tow. And later on, the remembering …. But at home as at the office, he preferred not to deviate, once he'd taken a position.

"I hadn't thought of that. Still, how often could we get to Paris in two years? Once? Twice at most?"

Julia shrugged as if she didn't much care. "I tried calling Joanne from work but she wasn't home yet," she said. "I'll try again after dinner."

"It usually takes a week or so to get test results." He made it sound like a warning. "Don't make her more anxious by pestering her."

"I just want to see how she's doing. Do you mind? Is that breaking any rules?"

Dinner was strained, with the unspoken suspended between them like a murky scrim. Julia's skin felt so tight that she retreated to a hot bath, using the aromatic oils Joanne had given her. Lavender was the most soothing. After a while the tension began to seep out of her and her strength returned. She wouldn't be sabotaged. Even if they'd started out as his idea, they were her children too. And it was her life. She would hold fast, using discretion until she knew just how far he was prepared to go. Suddenly Nick knocked on the door, then came in. "Sorry, babe, but I had to tell you." He sat on the edge of the tub, dipping his fingers in the scented water. "Joanne's news wasn't too good."

"You spoke to her? I said I'd call when I was done."

"She beat you to it. They suspect something but they're not sure." He waited, as if it pained him to go on. "They mentioned MS. Or something along those lines."

Julia sat upright. Another blunder. If only she'd called before her bath ... "How can they know already? You said it would take a week."

"I guess when the results are bad they call right away."

That was a nasty trick, she thought. He hadn't been so devious before. She felt too exposed and wished there were some way to cover herself. Of all the dire fantasies mothers were prone to, she'd never imagined anything like this. "How'd she sound? I mean, how's she taking it?" She lifted the stopper to let the water out, rose and wrapped a towel around herself, ran her fingers through her damp hair.

"She was pretty calm, considering. Until they know for sure, she'll try to go along as usual, keep up with her work. She said not to panic. It may still turn out okay, but ..."

"I've got to get out of here. It's too hot." As she opened the door, the shock of cooler air hit her and she went weak, overcome by heat from within. She stretched out on the bed. "Could you open a window, please? And turn on a light?"

He did, then stood staring down at her, huge and relentless, as if offering a challenge. If she didn't remember their games so vividly, she might fear he'd actually leap on her, pummel her. Take her in one of his old wrestling holds for real and grip her hard till she gave up, gave in. In their early days he'd sometimes stare, too, but that was a different stare. And if he suddenly seized her and pinned her down ... well, she had liked that. There was no wanting in this stare. It was hand-to-hand combat now, and he was the expert.

"Why do you keep looking at me like that? Stop it."

He backed off but kept staring. This wasn't fair. Joanne! Her precious baby! Kevin's moving to Paris was benign, but this is going much too far, Nick. This is cruel. Those were the words to speak, but she felt too weak to say them.

"I told you," he said, "nothing is written in stone. The doctors have to study the results. They can misread them the first time." He paced back and forth to the window, glancing down at his garden. "Besides, lots of people have these diseases with barely any symptoms. Only an occasional flare-up."

The time for cunning was past. He'd matched her in cunning. Now he was proposing a crude bargain. If she backed down on Kevin, he would back down on Joanne. Of course she must save Joanne—it was unbearable to think of her deprived of her promising future, in pain, confined to a wheelchair or worse … They might have to visit her in an institution, where Joanne might not even recognize them. Her own life, their life together, all their blithe indulgence in what they had brought into being, would become a pathetic joke.

"Nick, please. I didn't mean for anything like this to happen. I tried so hard …"

He stood gazing out the window with his back to her. "You never really wanted them."

She had, she protested. She'd been a good mother.

"Maybe so. But you've always tried to get rid of them. Colleges far away, trips abroad. You even wanted Kevin to take that UN job in Africa. I'm surprised you never suggested boarding school."

She sank deeper into the pillows. She'd thought of boarding school but knew he'd never agree. "I thought those were all great opportunities. Other kids were doing those things."

"Maybe." When he turned around his face was dark, as if it had caught the darkness from out the window. "But our kids are different."

"They are. They're special. That's why we're free to—"

"You don't need to say anything about it. Do you hear?"

"Okay! I hear. Look, Nick, you're right, in a way. I only went along with it in the first place to humor you." She was whispering, as if they might be overheard.

"Humor me! Humor *me*?" He was not whispering but shouting. "When Joanne started that literacy program at the center you almost wept with pride. And Kevin's band? You put up with those rehearsals day and night and then cheered yourself hoarse."

"So what if I did? I liked it. I got caught up. Isn't that what you wanted? But now that they're ... grown, we can ... You know. We can do other things. We've done the children."

"Do you know what you're saying? I don't believe it. You can't just give children up. It's not like some job where you take early retirement."

"I don't mean give them up." That was a lie, she knew as soon as the words were out. She could give them up, provided they were well, and well launched. "I just mean we could be a little less involved. Gradually. Like in most families."

"But we are, aren't we? We have been for a long time." He poured a drink from the bottle he kept in the night table and didn't offer her any. She always refused, but still it was a petty revenge. "How much less involved can we be, with each of them miles away? Where you wanted them," he added bitterly.

"I'm not enough, am I? I've never been enough. Not after the first few months. You just wanted someone to ..."

"I never said that. No. But you knew from the beginning how I felt about having children. You knew how I felt about losing..." He could never say his son's name without pausing to swallow. "Tom."

"Why didn't you leave, then? Find some woman who could give you what you—"

"Julia!" His face twisted like a rag. "I would never use that to hurt you. We made a good life together. We found a way ... Don't ruin it."

"You can pretend all you want, but you can't change the facts, Nick. Our children aren't—"

With a swift leap he was standing over her again, and this time she knew he could pounce. "Don't say it." He leaned down and gripped her arms so tightly that she winced. "Do you understand? Don't ever say it."

"All right, all right. Let go."

"You'll speak to Kevin about Paris?"

"All right. But only if Joanne, you know, the tests ..."

He nodded, released his hold, and sat down heavily alongside her.

"It's a pity, though," she murmured. "To live in the City of Light..."

He seemed not to have heard. "I wonder if it'll be a boy or a girl. Which would you rather have? You choose this time," he said.

The children would be with them till death, Julia thought. It was too late for change. In her future was a growing family—first words, first steps, the story all over again. It would go by in no time at all, just as before. Any day now the grandchildren would be visiting for holidays, starting school.... At least Joanne would be well. She could count on that—Nick kept his word. Joanne would be well and finish her studies and probably marry too.

"Julia?" he said, touching her arm again, but gently. "Boy or girl? Your call."

She shook her head. "Either one is fine with me, as long as it's healthy." She felt sick with defeat. "We'll know soon enough anyway. The women all have that test now."

"Of course, you're right. We can wait to hear."

Something in his voice made her glance up. He was smiling, the old smile, the smile from when he thought her body held hidden treasure, the smile that promised he would give her everything she wanted, for as long as she wanted, if she would play the game his way. And after all the ugliness of the past days, she found she still wanted him. It drifted through her like a fever gathering momentum, the slow onset of a furious virus. It was insistent. She had to cooperate, let it have its way.

"Same as we did, remember?" She shrugged off the towel and reached to stroke his leg. "Remember we went for the amnio? Remember you saw it on the screen? You were so excited. I remember the look on your face."

Twisted Tales

There once was a woman who could not abide clutter. A thing out of place, intruding on a bare surface, vexed her like a hair on her tongue, a stone in her shoe, a lash in her eye. Clutter kept her from thinking, as if the clutter were not merely around her but in her mind, or rather, as if her mind were nothing but a mirror reflecting her surroundings. When every surface was bare, then, she thought, she could begin to think, though what she would think about she didn't yet know: there was too much clutter to tell.

She spent her time throwing things away and putting things out of sight, but there weren't enough places to put all the things. Finally she persuaded her husband that they must move to a bigger house.

"Very well," he said. "Now you'll have enough places to put all the clutter that bothers you so." Her husband hoped she would be happier in the bigger house and stop darting nervously about, looking for places to put things.

They settled in the house with their children, and the woman arranged everything in its place—there were plenty of closets and shelves. But after a few weeks, when she felt almost ready to think her thoughts, whatever they might be, clutter began to appear again, as it will despite closets and shelves, reproducing and growing like a species with varied incarnations, so that she had no space to think.

She began tossing things down into the basement, a cozy basement with a window near the ceiling and a small bathroom and small kitchen with a tiny stove and refrigerator. First she tossed down newspapers and magazines. Then sweaters and gloves and notebooks and candy bars the children left on chairs and tables. She tossed down vases and photographs and souvenirs from trips. Soon she was tossing down anything left on a surface, coffee cups with their dregs, mail, scraps of paper, books, pencils.

Each night as she lay down in bed, she planned to begin thinking, but she was distracted by the possibility of clutter and would get up to check the house one last time. Invariably she would find some object on a surface and toss it down into the basement, and when she finally climbed back into bed, the thought of the clutter that might accumulate the next day made her too anxious to think.

She never went down to the basement. Sometimes her husband and the children went down to clear away the things heaped at the foot of the stairs or to retrieve some object they needed, for she had tossed down the children's toys and told them if they wanted to play with them they had to play in the basement. She tossed down the combs and brushes and coins and keys her husband left on the bedroom bureau. She was about to toss down the CD player, but her husband rescued it from her arms in time and carried it down along with the CDs. He carried down the computers and TV sets and radios and telephones too, before she could toss them.

She needed to see the walls bare; the pictures and hangings and clocks were preventing her from thinking, though what she wanted to think about she didn't yet know. She knew only that her mind must be empty in order to begin. Her husband had arranged a nest of blankets and pillows at the foot of the stairs so that the tossed-down things would not break. Still, there was a shattering of glass as one picture after another hurtled down.

Her husband was distressed by the bare walls but was afraid of what his wife might do next if he challenged her. Without a word he swept up the glass and stacked the pictures against the basement wall. Meanwhile she rolled up the rugs and sent them bumping down the stairs. Down went pots and pans, sheets and towels. She stripped the windows of curtains and shades. She tossed down furniture. She was beginning to enjoy the bareness of the house and felt almost ready to think.

The children complained that they had to keep running down to the basement to get what they needed to dress and go to school. She picked up the children one by one and tossed them down onto the nest of blankets and pillows, where they landed with no injury. From then on, in the morning she would toss down their breakfast and their lunchboxes, and in the evening, their dinner. With the children in the basement the house was much less cluttered, and she felt the faint stirring of what might have been a thought or two.

The house was almost bare now, except for the double bed and some furniture too large to toss. In the evenings her husband would spend some time in the basement with the children, then come up to bed. One evening she stood waiting for him at the top of the stairs. She stretched out her arms, but they both knew he was too big for her to toss. She simply pointed and he understood. He turned and went back down the stairs.

Now she was alone in the empty rooms. She sat on the floor and began to think. She thought about what it must be like in the basement, from which she could hear the lively sounds of talk and laughter and music. She thought of leaping down the stairs and landing softly on the blankets and pillows and saying, "Can I join you?" Then she thought that this talk and laughter and music were not meant for her. She would need to live a long time in emptiness before she was ready to return to talk and laughter and music, if ever.

౭ఠ

There was a man who never wanted to go to sleep. Like most people, he grew tired by nightfall, but he resisted going to sleep. He did useful work all day but the work was demanding, and when he came home he wanted the satisfaction of peace. He was glad to have dinner with his wife and children and share in their chatter; afterward there were always matters to attend to—homework or phone calls or minor repairs, bills to pay and letters to answer—and though these things were necessary and important and made up the fabric of his life, they did not give the satisfaction of peace but only delayed it.

When the children went to sleep he and his wife would talk for a while, or read or watch television in the living room, and soon she would yawn and go off to sleep. "Come to bed," she sometimes called from the bedroom, and fairly often he went to bed and made love to her, which was satisfying but not with the satisfaction of peace that he craved, and so he would return to the living room and read about the events of the day in the newspaper. The events of the day were never peaceful, so he would turn to a book; by this time it would be quite late and he would be quite sleepy, but he was reluctant to give up consciousness; it felt like admitting defeat, though by whom or what he didn't know.

He only knew he must keep vigil, waiting for a certain feeling to descend on him, not simply the satisfaction of peace but also a feeling of accomplishment. He had already accomplished everything necessary for the day both at work and at home, yet there was something more, something unknown and mysterious he wished to accomplish. To go to sleep unsatisfied would be a concession, and this concession to he knew not what felt treacherous and dangerous.

Sometimes his wife came into the living room and asked why he wouldn't go to sleep, and he tried to explain what he was waiting for. She said those vague needs were just signs of weariness and frustration from lack of sleep. She said the state he craved did not exist in life: was he keeping vigil for death? But he thought it was life, his real, not-yet-lived life, he was waiting for.

He stayed up later and later, waiting, and once in a while, when the house had been still for some time, he would feel the satisfaction of peace approaching like a cloak settling gently on his shoulders, and even a faint feeling of accomplishment, like a suppleness in his muscles. But by then he was so tired that as he tried to cling to these stray feelings, elusive as daydreams, he would drift off. Then he roused himself to go to bed, since he knew he couldn't manage a new day after a fitful night on the sofa. Even as he lay down, his body begging for rest, he fought against giving up unsatisfied. But sleep overtook him; he slept soundly for the few hours remaining till break of day, when he would begin again.

He went on this way, keeping vigil and growing ever more fretful, until the days became a burden and his mind was not clear enough to accomplish what was necessary at work and at home. He realized at last that he couldn't continue. He admitted defeat and began going to bed at a sensible hour like most people, without having attained the satisfaction of peace at the close of day or the feeling of accomplishment of he knew not what. He learned to live unsatisfied. Outwardly he seemed more at peace once he began to sleep regularly, and his wife was relieved, but what he truly felt was the resignation of defeat.

All his life he longed to know whether the cravings whose satisfaction he had renounced were his alone, or whether others felt them too and learned to suffer them quietly. He never found out because this was not something anyone really talked about.

ൟ

A husband and wife invited a bunch of people over for a party. The man liked to get things organized well in advance. The night before, he suggested to his wife that they go out to buy food and drink for the party. She said no, she was busy and they could wait until tomorrow. The next morning, he wanted to get an early start, but she wanted to sleep late. "Okay, I'll go myself." "Please wait," she said. "I want to pick out what we'll serve."

Early in the afternoon, he said, "Let's go. There's not much time." But she said she had things to do. All day he waited and fretted, while she kept finding things to do. "We have plenty of time," she said.

An hour before the guests were due to arrive, the man was agitated: there was nothing in the house to feed them. "There's still time," the woman said. She needed to rest before the party started.

The guests arrived and the hosts were busy with greetings and embraces. They'd be going right out to get food, they told their guests; they were sorry to be so unprepared. But they got caught up in conversation and never did manage to go out for food.

Time passed and no refreshments were served. The man was very embarrassed. Luckily some of the guests had brought offerings of snacks and bottles of wine. They put out the snacks, opened the bottles and drank, and in the end, even with such sparse fare, everyone had a good time.

The guests had such a good time that they suggested coming over the next night to do it all again. This time more people brought wine, and some even brought pizza and salads, and again they had a rousing good time. "You see," the woman said to her husband afterward, "you can throw a good party without giving people anything."

A few weeks later, when they had just been to the market and had plenty of food in the house, the man said, "How about calling everyone up and having them over for a party? Since this time we have plenty of food around."

"No," his wife said.

"But why not? We had such a good time before, and now it would be even better."

"This time," she said, "we have too much to lose."

35

∽

There are people who cannot a resist a mirror, and vanity is not the only or even the principal reason why. They look to make sure they are still there: this is widely known, though not always to those with the mirror habit. For one such person, glancing in mirrors had become an obsession. He was not vain and didn't seek to admire or assess himself. But he had no one to reflect or acknowledge him, and so he sought and found acknowledgment in mirrors. He would look first thing in the morning, greeting himself after sleep's prolonged and pathless exile, and then while shaving and dressing, and then just before leaving the house. On the way to work, he checked in shop windows, where his reflection was shadowy and transparent but still reassuring. Certain windows provided real mirrors, for instance the drugstore with the tall narrow one that he passed morning and evening, and at these places he would slacken his pace ever so slightly and sometimes give a furtive nod of recognition.

His office, where he was known generically but not individually reflected, had no wall mirrors but it did have a plate-glass window in which he could steal glances, and in the top drawer of his desk he kept a small hand mirror facing upward, which he could glance at by opening the drawer a few inches; this he could do even while conducting a meeting or an interview from his desk.

There was always the briefest instant of panic before he confronted a mirror, and then the briefest instant of relief at the same reliable image. He had never much dwelt on what he was panicked or relieved about; a habit is a habit and takes possession like a parasite, the host often compliant until forced to take notice. One day he was forced. It happened as he was passing the drugstore with the tall narrow mirror, not far from his apartment. He checked, as always, and he was not there. Instead he saw a display of colognes and aftershave lotions. In that terrible instant of not finding himself, before he grasped that the mirror had been replaced by a display case, he understood the meaning of his fear. That he could see and feel his own body did not ease the panic. His physical existence was not in doubt—he was its witness—but his own testimony did not answer the larger question of whether others could see him. What if he cast no reflection in the world? Only mirrors could say for sure. What good was having a physical existence if he was its only witness?

And yet that moment of seeking and not finding himself in the drugstore mirror was so profoundly unsettling that he was reluctant to look in mirrors anymore for fear he would find nothing. Even if his absence turned out to have a simple, rational cause like the replacement of the drugstore mirror, the instant of panic at that nothingness, which was the precise shape of his fear, was too dreadful to risk again.

He stopped looking in mirrors. He trained himself to walk down the street looking straight ahead, avoiding all the familiar store windows. He removed the hand mirror from his desk drawer and avoided the plate-glass window of his office, and at home he dressed and shaved as best he could without the aid of mirrors. This was difficult and often impossible; when now and then he had to consult the mirror or inadvertently glimpsed himself—unfailingly present—the minuscule instant of terror was almost too much to bear.

Now he no longer had his peculiar habit. Now, outwardly, he was like everyone else, except for his peculiar habit of avoiding mirrors. He tried to trust his own testimony as others seemed to do, and sometimes he succeeded; still, for the rest of his life he would feel an outlandish surge of gratitude when strangers on the street stepped out of the way to avoid bumping into him.

ைୡ

A certain woman never felt entirely comfortable speaking her native tongue. She spoke ably enough, her vocabulary and grammar were adequate to say all she needed to say, but she didn't feel at home either in her mind or in her mouth. Since she had never spoken any other language and couldn't know what degree of comfort others felt, her discomfort was vague and amorphous; she knew only that she had to search uneasily for words and phrases as if they came from a second language and not a first, that the contours her mouth formed and the paths her tongue traveled did not take shape as readily as she imagined they should. She even suspected she might speak differently were her tongue more at ease. She would express herself with richer and more subtle nuances, and in the process her opinions and attitudes themselves might change and grow more subtle. In other words she might be a different person, or more precisely, a self waiting inside her, speechless, would find speech.

One day while riding on a bus she overheard a conversation in an unknown tongue between a man and woman sitting behind her. Though she couldn't understand what they were saying, the sounds of the language seemed familiar, like the features of a distant relative. The broad, lingering vowels, like amber deserts or rose-tinged skies, called up dormant affinities in her vocal cords and in the pathways of her brain; the harsh, craggy consonants suggested jagged cliffs or surf hitting rocks, unlike her native language whose vowels sounded like cream and custard, the consonants like pastry crusts.

From the strangers' tones she could distinguish questions and answers, interjections and phrases of surprise or dismay. After a while she could make out the shapes of sentences, syntactical groupings that fell into patterns. She felt she was starting to grasp the curves and the trajectory of their conversation—she lacked only the subject matter. The more she listened, the more she had the uncanny sense that at any moment she would understand what was being said, as if what barred her from understanding was not her total ignorance of the language but rather a thin veil she could almost, but not quite, see through. She had the excited feeling that at any moment the veil would be lifted, or else she would penetrate it. Before the couple got off she turned around to ask—in her native tongue, the only one she knew—what language they were speaking. It was the language of her ancestors; she had never heard it spoken because her grandparents had died before she was born and her parents either could not speak it or didn't wish to.

Some time later, in a taxi, she heard the dispatcher on the intercom instructing his drivers in what she recognized as the same foreign yet familiar tongue. Now and again she distinguished the name of a local street, and perhaps because of these intermittent known words and because the subject was obvious—where to pick up and discharge passengers—she felt even more strongly that at any moment the veil would lift and she would understand everything.

When she reached her destination she told the driver she'd changed her mind and wished to be taken elsewhere, just so she might keep listening. She tried to fix certain syllables in her ear—rough and pebbly, yet musical—repeating them under her breath to see how they felt on her tongue, wondering what as-yet-unknown nuances of herself they might be made to articulate and who she would be as a result. This pleased her, yet the pleasure was frustrating: the veil did not lift or become transparent. Still, if she listened long enough, maybe it would happen. Or if the veil did not lift, she would burst through it.

She yearned for the feel of words coming instinctively to her tongue and for the new self that would emerge along with them. Meanwhile, her native language was feeling more and more cumbersome. Rather than study the alluring language in books, she decided to go to the country where it was spoken. Once there, she acquired the most essential words and phrases and picked up others from signs or shop windows, as strangers do. But she resisted studying the language in any methodical way. She felt it was already wholly inside her, and once the veil had lifted, the words would spring instantaneously to her tongue.

She wandered through streets and shops and parks, her ear taking pleasure everywhere in the sounds it had longed for. Always she felt that the veil was about to lift. And she did begin to grasp fragments here and there, but simply as strangers do, not in the instantaneous way she expected and thought she merited.

She stayed a long time, learning to shape the craggy consonants and the broad amber vowels. The language required that her mouth take new positions, more open and flexible ones, and that her tongue, moving in new patterns and at different speeds, strike against her teeth and palate at new angles and with different degrees of force and subtlety. All this she did well; her accent was good, and over time her vocabulary increased and her grammar improved. She was able to say most of what she needed to say, although she was not aware of saying anything she might not have said in her native tongue.

After some years she was fluent, and her mouth and the pathways of her mind felt comfortable as they had not with her native tongue, which she remembered but rarely used: that felt like a foreign language now. She even began to think and to dream in the new language. And the nuances of her manner of expression did change somewhat—but she could never be sure whether this came about through the new language on her tongue or simply through the passage of time and the effects of leading a new life in a new place.

In the end she came to speak the language of her ancestors as ably as she had wished, but she never had the satisfaction of seeing the veil lift and understanding everything instantaneously. Now, when she overheard conversations on the bus, she understood perfectly, but without the sense of wonder she had anticipated. Nor did the self she now was strike her as wondrous either, since she had been present at its gradual evolution—as she would have been in any language. So while she was contented speaking her adopted language, her contentment was marred by uncertainty: had she learned to express herself so well because of an ancestral affinity in the pathways of her brain, or had she simply mastered a new language by proximity and long residence as any stranger might? Perhaps it was a mistake to have come. If she had remained at home, listening to occasional random snatches of the ancestral tongue, waiting and trusting, perhaps the veil might one day have lifted to reveal its entire lexicon and structure. And if so, then she had spent years earning what would have been hers effortlessly, and laboring to become the person she would naturally have become in time.

Referred Pain

These may seem dramatic effects for such a tiny cause, but each person knows how much it hurts and where.

—JOSÉ SARAMAGO,
THE YEAR OF THE DEATH OF RICARDO REIS

In December of his thirty-second year, sturdy Richard Koslowski, musician and computer wizard, attended a party in a downtown loft. His girlfriend, Lisa, a red-haired, studious beauty, was home with a bad cold and Koslowski missed her. He would miss her more if there were dancing later. Others would be willing, sure, but Lisa was the best, sinuous and lithe as a mermaid blessed with legs. Meanwhile there was food; most of the guests had contributed a dish. Even Koslowski and the members of his band, arriving straight from a gig at an East Village club, had stopped off for six-packs and barbecued chickens. He was hungry and helped himself to a colorful spaghetti dish with green and black olives.

Balancing his plate and his beer, he spied an empty chair and found himself listening to the woman on his left, a human rights attorney, tell appalling tales of torture and abuse; she had just returned from an investigative trip to China. "Hi, I'm Cara," she said briskly when he sat down, then resumed her narrative. Koslowski was all for human rights, in China as anywhere else, yet was not overjoyed at the conversation he'd stumbled into. He had heard such stories all his life, in more pungent language. Human rights abuse, he could have told the attorney, was a euphemism. Still, he paid polite attention, not only out of innate civility, but for Lisa's sake as well. Her focus in law school was women's issues, but maybe he could pick up some useful information, even make a contact, while she lay coughing and sneezing in bed.

Not only in China but all over the world, people were suffering unjustly, and Koslowski's neighbor was doing her best to help them. He nodded and chewed absently. What did she mean, suffering unjustly? Is any suffering just? Well, maybe criminals, torturers ... Something in his head exploded. Koslowski raised a hand reflexively to his cheek and a moment later spit pieces of crushed olive pit mixed with human tooth into his napkin. The room around him, furniture, walls, the laden table, grew dim and receded into a gray mist.

"I think," he murmured, "I cracked a tooth."

There was a sudden hush. Everyone stared. An outlandish pain bloomed in the upper right side of his mouth. His heart pounded and he trembled as with the aftershocks of a quake. He had never shaken this violently, even in the subway accident three years ago, and that was more from shock than pain—he had suffered only minor bruises.

"I'm going to pass out."

He was led to a couch where he lay prone with his head hanging over the edge. Through the mist penetrated the deep voice of the human rights attorney's husband, Jeff, a man somewhat older than the rest: "I heard that crunch. I thought it was my own bridge breaking."

Bridge? Wasn't that something engineers built over a river? Koslowski thought as darkness swallowed the mist. His final thought: This must be the darkness his father meant when he described his recent blinding headaches.

The next thing he knew, Hal, the band's singer and guitarist, was waving a bottle of Top Job under his nose; there was no brandy around, only wine and beer.

As soon as he had revived, Koslowski excused himself and took the subway home to Brooklyn. Every now and then he poked his tongue around the injured tooth, its edge sharp and ragged as splintered wood. When he poked, a pain for which he could find no words shot through his head. It reminded him of the sound made by the unwilling trumpeter in his high-school orchestra years ago. Koslowski, quite the contrary, had practiced the piano happily in his parents' Brighton Beach apartment, gazing out at the rhythmic waves far below.

Despite the indescribable pain, he couldn't resist poking: the sensation was so rare, so eerily alluring, a glimpse of the legendary realm he had heard about but never before been invited to enter. So this was pain. A small dose was more illuminating than a lifetime of secondhand stories. But for this pain, so small in the scheme of things, there was a remedy. Tomorrow he'd go to the old family dentist in Brighton Beach. No, tomorrow was Sunday. Monday then. Mild, white-haired Dr. Blebanoff, with his long pink fingers, would know what to do. He had filled three cavities in

Koslowski's mouth over the years. Koslowski had excellent teeth, as did his parents, which in their case was miraculous considering the malnutrition and deprivations suffered in their youth. Dr. Blebanoff used to joke that if all his patients were like the Koslowskis he could never make a living.

At home, he found Lisa sitting up in bed with her law books. "Feeling better?"

"A little. What's the matter? You look terrible."

He told her about the chewing accident.

"Oh no! That's awful! Does it hurt a lot?"

"Mostly when I poke it." Having been reared to stoicism, he offered amusing details about Hal and the Top Job, and Cara, whose narrative had distracted him from chewing more attentively. Lisa picked up on his levity and suggested he might sue the maker of the spaghetti for negligence, since he or she had not pitted that one olive on which Koslowski had had the misfortune to bite.

"I don't even know who brought it."

"You could find out. Maybe hire an investigator?"

"But whoever it was didn't do it intentionally."

True, the case would be ambiguous, she said: he couldn't prove the spaghetti maker had willfully caused harm; with so many olives to pit—this was clearly a gourmet cook who wouldn't stoop to canned olives—it was conceivable to miss one. Nonetheless the perpetrator might still be found liable.

"How so?"

"If you could successfully demonstrate that he or she didn't take the routine precautions against danger that a reasonable person would take."

"I see," said Koslowski, who had meanwhile undressed, moving his head as little as possible, and now crawled into bed beside her. "Maybe you could handle the case. No, don't touch. At least not there."

"It'll be all right, Richie. It's just a tooth."

Of course Koslowski had no intention of suing any-body, much as he enjoyed hearing Lisa show off her new legal savvy. But with no evidence at all he suspected Cara, the human rights attorney, of bringing the spaghetti and olive dish, even though she hadn't owned up to it or shown regret, as one might expect. Maybe guilt kept her silent. Or an educated sense of proportion. After all, this was trivial compared to what she had on her mind.

Koslowski spent the snowy Sunday holed up in the apart-ment, trying not to lick his wound. Huddled in an armchair, drinking warm broth. Hot hurt. He was in shock, a parallel universe, a state of prolonged amazement, his every move determined by the pain.

"Go to the emergency room," Lisa advised. "They must have emergency dental care."

No, he was atavistic; he would wait for Dr. Blebanoff. It was only a tooth. It was not like having one's father car-ried off by the KGB in the middle of the night, or having one's house looted, then being enslaved and starved and beaten and worked half to death, the kinds of calamities that Koslowski had heard so much about in childhood and that Cara (who surely had not—she had the zeal of a con-vert, not one to the manner born) had described with indignation. At some point he roused himself to call his parents.

"How's Dad? The headaches any better?"

"The same." His mother paused. "He gets these spells—he forgets where he is, I think he blacks out for a minute. But he insists it's nothing. What's wrong? You sound funny."

"I broke a tooth." He described how.

"That's too bad. So go to a dentist. Did you read the paper this morning? What's going on in Bosnia? Torture, bodies, barbed wire. Same thing all over again."

Koslowski was in charge of computer systems at a small music company—the best in the business, the human resources director called him—but he took faint interest or pride in his skill. He served his time in the hope that some-day, through his contacts, his band would be recording in one of the studios. He rarely missed a day, but when Monday came at last, he called in sick.

Dr. Blebanoff, greatly aged since Koslowski's last visit, peered and probed and declared the tooth would have to be pulled. In his state of shock, Koslowski nodded mutely in submission and gazed out the window at sleet drifting into the Atlantic. With a force Koslowski wouldn't have attrib-uted to the old man, Blebanoff began tugging at the tooth while Koslowski, to his surprise and embarrassment, resis-ted with all his might, like a captured animal.

"Come on, Richie. You can't be feeling pain, not with the Novocain." That was true. He didn't fight back out of pain. Simply, the assaultive yanking of those bare pink fin-gers called forth a feral response, as if the tooth itself refused to be torn from its lifelong home.

This was the most prolonged physical assault of Koslowski's life. Peaceful by nature, he had been in the usual scuffles as a boy when they were unavoidable. He was big and solid and came out well, with the occasional bruise or bloody nose. Once he was mugged on a deserted street by three older boys who knocked him down and took his wallet; he was sore and humiliated but otherwise intact.

How lucky he was, as his parents never ceased to remind him. Millions of people had known agonies he couldn't conceive of. Beyond the obvious victims of war and torture, more to the point right now were all those hapless souls in the dark reaches of human history who had had teeth pulled before Novocain. To stop his involuntary struggles in the chair, Koslowski tried to picture them thrashing about. It didn't help. This was his alone. In desperation, he conjured up images, always available, always suppressed, of his now portly father, skeletal in the striped uniform of the camps, of his mother a ragged, famished waif hunting for food on the icy streets of wartime Leningrad. All through childhood these images had kept him up at night longing to undo history, to pluck his parents from its claws; he learned to fend them off by playing music in his head. But even they lost their potency under the dentist's relentless assault. At last, to their mutual relief, Blebanoff prevailed. Shyly, like a neophyte lover, Koslowski poked his tongue in the tender hole.

Dr. Blebanoff outlined his options. He could have a bridge made, and when Koslowski inquired, he explained what a bridge was. Or—and this was Blebanoff's recommendation—he could have a removable bridge. "I'll show you." Like a magician, the dentist reached into his mouth to remove a small object—a tooth, girded by wires!—and held it forth for inspection. Koslowski was nonplussed, almost as if the dentist had made an indecent gesture. The too-intimate display of this odd object recalled childhood games of doctor under the boardwalk with Sonya, his next-door neighbor. Modestly averting his eyes, he said, "Oh, no. I'm too young for that."

Dr. Blebanoff shrugged and reinserted his device. "Either way, you have to wait six weeks for the hole to heal. So, how are your parents? Did you read what's happening in Bosnia? It never ends, does it?"

At his weekly gig at an East Side piano bar that night, he gave the diners three hours of old musical-comedy favorites— Cole Porter, Irving Berlin, Stephen Sondheim; while his head swam, his fingers moved on automatic pilot. Later, the numbness gone, he made love to Lisa, something he did as expertly as playing the piano or fixing computers but had not felt up to since the accident. In the midst of it, he was assailed by a long-forgotten image of the nine-year-old Sonya's pink panties, which she would not remove, he recalled, only pulled down for a searing instant. Afterward, as he and Lisa caught their breath, he described the pulling of the tooth.

"You mean he didn't give you Valium?"

"No. Was he supposed to?"

"Sure. I had two wisdom teeth pulled and didn't feel a thing. I hope he wore gloves, at least."

"Gloves? No."

"Richie, this guy is out of it. All dentists wear gloves these days. Didn't you read about that girl who got AIDS from her dentist? Find someone else. Or leave it alone. It doesn't show. Smile. Well, hardly."

"It feels funny. Like something's missing."

"Well, we all know about the symbolism of teeth, don't we?" She reached down to stroke him. "Don't worry. Everything's still there. Safe and sound. Very sound."

"I never thought of that."

"You're so innocent. Like a virgin, you know? Dental virgin."

While the bloody hole healed, Koslowski made inquiries about bridges. Many people had them, apparently. Even his parents, as they revealed when he and Lisa went over for dinner. He listened in wonder, as if they had undergone major surgery without informing him. "When was that?"

"I can't remember," his father said. "When you were a kid, I think. Maybe when you were away in college. What's the difference? Did you hear the latest? Ethnic cleansing, they call it now. Makes it sound almost respectable."

"Don't get yourself all upset," his mother said. "You'll bring on one of your spells."

He waved away her cautions with his hairy left hand, the one missing the little finger. "A disgrace. And we just stand by and watch."

"Hundreds of Muslim women are being brutally raped," Lisa put in, "and as if that's not bad enough, they're afraid to tell. It's used as a weapon."

Koslowski let Lisa handle this conversation. His parents intrigued her: their penumbra of endured catastrophe, the gruesome details they let casually drop if encouraged. He suspected that his history—their history—made him more attractive to her. Exotic. Even privileged. He would try to ignore her hushed awe as they told their stories, yet he too knew the lure, the sickly fear and sickly envy of that priceless knowledge. As a boy, lying awake in the dark, he would overhear his parents in the living room talking to friends, many of them Russians newly settled around them in Brighton Beach. He caught snatches of garish, enigmatic stories like the fairy tales in Sonya's books, where people bled their fingers raw sewing shirts out of nettles or furiously weaving roomfuls of straw. Had his mother really chewed on wood? His father's frozen finger been chopped off without anesthetic, the stump wrapped in newspaper? "The corpses lay in the streets." That was his mother's voice. "Everyone raced to strip off their clothes. If they didn't fit we could trade them for bread." He heard disputes about how much to tell the children.

"It was wartime," his mother would say. "Those things happen. Why do they have to know? Let them have a normal childhood."

"Why?" came his father's voice. "It's not a normal world."

How, then, could Koslowski expect his boyish tribulations to stir them, his scrapes and cuts and broken arm from leaping off the boardwalk, his little disappointments like losing a school election or a football game? Don't be a baby, Richie, his father would say. There are worse things in the world. He didn't need to enumerate; Koslowski could choose from an abundance of family legend.

How lucky he was, they told him. He understood nothing of suffering. How lucky he was, until he hated the sound of the words that set him apart in his ignorance. "Okay, so maybe I don't understand," he shouted back one awful night. "So I'll never know what you know. So what do you want me to do about it?" His mother looked at him sadly—what he called her martyred look—and turned away.

In truth he was lucky by any standards: handsome, athletic, musical, popular. Girls liked his effortless charm, his curly hair and gray eyes, his slightly lopsided smile and beguiling air of both needing and offering protection. He was grateful for his blessings and tried not to dwell on the lore that became his bedtime stories, like the time meat appeared on the table and his mother ate it, then vomited when she discovered it was a stray cat. She was slapped for wasting a meal.

He took it all in, though, then woke up choked by nightmares in which he rushed after his parents, chasing them through time, not space, to catch up and carry them to safety. But he was helpless: they were always swallowed up, by the earth or by the sea, or in tornadoes and hurricanes and pillars of cloud.

All that was long ago. Now he simply tuned out as they reviewed the latest atrocities in the papers. Leaning back, he poked at the shrinking hole in his mouth. What had begun as a large round chasm that could accommodate the tip of his tongue was contracting daily, infinitesimally, leaving the new perimeter smooth; the tip of his tongue could just describe the circumference. The salt taste was fading too.

Koslowski's computer job might be merely his daily bread, a means to an end, yet its methods had taken root. If an imperfection existed, it must be fixed. He would have the bridge made: a new experience, maybe even a useful one. In detective stories, corpses were often identified by their bridgework. Maybe one day his teeth would save him from being tossed anonymously into a mass grave.

Six weeks later, leaning over Koslowski, Dr. Blebanoff explained that he would grind down the tooth behind the space and, in a week or so, the tooth in front of the space, then cover them with crowns. Crowns? Koslowski pondered. As in crowned heads? How could any such object fit on a tooth? And why destroy two more perfectly good teeth? That made no sense. But virgin that he was, he must bow to a higher authority. The dental plan at work would pay the bill.

"Why not do them both now? Get it over with."

"No, that's too much for one day."

Too much for the patient or for the dentist? The waiting room was usually empty. Perhaps Dr. Blebanoff, past retirement age, couldn't stand on his feet for long stretches, or suffered from attention-deficit disorder.

Winters had always been drafty in Blebanoff's office. Under his white smock, the dentist wore a long-sleeved knit turtleneck. As he approached, instrument in hand, he pushed up his sleeves. On the inside of his right forearm was the branded number—Koslowski had never noticed it before. It glared at him like a reminder of his own innocence, his meager pains, his easeful life. He moaned faintly, closed his eyes, and offered his open mouth to the drill.

When the dreadful noise was over, he was sickened to feel the smooth, razed stump of an inoffensive tooth. Nearby, the dentist bent over a tray and toyed with plaster and toothpicks—making a temporary crown—just as Koslowski, in kindergarten, had labored over clay statues of horses and giraffes.

At a club that evening, the crown slipped off into a nacho. Startled, he held it in his cupped hand like a live grenade.

"Oh, just stick it back in," said Lisa, and coaxed him back to the dance floor.

After the second such occurrence, he returned to Dr. Blebanoff. "Besides, it doesn't fit right."

Dr. Blebanoff ground the tooth down further. Once. Twice. Koslowski was missing hours at work. His machine blared messages of distress; his own patients weren't used to such delays.

"I can't grind any more," said the dentist. "Already it's almost like it's not there."

But it was very much there, and as he rose from the chair, a bolt of pain shot up into Koslowski's cranium and lodged there, reverberating. Concentric circles hummed around his head. Haloes, he thought, like a martyr in a medieval fresco.

"Relax, Richie. You must have bit down in a funny way."

On the subway and during the walk to his office, the reverberations gradually subsided, leaving a grainy tingle like the ebb of crashing cymbals.

"So, how's the tooth?" asked the human resources director, sauntering down the hall.

"I have this pain, I don't know what to call it. It's like nothing I've ever felt. Sort of like chalk on a blackboard."

"I know what you're talking about," she said. "There's a name for it. It's called exquisite pain. You probably need a root canal. By the way, Joe Bracco's been asking for you. They're having a problem with downloading."

Exquisite pain. After he ministered to Bracco's computer, he called Lisa, but she was out at a class. He called his mother.

"That idiot Blebanoff must have hit a nerve or something. He ruined another good tooth. And tonight's a big rehearsal."

"Blebanoff? You still go to him? He's getting old, you know. That's too bad, Richie. Take some aspirin and find someone else."

"Too bad! The jerk doesn't even wear gloves. I could get AIDS. Oh, never mind. How's Dad?"

"The same. The doctor asked him questions, like what do you call the things you wear on your feet. He got everything right," she said dryly. "Now they want to do an MRI. They put you in a closed coffin and take pictures." She paused to sigh. "Don't worry, I don't think you'll get AIDS from Blebanoff."

The exquisite pain consumed him. It was dormant except when he poked the tooth, hoping it might miraculously have vanished. But it pierced his brain like a spear. Still he kept poking, perversely reviving the sensation like an epicure craving arcane, stinging delights. Lisa recommended her dentist. State of the art. Sexy, too.

"Oh yeah? Does he turn you on? With his big drill?"

"Richie, I was only kidding. What's with you? Listen, one of my professors is going to Sarajevo this summer. They're putting together a team of lawyers and social workers to interview the women who were raped. They may take a student along to do the scut work. I'm applying. Wouldn't that be great?"

"Great," he echoed.

After releasing Koslowski from some weighty armor used for X-rays, Lisa's dentist inspected each of his teeth one by one with a measuring instrument that filled his mouth to bursting. Like a bingo host, the dentist called out numbers to the hygienist, who wrote them down. "Before you can get a bridge," he said, "I have to assess your periodontal situation." Baffled but submissive, Koslowski looked around. On the facing wall hung an enlarged copy of a letter from a first-grade class in the teacher's neat chubby print. "Dear Dr. Rodriguez, Thank you for letting us visit your office. We learned a lot and had a very good time." Below, above, and around this message, the children had scrawled their names at odd angles, using all the colors of the rainbow—Melissa, Keisha, Jared, Esteban.

The light out the window was a dreary March gray. Opposite, a brick wall. Mengele came to mind: his father claimed to have seen him once in the camp. Mengele was inspecting a row of naked women, pacing up and back and brandishing a stick, like a general reviewing his troops. You could tell he was evil by the way he twirled the stick, his father said. The image was a part of family lore.

Dr. Rodriguez looked nothing like Mengele, though. More *Miami Vice*—slick and shady, a style Koslowski was surprised could appeal to Lisa. "By the way," he said, "quite a few of your teeth need bonding. You should consider that at some point."

"Really? How many?" And what on earth was bonding?

"Eighteen." With a gentle tap, the probe arrived at Koslowski's ground-down tooth. The exquisite pain shot through his head and he levitated two inches from the chair.

Dr. Rodriguez and his hygienist exchanged a stunned, meaningful glance. "Root canal," he announced. Not in his purview: he recommended a Fifth Avenue colleague.

Dr. Callahan, the endodontist, thrust long needles deep into Koslowski's tooth. As his jaw locked into position, panic clutched him. What if his jaw stayed locked this way forever? What if the dentist couldn't get the needles out? He was puny and seemed to be yanking rather hard to remove them. Koslowski broke out in a sweat and feared he might throw up and choke. His usual remedy, devising keyboard arrangements in his head, was no help. Only with great effort could he keep from leaping out of the chair.

Koslowski was no coward. In the past he had shown exceptional courage. At college in Vermont, when fire broke out in the old house he shared with seven other students, he raced around waking his housemates, then went back inside to carry out two girls overcome by the thick smoke. At the service held for the one student who died, the president of the college publicly commended him (though mispronouncing his name, with a "w" instead of a "v"). The dean asked him to dinner and the school paper ran an article about his heroic rescue, with a large photo. His parents flew up—fire was something they took seriously—and his mother clasped him to her breast and sobbed. Then she looked so angry he thought she might slap him, big as he was. "You don't take such chances! In an emergency it's enough to save yourself." But she cut out the photo and hung it in the bedroom beside her wedding picture.

He knew there were worse things in the world than a root canal. He knew them like a litany. Civilian suffering in wartime. Political prisoners. Victims of famine and earthquakes ... But this thing, right now, was the thing that was happening to him. Still, what right had he to complain? Tomorrow his father, whose "spells" were becoming more frequent, was scheduled for the MRI in the coffin. This very minute, as he sat helpless in the chair, the news on the dentist's radio told of mass graves filled with mutilated victims discovered near Sarajevo. Koslowski gagged. Could the endodontist concentrate with such news in his ear?

"Expect some discomfort," Dr. Callahan said. "Call me if the swelling and pain don't go away in two days."

He walked along the park benumbed, past the bannered Plaza Hotel with its caravan of taxis and bustle of baggage, past the carriage horses, still in their winter wraps, pawing the ground, past uniformed doormen opening doors with a practiced flourish. He saw it all, yet his eyes were as numbed as his mouth. As he trudged the mile back to his office, the

Novocain ebbed, and an ache at the site of his murdered tooth blared in outrage.

A message from Joe Bracco awaited him. "Hey, Richie. The computers are wacko again. I thought you fixed everything. Would you get down here soon as you can? We're all jammed up."

He answered the summons and found his error. Unlike him to have overlooked something so simple. He was slipping; it was the tooth.

That night the band had a gig in a downtown club. Here he wouldn't slip. The music was safe, not in his head anywhere near the tooth, but in his blood, his marrow, the strong pads of his fingers. Luckily he wasn't a horn player— that might be a problem.

"How's it going?" Hal asked while they set up the amps.

"I just had root canal."

"The pits. Oh, sorry, no pun intended. So, are you okay? Can you do this?"

"Sure I can do it." Hadn't there been chamber orchestras in Auschwitz? Composers, operas, concerts? The words were unspoken, barely thought, yet he winced with shame at so gross a comparison. He couldn't wait to begin playing, to escape his own errant mind. And soon enough, all thought was extinguished. His mouth forgotten, he lived through his hands and ears. He was restored to himself, the self he had owned before he crunched on the olive pit. Lisa, gorgeous in black Lycra and streaming red hair, clapped and whistled from a front table. When it was over she climbed onstage to throw her arms around him. "You were great. I love to hear you play," and she took his face in her hands to kiss him.

"Ow! Don't."

"Oh, I forgot. How was it?"

"There are worse things in the world. Only right now I can't remember what they are."

"You're cute, Richie. You're such a big baby."

The next morning, as he drank hot coffee, Koslowski noticed a strange sensation. With each sip, his tooth, or what was left of it under the loose temporary crown, expanded like a living organism, a cell gone wild. Soon he would barely be able to close his jaw around the rapidly growing thing in his mouth. It was supposed to be dead, its nerve destroyed. He must be hallucinating. This was the stuff of his childhood nightmares, where innocent toys came to menacing life, assaulting and carrying off his parents while he stood by helpless.

Teeth did not grow after childhood. Koslowski knew that. But was it possible for a ground-down tooth to regenerate? He wished Lisa were home—she was the only one he could ask this absurd question. Why was she never around when he needed her most? Had she been at the party, the whole thing might not have happened. It wasn't supposed to happen—not to him, anyway. Not with his teeth. She had a cold that night, true, but she was well enough to be sitting up studying when he got home. With Lisa there, he might not have found himself next to Cara, the human rights attorney. They might have eaten later. The portions of spaghetti would have been allotted differently, with some other guest getting the lethal olive. Not that he wished such misfortune on anyone. But someone else might have detected the pit, someone with a different heritage, someone not so liable to be distracted by tales of human rights abuses offered as party chitchat.

Over take-out Chinese food that night Lisa groaned about all the papers she had to write, the exams to study for. The term was more than half over, the work at its peak. Plus the extra projects she'd taken on—the Women's Caucus that was investigating gender discrimination in academic hiring, the Harassment and Rape Advisory Center.... And the application for the summer mission to Bosnia. If she didn't get that, she'd have to hunt for a summer job and psych herself up for wearing suits and panty hose every day. Koslowski decided not to raise the question of whether teeth could grow.

Instead he called his mother. "How did the MRI go?"

"They won't have the results for a few days."

"Oh. Well, how'd he take it? I mean being closed up in the tube."

"You know him. He said it was nothing, it's all relative."

In bed, in the dark, he felt the tooth expanding. He tried various positions and found it best to lie on his back with his mouth open, even though he disliked breathing open-mouthed. But each time he woke and shifted around, it grew again. At this rate it would get so huge he'd be unable to move his tongue to call for help. He would choke, asphyxiated by his own tooth. Exhausted by panic, he plummeted into a mire of dream and recollection: soldiers in white smocks and high boots hurtled up the sands of Brighton Beach on rampaging horses, and he ran from the window to hide in the closet and gnaw at the doorframe. Peering out, he spied his mother as a child, the last living child in her family, being grasped roughly by the shoulders and forced to drink the milk from her mother's breasts. At her age, seven, it was a humiliation, but she'd be beaten if she didn't obey. She took the nipple in her mouth and gagged, but she sucked.

He woke in a cold sweat, pulled Lisa close and made love hastily with no words and no kissing.

"That was not so nice, Richie," she said mildly.

"Sorry," he grunted.

By morning the tooth had shrunk to normal size. Blessed relief. So it was all an illusion, a brief episode of madness. But as he stood up and moved around, it began to grow again. Hot coffee, especially, made it grow, like watering a plant.

Dr. Rodriguez was puzzled. He gave Koslowski a curious glance and said the feeling would probably go away. Meanwhile, the results of the periodontal exam were dismaying. "You can't build a bridge in sand. No reputable dentist would make you a bridge until you attend to your gums." Koslowski left in disbelief, holding a card with the periodontist's name.

"He can't build a bridge in sand?" Lisa echoed. "Sand! I don't mean to laugh, Richie, but it is funny. Look, don't start with all that gum stuff. Just go to someone else."

"You recommended him. You said he turned you on."

"You're losing it, you know? Like, I'm really sorry this is happening, but I've got to work now. Oh, what about your dad? How did the MRI go?"

"They don't have the results yet. But they can't be good," he said glumly. "It's probably a brain tumor."

Night after night in the dark, his tooth grew, while he lay overwhelmed by the obscene mystery in his mouth, fearing for his sanity. But he said nothing; his friends in the band and at work frowned when he mentioned teeth, as if he were complaining of a hangnail. Everyone had had dental work—they rolled their eyes and cited their abscesses, their infected gums and impacted wisdom teeth—but no one took it seriously. No matter. Pain was subjective. For his part, he understood suffering now, not only physical suffering but the intangible anguish of the mad. Those periodic news items about ordinary men who went berserk and murdered their loved ones: a nice guy, the neighbors always said; he greeted us on the street, he liked to wash his car on Sundays...

He took Lisa's advice and consulted another dentist, recommended by the human resources director at work. Muzak from the office speakers, a bad sign. Dr. Olafson was intrigued by his bite. "Click your teeth together," he commanded, "and listen to the sound. Okay, now listen when I do it. Do you hear the difference? The two sides of your jaw don't meet simultaneously the way mine do." With his musician's ear, Koslowski clearly heard the nanosecond of discrepancy. "So, what does that mean?" "I'd have to grind down one side before I could make any bridge. Otherwise you'll start getting headaches. Maybe you already do." Indeed, a headache was coming on.

His worst fears were borne out. His father had a brain tumor. Koslowski rushed to Brighton Beach as soon as he heard the news.

"Don't bury me yet," said the elder Koslowski in his gruff way. "They make mistakes all the time. If they were sure, they'd have me on the table cutting my head open. Why can't they just give me something for the headaches?"

Koslowski looked mutely at his mother. He must defer to her, but he hoped she wouldn't insist on the truth. Why labor to convince a man he was dying if he chose to think otherwise? Especially as the doctors found him too far gone for any remedy.

"Take the pills you have," she said evenly, "and I'll call tomorrow and ask them for something stronger."

"They make me groggy, and when I wake up the headache is still there. If I'm too groggy I can't drive to work."

"You can't drive, period. They said it's dangerous."

"I'll decide that. They're only doctors. They're not the law."

"So," Koslowski asked when his father went to lie down, "what do they expect will happen?"

"He'll deteriorate, they said. They can't tell how soon. They said to take one day at a time." She made a wry face. "Deteriorate."

He agreed it was an ugly word. Unbearable, in fact. And yet his father seemed as forthright and irascible as ever. Maybe he was right. Doctors had been known to make mistakes. Tests could be misinterpreted. "We'll manage, Mom. We'll get through this all right."

She smiled wanly. Koslowski knew now that what he used to call her martyred look was merely patient desolation. She had lost one husband already, ages ago back in Leningrad. Killed on the job when a scaffolding collapsed. She'd felt crushed herself, she used to say. So crushed under a cloud of gloom that she had to get away. Even if the cloud followed her, at least it would be in a new sky. And somehow she had managed to persuade a distant relative in New York to sponsor her passage. Once she was there, rumor had it, the new world would not send her back. But where could she go now?

She patted his hand as if he were a boy. "Dying," she said, "everyone gets through. I only hope he doesn't suffer too much."

She must have looked this way when she first arrived, barely speaking English, and the only work she could find was cleaning office buildings. Koslowski could imagine his father, who worked in one of those offices, being drawn to her sallow face, her thin, tense body bent over the mop and pail. He had expected to brood alone forever, but must have sensed that with her he needn't give up his nourishing bitterness. He felt at home with her misery; he wanted to live with whatever had carved the hollows in her cheeks.

By chance, the periodontist's office was right next door to Dr. Callahan's, the root canal man. Was it truly chance, or was he in the toils of a dental cabal? Dr. Dahlberg, barely older than Koslowski himself, had officious little wire-rimmed glasses and an ashy, pursed face, like Mengele. But he was short and stout, which was not the way Koslowski remembered Mengele. Or rather, the way his father remembered him. In a high, nasal voice, he pronounced Koslowski's periodontal situation grave indeed. Lots of "pockets" in which food could be trapped, rotting the teeth. He would have to undertake a series of deep gum cleanings, one "quadrant" of the mouth each week, with Novocain to get at the remoter places. Then he would decide if surgery were required. He also recommended, in passing, that Koslowski have all his wisdom teeth removed.

He listened in a daze, his eyes fixed on a poster with bouncy red letters, some of them shaped like teeth: "Be True to Your Teeth or Your Teeth Will Be False to You." Could these be his excellent teeth the creep was describing? He, with his superior dental legacy, his stellar record? His very identity was being denied. But he must hold fast to reason, and to his goal: the bridge. If his gums were sand, it followed that they must be shored up. Beyond reason, some obscure impulse drove him on. He was embarked on a process, a kind of quest, that must take its course, stage through wretched stage.

After the second week of periodontal cleaning, the human resources director called him in for a conference.

"We know you're the best in the business, Richie, but you're getting careless. Is something the matter?"

"No, nothing," he mumbled. "I'll get it together."

"You do that. Things are getting backed up. We can't afford that, you know."

Nor could Koslowski afford to have his job at risk. The dental bills took his breath away, but the human resources director had taken special pains to intercede on his behalf with the dental plan.

On the third visit, when Dr. Dahlberg exultantly held up a tiny brown shred dug from the upper reaches of his gums—"See? See what I found in there?"—Koslowski knew the man was mad. But he couldn't turn back. He was trapped in the process, a maze with no exit in sight. The dentist's white brick building itself resembled a sinister mound of teeth, and its very slow elevator and pristine halls, their sleek doors bearing plaques for polysyllabic medical services, grew more eerie with each visit. Even the familiar sights of Central Park—the traffic, the horses in bondage, the kiosks, the children tottering on the jungle gyms in the first bright days of spring—seemed full of peril. He saw it all through the prism of his battered jaw, the walks back downtown drenched in Novocain.

Throughout, his father's condition was unchanged. "What about the driving?"

"The car's in the shop," his mother said. "The transmission. It may take a while to get the parts. Maybe never."

She was nothing if not resourceful. This was the woman who had gotten herself to Brighton Beach a decade before the wave of emigrants. "How'd you manage that?"

"I fiddled with a few wires under the hood. It was easy. I have a car service taking him to work. Who knows how long he'll be going. Anyway, he likes it. No hassle."

That night in the piano bar, he abandoned the old favorites and indulged himself with Ellington and Thelonius Monk. No one paid much attention either way, and it eased his mind. The owner, a dapper old man with a fondness for Koslowski, liked it too. "Nice, Richie. Very nice. Gives a touch of class. Not every night, but once in a while it's fine."

After the final week, Dr. Dahlberg said that surgery was needed in several areas.

"Only where the bridge goes," growled Koslowski through clenched teeth.

"Sit very still now," he ordered during the surgery. "I'm going to scrape off a bit of bone."

"Wait just a minute. What do you mean, scraping off my bone?"

The periodontist smirked. "Do you want me to put up a mirror so you can criticize the whole procedure?"

Fuck you, Koslowski longed to say. But the lunatic's hands were in his mouth.

He left with two strips of gray putty, makeshift Band-Aids, on his gums, and a printed sheet of post-operative instructions for daily rinsing and compresses. In his Novocain haze, he felt at one with the dour horses, shuffling through the park in their abject servitude. He'd lost weight; his pants needed pressing; he needed a haircut. He probably looked as wretched as his father when he first arrived at the age of nineteen, scrawny and enraged after months in the camp. If he held out a Styrofoam cup, he thought, people might just drop coins in.

In bed, when Lisa read him a newspaper article about the rape victims in Bosnia, he said, "I feel raped too."

"What are you talking about? You're doing this by choice."

"It doesn't feel that way. Those hands in my mouth. It feels like something I've been sentenced to, I don't know why. First it was just an accident. Then it became my destiny."

"Richie, don't you know the difference between oral surgery and being raped by a troop of soldiers?"

"I guess not."

"You're sick, you know? You should get help." She barricaded herself behind the paper.

He didn't need help. He was someone who gave help. Not only in the dormitory fire. The subway accident three years ago: he was working as a computer doctor for a large chain and roamed the city on house calls. Just over the Brooklyn Bridge, the speeding train heaved and veered, then crashed maniacally to a halt that tossed the passengers out of their seats. The lights went out. People shrieked. Koslowski, on the floor but unhurt, felt around for the howling baby who'd been opposite him and managed, in the dark, to set the stroller upright and get him back in it. He urged people to try to find seats and stop yelling. When a conductor with a flashlight appeared and began to restore order, Koslowski helped the baby's grandmother to her feet. He soothed a whimpering boy, then carried an injured old man along the tracks to the next station, a quarter of a mile away, where emergency medical workers awaited them. His mother saved the small item in the paper that cited his deeds. All that could be seen of him in the photo was a leg and an arm: he was helping to raise a woman onto a stretcher.

When the putty was removed a week later, Koslowski was aghast at the new configuration in his mouth. It was no longer the mouth he had lived with so intimately for thirty-two years, but an alien mouth with cavernous spaces between the teeth, big enough for a grain of rice. Against his specific directions, the periodontist had left a gaping space between two front teeth, marring his distinctive smile. The man had deformed him, mutilated this most private part of his body—irreparably, he was told when he demanded a reversal. He protested vehemently. Food would lodge in the spaces. He would have discomfort forever. His body, his material being, his very essence had been violated. "Don't you understand what you've done?"

The dentist stared as if he were a nut case. Everything he had done was necessary and therapeutic, he said; he did it all the time. It was imperative to raise the gum line. If Koslowski didn't like the space in front, he could have the tooth capped.

"Go to hell." As he walked through the park he devised excruciating tortures for Dr. Dahlberg, involving the soft, generative parts of his body, which he imagined as small and ineffectual. Mengele, he thought, where are you now that I need you?

Rage was energizing. He strode quickly past the captive horses, his strength resurgent. He would live with the mutilated mouth the way people lived with disabilities. He knew plenty of disabled people. A boy at school had been a thalidomide baby with flippers instead of arms; he went on to become a biogeneticist. The bass player in the band had lost an eye in the Gulf War and wore a black patch; he was jaunty and uncomplaining. Right this minute a young woman in a motorized wheelchair was speeding nimbly through traffic on Central Park South. She was luscious, with dark skin and amber corn rows. Koslowski stared until she was out of sight.

Be a man, he told himself, even as he felt the tooth growing in its maddening way. He called in sick and got a haircut. He bought two pairs of pants. He paused at a store window full of tennis rackets, basketballs, sneakers, hard shiny Rollerblades. The customers going in and out were breezy and muscular. He too had had that resolute air, not so long ago. Straightening up, he went in.

"I'd like to try on some Rollerblades."

A genial West Indian sales clerk brought out several pairs. "Ever skate before?"

"Not on these. But I ice-skate."

"You should be okay, then. Go on, try them out."

He got to his feet and slowly skated around on the polished floorboards with the three clerks cheering him on—"Go, man, go!"—even when he stumbled and nearly overturned a rack of sweatsuits. He pretended he was on ice skates and the floor was ice. Long ago, his mother would take him skating on the lake in Prospect Park. When she was six, she told him, she could already zip around on the canals and the frozen Neva. That was before the Germans surrounded the city. After, they had to cut holes in the ice and lower buckets for water, with luck catch a fish, then hunt up enough wood for a fire in the stove. One morning when she was sent out to find wood, or scraps, or anything at all, she saw blackened holes and ridges in the huge columns of the cathedral, stone columns so thick they had seemed impermeable. Shelled during the night. And as if transfixed by memory, she would stare out the window at the churning, unfreezable Atlantic.

He left the store with a pair of very expensive skates and the knee, wrist, and elbow guards to match, all black and hard and gleaming.

"Blades?" asked Lisa. "How come?"

"Why not? You could get a pair too. We'll go together. It's spring!" He hugged her, but she stood impassive.

"I don't think so. It looks dangerous."

"So let's live more dangerously!"

He took readily to the skates. As skater rather than sufferer, he zoomed through Central Park, claiming and detoxifying the paths he had trod in misery, reclaiming his life. His father was feeling better too—the new pills were working; he'd known all along it was nothing serious. His mother's reports were less sanguine. Yes, in a way he seemed better, but he wasn't himself. "He has moods, up and down. He forgets things, he gets mixed up." Well, his father was over seventy. It was only natural.

For skating company Koslowski had his tapes and Walkman. Lisa never joined him. They barely had time to talk, she was so busy with her studies and projects. Too tired even for love, most nights. And she never asked about his tooth.

It still grew during his waking hours and shrank back to size by morning, and this continued to terrify him. But the terror was familiar now. It was possible to live with terror, he discovered, to accommodate it and find a place for it, like keeping a snarling beast locked in the basement rather than giving it the run of the house. You heard its snarls, and you had to toss down some meat once in a while, that was all.

Each morning he would probe the root canal area with his tongue to test for pain. One day he noticed a nasty taste coming from the spot where the needles had been thrust, as if something noxious were dripping down from the cavity around his brain. The next day, during his reconnoitering, he felt a sore bump under his gum, the size of a pea.

He missed work again to have the cyst surgically removed.

"How does the tooth feel?" Dr. Callahan asked. "Does it hurt if you tap it with a fingernail?"

Koslowski tapped. It hurt slightly, perhaps no more than reasonably, given its recent ordeal. What degree of pain was worth acknowledging? Reporting? In the realm of pain, too, he was a virgin, lacking all sense of possibility: height and depth, scale and proportion, subjective and objective. "It still hurts a little, I guess."

"In that case I'd better do the root canal again, as long as I'm going back in. You can't get a bridge if it still hurts."

What could he do but submit? But as the needles dug deep into his head, maybe his brain, it struck him that Callahan might be another madman, injecting toxic fluid for some insane research project. He'd read of shocking experiments performed down South on unwitting subjects, mostly black men, in the name of research. That was years ago, of course, but still... Maybe the dental cabal didn't like his name.

"By the way, I'm doing a bone graft. You have, what can I call it, mushy bone. Sorry to use such an unpleasant term, but it's the simplest way to describe it to a layman. Strange that it still hurts. It looks like a perfect root canal."

In his drugged state, he hailed a taxi to speed him to work—six dollars and twenty cents in midtown traffic. He handed the driver a twenty, but found he couldn't calculate the tip; the numbers lurched and jostled in a mind befogged. He struggled to think: a dollar and a quarter seemed about right, which would make the total ... seven forty-five? Right. Say seven fifty. But how much change to request? As he faltered, the driver reached back and put a pile of bills and coins in his palm. Koslowski stared at the money. It seemed less than he should have received, but he couldn't manage to count it, couldn't assemble it in his mind. Was this milky fog what his father felt all the time, behind his brash, valiant denials? Was this how madness clawed away the mind?

Horns honked behind them. He thrust a bill and some coins at the driver. On the street, he studied the five and few singles that remained in his hand. Had he been shortchanged, or had he mistakenly given the driver a five or ten instead of a one? He stood on the sidewalk straining to make sense of it all, then gave up in despair. Tears blurred his eyes. Through them, he pictured a straggly crew of bony men moving piles of sand from one end of a barren field to the other. His father, very young, was among them. The sun was broiling hot and his father's head was pounding. He wasn't trying to figure anything out, just doing the task required to live to the next day. His resilient father had managed to live. And not only to live, but to thrive: to go through night school and become an accountant. He, Koslowski, could barely live through a root canal and handle a short taxi ride. He would never have come out of there alive. Never. He was made of weaker stuff.

At the piano bar that evening he soothed himself with a medley of Scott Joplin and Scarlatti improvisations. An older woman with ash-gray hair and diamond earrings stopped on her way out. "Let's see your hands," she said, and ran a finger along the tops. "Very nice hands. Where else do you play?" This happened from time to time; women found his faintly foreign look and off-center smile appealing, though the smile, since Dr. Dahlberg, was not all it had been. Sometimes he told Lisa, if the approach had been unusual. The woman dropped a ten-dollar bill in the tips glass on the piano. With this windfall Koslowski bought two bunches of daffodils at the all-night deli on the corner.

Lisa was still at the computer, finishing her paper about the division of assets in divorce cases. She flipped on the screen saver, a quote from Margaret Fuller: "We would have every path laid open to Woman as freely as to Man." "I see why lawyers are so nasty," she sighed. "They get traumatized just trying to survive law school. How'd it go tonight?"

"Fine." He wouldn't, after all, make an amusing story of the fifty-year-old woman. Lisa would say there was nothing laughable about a woman asserting her sexuality at any age—so long as he didn't take her up on it. He presented the flowers.

"They're beautiful. Thanks. What's the matter? Your face is a little swollen."

He confessed to the second root canal.

"Richie! Why can't you let it alone? Give it a chance to heal. You're into some kind of, I don't know, like masochism. You don't have to go along with everything they say. They'll do anything for money, especially if you don't protest."

"Calm down, okay? It's too late. It's done."

He persuaded Lisa to take a late-April Sunday off. They rode bikes in the park, ate hot dogs and ice cream, danced to music in the band shell. They lay on the grass, his head in her lap, and spoke loving words, as they had not done in months. In the evening they rented an old movie: Tallulah Bankhead and a half-dozen other stars were marooned in a lifeboat in mid-Atlantic, their ship blown up by a German sub. There was no escaping the war. The best old movies were inspired by it. William Bendix's wounded leg was infected, and the only way to save his life was by prompt amputation. Tallulah Bankhead proffered her bottle of brandy to dull the pain—more comfort, Koslowski thought, than his father had had when they chopped off his frozen finger.

He fell asleep in awe of William Bendix's bravery in submitting to the knife and awoke charged with clarity and vigor. If William Bendix could sacrifice a leg, he could sacrifice the accursed tooth. It was corrupting his mind, spewing wretchedness and confusion. He must be rid of it. Excise it, like a tumor. Exorcise it. Once it was out, all would be well. The life he had led before the olive pit would be restored. He would play his music and love Lisa and skate: his lucky life. True, he'd be missing two teeth in his upper jaw, but he could get a little removable bridge of the kind Dr. Blebanoff had shown him months ago. In his ignorance he had rejected it out of hand, but he'd learned a lot since then. So what if the bridge symbolized old age and decrepitude; it was better than obsession and paranoia. Years from now he might look back on the whole nightmare with serenity, even amusement. Though just now he could hardly recall how life had felt before the accident.

Dr. Callahan agreed it was a wise, if hasty, decision. "We do all we can to save a tooth," he said gravely, "but sometimes a tooth can't be saved." He paused to emphasize the philosophic import of his words.

"Right. I get it. Can you do it today?"

"I don't pull teeth. I'm an endodontist." He recommended a colleague in dental surgery, Dr. Fisher.

Koslowski dreaded the appointed hour—the exorcism—recalling all too well the mortifying battle with old Blebanoff over the first tooth. A needless dread, as it turned out. Dr. Fisher, a tall, stooped man whose world-weary face was lit by intelligence, administered a deft shot in the arm. Before Koslowski could fully savor the glorious well-being conferred by intravenous Valium, the dentist announced he was finished. The tooth was out.

"Already?" No yanking, no struggle?

"The Valium distorts your sense of time."

"Well, can you see what was wrong with it?"

"There doesn't seem to be anything wrong with the tooth." Dr. Fisher shrugged. "Sometimes teeth hurt and we can't figure out why. It could be referred pain."

"Referred pain?"

"That means the place where it hurts is not the source of the trouble. The source of the trouble is somewhere else."

"Where?"

Dr. Fisher shrugged to signify ignorance. Dentists, Koslowski noted, had in common a tendency to shrug.

"So where is it? My tooth, I mean."

"Now?"

"Yes." He needed to see the thing that had caused such grief yet might be innocent after all. Was it callously dumped in the shiny stainless steel trash can, or heaped on a shelf with others that had met the same fate? For all he knew, there were mountains of teeth concealed in the office, like the mountains of shoes and suitcases...

With tiny tongs, Dr. Fisher plucked something from the counter, placed it on a tissue and brought it to Koslowski, like displaying a jewel on its velvet bed. His tooth. It was larger than he expected—the bulk of it, with its two tiny tusks, had been concealed under the gums.

"Okay, thanks."

"Do you want it?"

"No."

"Just for ... closure?" Dr. Fisher said with irony.

"Yes." And they exchanged a comradely smile.

"They say people who lose loved ones do much better later on if they actually see the body being buried. Then they know for sure. It's easier to accept, somehow."

Koslowski nodded, grateful for this knowing, subtle man.

He left with a new bloody hole in his mouth and the usual instructions for post-surgical care. When Lisa saw him gargling with salt water at the bathroom sink, she grunted and moved on in silence. She didn't need to speak; he knew what she thought. Later she told him she'd been offered a place in the group going to Bosnia. She'd be leaving in less than two months.

"Terrific. That's just what you wanted."

"I know. But now that I'm really going ..."

"You're having second thoughts?"

"No, I definitely want to go. I'm just ... scared, I guess."

"You'll do fine. Only I'll miss you."

When his new bloody hole was healed, Koslowski explained to Dr. Eng, recommended by Joe Bracco at work, what he wanted: the removable device Dr. Blebanoff had displayed. The atmosphere in Dr. Eng's office was promising. Chopin nocturnes played softly in the background, and a photo on the wall showed a benign domestic tableau: two small boys, presumably the young Engs, romping in a plastic backyard pool.

"No way," said Dr. Eng. "They're not used anymore. Maybe in Europe or Asia. But no reputable dentist here would make you one."

"Why not?"

"Well, for one thing, you could swallow it."

"Oh, I'm sure I wouldn't swallow it." Koslowski's heart thumped in frustration.

Eng was adamant. However doting a father, he was an exacting dentist. He proposed instead a plastic plate that would extend over the roof of the mouth and hook on to the teeth on the other side.

Koslowski fought down a wave of nausea. "How much will it cost?" he blurted out. "Because I'm not sure the insurance will keep covering all this."

"Around two hundred fifty dollars."

Two weeks later, to the syncopated sounds of Poulenc, he was presented with a large and hideous pink thing, gleaming and nacreous like a polished seashell, with two teeth wired onto one end. As he opened to receive it, his throat constricted and his guts heaved in protest. He knew, the way he knew his own name, his own history, that he should not be submitting to this violation. But how could he retreat? He was lost in an alien land; he didn't know the language or the customs. In such circumstances people submit to anything, out of confusion and terror, ignorance and powerlessness, all of which engulfed him.

"Keep it wet when you're not using it," said Dr. Eng. That, Koslowski knew, meant keeping it in a glass of water overnight. He had spied Sonya's grandmother's teeth once, sunk in a tumbler beside the couch where she was napping:

a moment of comic horror. Teeth belonged in mouths. Anywhere else, they became grotesque.

"You won't be able to chew most things with it," Dr. Eng said with satisfaction.

"What do you mean, most things? Like what?"

"It's plastic. It can cut about as much as a plastic fork. I made one for my father-in-law, and he wanted to use it to chew. What do you expect? I told him. It's plastic."

Why, Koslowski wondered, should he be condemned to the same fate as Dr. Eng's father-in-law, surely a much older man, a man perhaps with no alternative, with a mouth full of bloody holes.

"Wear it a little longer each day to get used to it. If you want, you can remove it when you eat."

He mumbled a hasty good-bye. He wouldn't be returning, despite the dentist's good taste in music. Eng had been revealed as one of the enemy.

Lisa grimaced when she saw it. "It's like the bite plate I had when I was twelve years old. A torture instrument. You're not really going to wear it, are you?"

"What else can I do? I can't get a real bridge until six months after the root canal. Meanwhile ..."

"Meanwhile you're on this weird trip. It's creepy. I mean, people like your father were forced to submit on pain of death. But with you it's some kind of perverted ... What are you trying to prove?"

Dinner that night—they went out to celebrate three years of being together—was a disaster. With his tongue he tried furtively and in vain to dislodge the bits of spinach that crept beneath the plate. The linguini deposited pasty lumps all over the plastic on the roof of his mouth, and the slippery texture of the clams was defeating.

"I'm not very hungry, actually. I had a late lunch."

Lisa glared. Koslowski regarded the inviting food in front of him: he alone was excluded from this most ordinary of human pleasures. And he had brought it on himself.

No. A gross cosmic error had been made. Stop! You have the wrong man, he screamed silently, like a prisoner led to the torture chamber. Others might have to wear such devices, but they had bad teeth and must suffer the consequences. He wasn't meant for this. He was lucky—hadn't his parents always said so? Hadn't he escaped unscathed from the fire and the subway wreck? And he was entitled to his luck. He, after all, was the designated beneficiary of his parents' investment of pain, was he not? The new-world heir to their untouched capital of good luck?

In the bathroom at home, he struggled to pry the thing from his mouth.

"Oh, great. Why didn't you take the fucking thing out before?" Lisa said. "It ruined the whole evening. It's ruining everything."

"It would never have happened in the first place if you'd come to that party. You weren't all that sick."

"Am I hearing you right? It's all my fault?"

"I'm not saying it's your fault. But it's true it wouldn't have happened."

"Leave me alone, would you? Get out of my life. You're not the same person you used to be. You're freaked out."

She sat up late finishing an overdue paper, then took her pillow and slept on the couch. Koslowski seethed.

An hour later, chastened by remorse, he tiptoed to the couch, apologized, and curled up beside her. The seed of resentment took firmer root in his heart. Like anyone shamed, he watered it with unshed tears. From then on he removed the plate for meals and kept the glass of water, its nocturnal home, concealed in a night-table drawer.

Dr. Eng's bill was not two hundred fifty dollars but seven hundred. Despite the intervention of the human resources director, the dental plan, thus far obliging, refused to pay more than the original estimate. How misleading had been that photo of the frolicking children. Never again would he be deceived by a cheap display of sentiment. Nor would he pay more than two-fifty: let Eng sue for the rest.

He had daydreams of cutting the plate with a miniature saw so that only the two teeth and their wires remained. Late one night after a rehearsal, he placed it on a carving board in the kitchen and held a sharp knife over it. He lowered the knife until it grazed the pink surface and kept it there for some moments. But his nerve failed him. Dentistry was a tricky business—he was living proof. He didn't trust himself to do the job right.

The knife in his hand felt good, though, and he gripped it until an idea struck him.

"I think we need some time together before you go off," he said the next night. "How about if we went to Italy first? Just a week, say. Maybe Rome? I'll put it on a card. Then you can go on from there."

Lisa hesitated an instant. "That sounds nice. But what about your father? What if he gets worse and they need you?"

"I called this morning. It's fine." Go now, his mother had said, while things aren't too bad yet. "Okay? I'll make all the arrangements. You've got enough to do."

He had feared, when Lisa said, Get out of my life, that she meant it literally. But she seemed to have forgotten her harsh words. On the plane, they raised the armrest dividing them and fooled around under a blanket. Koslowski felt calm, in command of his distress. He had a plan. Okay, so maybe no reputable American dentist would make a removable bridge—hard to believe, but never mind. Dr. Eng had let drop that such a device might be extant in Europe. Rome is in Europe, Koslowski syllogized. Ergo, he would get the bridge in Rome. Europeans, with their long, complex and bloody history, would not be daunted by the unlikely danger of someone swallowing a small plastic object. Or by the risk of bizarre lawsuits.

Their first day in Rome, while Lisa slept off her jet lag, he called the American consulate and got the names of three English-speaking dentists; he envisioned a mellow, urbane Italian, someone like Dr. Fisher, the dental surgeon. A man who would bring old-world esprit to his case.

Only one of the three could see him immediately: Dr. Habemeyer. Habemeyer? That didn't sound Italian. But he would not be foiled; no doubt there were reasons why an Italian might be named Habemeyer. After all, he was an American named Koslowski, which most people initially mispronounced.

"I have an appointment tomorrow," he told Lisa as they spooned up coffee granitas in an outdoor café opposite the Pantheon. He avoided the word "tooth," dreading her ire, yet he had to account for his absence.

"What kind of appointment?"

Her reaction was a surprise. "An Italian dentist? That's cool! Maybe he'll fix you up so you can forget teeth and get back to your life. Can I come? I'd like to see what an Italian dentist's office is like."

With Lisa along, the excursion felt almost like a lark. They took a circuitous route, strolling through the piazzas and climbing the Spanish Steps. Their destination turned out to be an august old building in the heart of Rome, studded with magnificent stonework. They stroked the wrought-iron curlicues of the elevator and admired the elaborately carved ceiling of the waiting room. The shapes of the ancient velvet-covered chairs blurred in the dim light. How far from the streamlined plastic waiting rooms Koslowski had grown accustomed to! The receptionist, even with her minimal English, was courteous, as if he were an honored guest. Ah, the old world. For a forgetful instant he wished he had been born here.

Before long he was summoned, leaving Lisa behind to leaf through an Italian fashion magazine. The dentist had pale mottled skin and wiry tufts of sandy hair. He spoke English, as the consulate had promised, but not with an Italian accent. German, unmistakably. Laurence Olivier in *Marathon Man* flashed to mind. But this was no movie, and anyhow it was too late. The dentist waved him to the chair.

Prejudice aside, Koslowski found Dr. Habemeyer's manner graceless, his probings clumsy. He interrupted the examination several times to bark into the phone, dealing at length with what appeared to be personal matters. Yet with all that, he offered a lucid analysis.

"I understand your situation. You have three options regarding this space. One: leave it alone. Two: have a permanent bridge made. Three: get implants. Each of these options has advantages and disadvantages. The first option is self-explanatory. The second option would mean grinding down two more teeth—"

Koslowski shook his head vigorously.

"However," Dr. Habemeyer continued, unregarding, "the two teeth left in back might not support a bridge."

He began describing implants and their attendant surgery, but Koslowski's mind fogged over at the very thought. "Can't you make me a removable little bridge?"

"Certainly." Koslowski's heart skipped a beat. "I do it all the time, but it would be expensive and would take several weeks. How long will you be here?"

"Six more days."

"In that case," said the dentist, as if it were the most casual thing in the world, "I can cut this one down to what you want."

Koslowski almost sprang from the chair. Cut it! Just what he had so often contemplated with the kitchen knife. And he had thought it a rash notion born of hysteria.

"Yes! Cut it! But," he added boldly, "be careful. It cost a lot of money." He gave a weak little laugh.

Merely raising a bushy eyebrow at the imputation, Dr. Habemeyer produced a miniature saw, the embodiment of Koslowski's fantasies, set the plate on a plastic tray, and began sawing away. Vengeful pleasure warmed Koslowski's innards as he watched Dr. Eng's work being destroyed, or at least humbled beyond recognition. Dr. Habemeyer dusted off the remains, which resembled what Dr. Blebanoff had so unceremoniously removed from his mouth, and Koslowski opened wide. A small click signaled success. The cost, millions of lire, translated to seventy-five dollars, which he paid gladly.

He sailed out of the office holding Lisa's hand. On the hot street he picked her up and swung her around.

"Richie! I haven't seen you this happy in months."

"I'm delirious. It's a new world."

"All because you have a bridge that fits?"

"Yes!"

"Well, that's great. I'm really glad. I wish everyone's problems could be solved so easily. What was the guy like?"

"A mad scientist type. Not exactly a winning personality, but okay. German. Imagine that!"

"What do you mean?"

"I mean, of all the dentists, a German is the one who helps me. It felt creepy to have his fingers in my mouth."

She didn't answer right away. "Okay, I get it, but I really hate when you talk like that."

"Oh, come off the p.c. pedestal. Can't you relax even for a minute?"

"Can't *I* relax? I'm not the one who won't let go. Doesn't it ever end?"

"Listen, let's not spoil things, okay? He was fine. He was terrific. So maybe his grandfather gassed my grandfather, but what the hell? He fixed my teeth. I'm so grateful I'm ready to overlook everything."

Lisa stared as if he were a stranger. "You are truly appalling. But ... let's just drop it for now. Where to?"

They gadded about Rome all day and ate a splendid dinner. Koslowski chewed carefully because the bridge was slightly loose and jiggled on contact with food. At night they went dancing; with no words, with music and wine, they unearthed the old affinity. They held hands on the way back to the pensione, and Lisa mused aloud about the women she'd be interviewing: their shame, their reticence, their future. What would become of their babies, who would be forever marked?

"You're just the right person for this," he said. "You'll do a terrific job."

"Maybe, but that's not really the point. It would be better if it didn't have to be done at all."

She saw him off at the airport—she'd be leaving for Bosnia the next day. They embraced, but when Koslowski turned back for a last look, she was already hurrying away. He stood a moment, willing her to feel his glance, then went on. Well, she couldn't help being preoccupied. He tried to imagine what awaited her, but he was so relieved to have the gap filled, the mad growth—madder in the absence of the tooth—held in check, that the suffering of others eluded him. He would think about the Muslim women tomorrow.

On the plane, he helped a blonde girl across the aisle hoist her huge backpack into the overhead bin and nodded to his seatmate, an elderly man in Bermuda shorts who was already half asleep. He plugged in the earphones and took refuge in Schubert: *Death and the Maiden.*

Its final movement was interrupted by a voice in his ear: "Good afternoon, folks, this is Captain Riley. I hope you're having a pleasant flight. I just wanted to alert you that we've lost the use of an engine and will be landing in Paris in about half an hour. We'll keep you posted if there are any new developments."

Paris! Koslowski unplugged. Could this be dangerous? Probably not. These big planes have engines to spare. Assuming the pilot was telling the whole truth. He glanced at his neighbor, fast asleep, and wished Lisa were beside him. No, if anything bad were to happen, better that she was safe. A flight attendant approached, pushing the laden cart: service as usual. He bought a beer and found the crossword puzzle in the flight magazine. No point in worrying—it was out of his hands. Maybe they'd be held over in Paris and he could have a quick look around.

Moments later he glanced up and noticed the blonde girl across the aisle, the one with the enormous bag. She sat rigid, staring straight ahead, her hands twisting in her lap, tears rolling down her cheeks.

Koslowski leaned toward her. "Hey, what's the trouble? Can I do something?"

She turned slowly, just her head, not her body. Her hair was the gold of legend, short and straight, curving into her neck. Her face was creamy, her eyes green and wet. She wore a white tank top and khaki shorts. Her lips trembled. "It's nothing."

"Come on." He smiled. "It's something. Is it what the pilot just said? Are you scared?" She was just a kid, traveling alone. The Indian woman beside her was asleep.

"I think I'm going to die. I'm sure of it." She wiped her cheeks with a fist.

"No way. We'll be in Paris before you know it. There's no real danger."

"How do you know?"

"I just do. These planes have four engines, and they're designed so they can run on two."

"What if another engine goes?"

"That's not too likely. They build them carefully. The pilots don't want to die either. Look, there are two empty seats. Let's sit there, and you can help me with this puzzle."

Still trembling, she followed him. What if she were right? Koslowski thought. Well, at least death in a plane crash would merit respect, unlike dental work. Headlines all over the world. His parents would change their minds about how lucky he was. He turned to the girl. No, she didn't seem the type who would enjoy macabre wit.

"They said Paris in half an hour," she wailed. "It's more than that now. We're going so slow, it's like we're hardly moving. Like we could just drop out of the sky."

It was true; they were going very slowly. "Let's not think about it, okay?" he said. "Let's finish the puzzle. Do you know any geography? A mountain range in Russia?"

The plane began its descent, which felt labored and ponderous. The girl—Jody, she told him with a sniffle—grabbed Koslowski's arm, and despite himself, he tensed for the impact. It's not going to happen, he thought. It's not my destiny.

A soft bump, a surge and roar, and the air filled with applause, with gusts of held-in breath. Jody fell sobbing into Koslowski's arms. Around them, people hugged and congratulated themselves on being alive. Even the flight attendants, who had remained crisp and smiling throughout, looked relieved.

In the airport lounge, a festive air reigned. Strangers chatted like old friends. Koslowski, in a gregarious mood, found that many of the passengers, including his former seatmate, were members of a senior citizens' Baptist church group returning from a fifteen-day tour. Only Jody, pale and trembling, as if they still might perish, clung to him and spoke to no one.

"God was with us," a stout, white-haired woman said jovially. "We were praying with all our might. It's all right now, dear," she exhorted Jody. "Cheer up. The Lord takes care of his own."

Perhaps he could hand her over to this motherly woman? But it was clear she wouldn't leave his side.

He shepherded her through the process of lining up, first for buses to take them to a nearby hotel for the night (the plane would be repaired and depart the next morning), then for room assignments. The group was served a chicken dinner in the hotel dining room at large round tables. The mood was bright, with much mention of God's will, and the meal, if not up to Parisian standards, was more than adequate. Compared to a malfunctioning aircraft, everything was fine, even Christian fundamentalism, even Koslowski's teeth and the loose bridge. He drank two glasses of free wine, and Jody, too, perked up with a few sips. Minutes after they said goodnight in the hall, as Koslowski prepared to undress, came a knock on his door.

Jody stood there in an embroidered powder-blue Chinese robe, clutching her room key.

"Everything okay?" he asked.

"I'm still scared." She stared up at him, open-mouthed. "Can I stay with you?"

He took a deep breath. What did she mean, exactly? Could he refuse? He opened the door wider and she slipped past him.

"I was just about to—"

"Go ahead. Whatever. I'll get into bed, okay?" She smiled coyly and removed her robe. She was wearing a peach-colored baby-doll nightie with a strip of white lace at the bottom and white ribbons at the top. Lisa slept naked or in his t-shirts. It was some years since he had confronted a woman in a sexy nightgown. "What's your name again? I was so nervous on the plane, I forgot."

"Richard. My friends call me Richie."

"So isn't this better than being alone, Richie? I mean, it's been such an awful day, I figured, why not ..."

"I'll be right back." He took his carry-on bag and escaped into the bathroom. How to appear on his return? Not stark naked, surely. He pulled on a pair of fresh boxer shorts, washed his face, smoothed down his hair. This was so unexpected, but as she said, why not? At this point he could hardly turn back. He was about to brush his teeth when he remembered the bridge. He couldn't leave it in a glass of water for Jody to find if she went into the bathroom. He might hide the glass, but where? There was no medicine cabinet, no handy nook. He stared into the mirror—he looked overwrought. Grow up, he chided. Lisa would never know. These were exceptional circumstances. He decided to keep the bridge in for now; later, when Jody fell asleep, he could put it in water and stow the glass in a drawer. In the morning she'd have to return to her room.

This problem successfully addressed, Koslowski felt better, on the brink of adventure. He grinned into the mirror, leered, winked. She was awfully young, too young, but no one could say he lured her. His behavior was irreproachable. Could he help it if she wanted him?

In bed, she put her arms around him with a curious blend of shyness and boldness. "You must think I'm some kind of flake but, really, isn't it nicer this way?"

"Sure it is," he whispered. "Much nicer."

Jody was very different from Lisa, whose lovemaking was forthright and passionate. He suspected this girl had known only a couple of college boys. She offered herself with confidence, though, as a coveted object, and wanted, passively, to be made love to. Koslowski obliged. She seemed impressed by what he had to offer.

"That was fantastic," she said. "Really fantastic."

He smiled in the dark. Dental work had not eroded this talent, although with Lisa, of late, he had felt distant, had withheld something. But the question of comparative suffering, of the subjective and objective apprehension of pain, of mountains and molehills, did not come between him and this sweet but irrelevant Jody.

"You're a beautiful girl. How old are you?"

"Nineteen. Almost twenty. What about you? Thirty-five, I bet."

Thirty-five? Had he aged so much since his troubles began? What would she think if she knew he was missing two teeth? That he kept a little bridge in a glass of water? She might not find him so fantastic then. "Thirty-three."

"I never made it with such an old guy." She giggled. "I've only done it with two, no, three, guys so far, no one over twenty-four. Are you married?"

"No."

"But you're with someone, right?"

"How'd you know?"

"I can just tell. 'Cause you didn't come on to me, maybe."

"I wasn't thinking of that when we were up there. Besides, you're so young."

"You think you'll marry her?"

"Maybe."

"What's she like?"

He shook his head. "What about you? What were you doing in Italy?"

She had spent her junior year abroad—she attended a small college in Ohio—and stayed on for a few extra weeks. Her Italian was fluent, she declared, and spoke a few words to demonstrate. "Guess what I said."

"How can I guess? What?"

"I like the way you fuck."

"Well, I'm glad," said Koslowski.

"Except for today it was a great year. What an ending! Anyway, I feel better now. The only thing bothering me is, we have to get back on that plane tomorrow. What if it happens again? Can we sit together? So if we die we're not alone?"

"It'll go fine. Something like this is a fluke—it wouldn't happen two days in a row. Is someone meeting you when you get back?"

"My brother. He lives in New York and he's going to drive me back home to Pittsburgh. Thank God I don't have to fly there." She yawned. "I've had it for one day. 'Night, Richie."

Once he was sure she was sleeping, he got up stealthily to remove the bridge and put it in the bathroom glass, which he hid in the night table. It was barely light when she whispered, "See you downstairs, okay?" "Mm," he murmured, keeping his mouth closed.

The flight was overbooked and they were assigned seats far apart, Jody up front and Koslowski in back beside the stout, white-haired woman who thought the Lord took care of his own. When lunch arrived, he bit eagerly into a chunk of French bread. A jolt in his mouth, a hard lump on his tongue. He removed the damp, doughy wad in which the bridge was embedded. "Shit," he muttered. "Shit, shit, shit." He wrapped his head in his hands and groaned.

"Something wrong?" the woman beside him asked.

"Nothing. Sorry."

"You're upset," she said soothingly. "And no wonder. Sometimes we have to act brave, but sooner or later it all comes out. You had a frightening experience. Just let go, it's all right. I have children older than you."

"It's not that," said Koslowski.

"No? Then what?"

"Well…" Airplane friendships! He'd slept with one stranger and was about to bare his agonies to another. "It's this bridge that just popped out." He wiped it off on the napkin. "And I thought it was the answer to my prayers."

"It happens to the best of us. Look." She extracted a tiny tube from her purse. "Denture glue. You squeeze it on. You can buy it in any drugstore."

Koslowski studied the tube as if it contained a precious elixir.

"Here, you can keep it. Go ahead, try. Don't be embarrassed. I use it all the time."

"Thanks." He squeezed some onto the inner ledge of the bridge, turned away, and popped it in. He'd used too much; it oozed onto his gums and tongue but didn't taste bad, a bit like toothpaste. "What if I can't get it out?"

"Don't worry. It's usually the opposite problem. But let me give you some advice. A young man like you, you don't want to be fussing with that kind of bridge the rest of your life. Get implants. Half the people I know have them. I'd do it myself but I can't risk the surgery. I'm a hemophiliac."

His new friend settled in to watch the movie, and Koslowski fell into a deep, dreamless sleep.

As they filed out he looked around for Jody but didn't see her until the baggage claim area, standing beside a young man with the same golden hair. The brother. Koslowski approached.

"I just wanted to say good-bye."

"Oh, hi, Richie. This is my brother Bill. Richie was so great to me on the flight, Billy, when I was freaking out. Listen, we've got to run. Thanks again for everything. See ya!" She was gone. He'd been afraid she would want to keep in touch, had even thought up discreet ways to extricate himself. Now he felt hollowed out.

On top of the waiting stack of mail was a postcard from Dr. Dahlberg's office commanding that he schedule a routine periodontal cleaning. He tore it to shreds. Better a plane crash than that again.

Even before he unpacked he called his parents. The news was not good: his father had taken a sudden and dramatic turn for the worse. Going to work was out of the question. The headaches were more severe, his mother reported, the "spells" more frequent and more intense. He forgot where he was, he repeated the most ordinary actions, he had delusions. Koslowski took the subway to Brighton Beach and found his father calmly reading *The New York Times*. He seemed listless and weary, but there were no other signs. Perhaps his mother was exaggerating.

Lisa would be gone for six weeks. Koslowski embarked on his single life. Thanks to the glue of the friendly fundamentalist, his mouth felt bearable and he could concentrate at work. He skated in Prospect Park with his Walkman. He played twice a week at the piano bar and worked on new arrangements with the band, for their promotional CD. The clubs were less booked during July and August, so they got gigs readily. He would have liked to tell Hal about the bridge, but Hal's siege of lower back pain dwarfed any dental work.

He visited his parents whenever he could. "Take a walk on the boardwalk, Mom. I'll stay here."

The first two times, his father was fretful and sulky. Koslowski felt useful, easing his childish demands. Then one day he stiffened and went quite pale. "Let me be," he cried. "I was at the roll call. I wasn't late."

"Dad, it's all right. You're at home. It's okay." He bent over, his hand on his father's shoulder.

"Let go! My head hurts. I need a pass for the infirmary."

Koslowski drew back in horror. The thing he had been fleeing and seeking all his life was suddenly right there in the room with them, invisible and charged with power, like electricity. If only he could gather his father in his arms and carry him to safety. But rescue was impossible because the thing was lodged in his father's head where no one could touch it. He wouldn't even let Koslowski near, waving his arms to fend him off even as he protested, "It's me, Dad. Richie. I won't hurt you. Please!"

All he could do was watch him moan and mutter in his chair until the seizure passed. His ravaged face untwisted, his gaze cleared, and he looked around, blinking, like someone emerging from a cave.

Every few days Koslowski got an e-mail from Lisa, spare and uninformative. "Hi, Richie, how's it going? It's not easy here, but I'm okay. We're hearing incredible things. The papers don't begin to tell what's really going on. I can't write more—this is the only computer and everyone wants it. Love, L." He wanted to picture her at work but she gave no clues. Did she meet with the women in offices, makeshift tents, bombed-out buildings? Did they weep with grief and shame or sit mute and stoical? Where did she sleep? What did she eat? Was she dodging bullets in the street? Land mines? She told nothing. He thought occasionally of Jody, with mild curiosity. Soon she'd be back at school. Would she remember him, or had she forgotten already? Perhaps he'd become a funny story for her friends. Thank God she hadn't seen the bridge in the glass of water—he could imagine a clutch of blonde, creamy-faced girls gathered in some dorm room, breaking up in laughter at the very notion.

As the summer passed, the e-mails arrived less often. Much as he missed Lisa, especially at night, the absence of strain was palpable, more so than the strain itself had been. It was all the fault of the teeth.

No. Even in his extreme state he knew better. Not the teeth, not even the botched treatments had divided them, but his utter frailty in the face of it all. His rampant obsession. And beyond Lisa, it divided him from everyone else who didn't understand. Teeth were a joke. He'd need something far more significant to have his sufferings taken seriously.

And maybe not even then. His father used to say that when he first arrived in this country, no one, not even the relatives who helped him get started, wanted to hear the truth. "You couldn't talk about it. It was like you were talking dirty. Forget it, you have a new life, they said. Put all that behind you. Like it was something you could erase, just like that. Idiots. They liked their innocence."

Later, when the "holocaust," a word his father never used, was taken up by the media—the books, the movies and TV specials, the museum in Washington—the elder Koslowski was not appeased. "Now they can't get enough of it. Back then, forget it. History they like, sure. Better yet, a movie."

But of course there was no comparison. Of course not. He didn't really mean that, Koslowski pleaded as if to a shocked courtroom. It was just an analogy.

His father deteriorated so badly that his mother could no longer care for him. Besides the seizures and hallucinations, there were his physical needs: he was big and unwieldy and uncooperative. They tried a visiting nurse, then a home health aide, while the doctor helped them look into a hospice, which was, in his phrase, "not so far down the road."

The road was shorter than anyone imagined. Within two weeks Koslowski and his mother brought his father to the hospice, where he fought back and struggled as the nurses tried to get him into a bed. He'd always been a strong man, but now his son was the stronger. "Let me do it," he said, and lifted his father in his arms. At his son's touch, the old man looked at him with recognition and trust, and stopped struggling. This was a moment Koslowski would preserve forever, an instant of grace amid the grotesque. Once he was in bed, though, the struggle began again. The nurses had to tie him down in order to give the necessary shot.

His mother left the room, but Koslowski looked on, his heart withering in his breast. "They're nurses, Dad. They're trying to help you," he repeated uselessly. Now, he thought, now he understood. To see this was to know. But as his father stared accusingly, his eyes alien and opaque with rage, Koslowski had to admit he knew nothing of what he craved. All he knew was his own sorrow.

He took his mother home and stayed in his old room in the Brighton Beach apartment to help her through this first night alone. The bridge rested in a glass of water—its home away from home—at his bedside. He'd grown accustomed to eating with care and placing it in water every night like some delicate flower, although it more resembled a tiny embryo of an exotic species, all pink and white innocence, floating in its amniotic fluid. But seeing it in this setting jarred him. This was the room where he had been an intact child never dreaming of such indignities. Or rather he did dream of indignities, but only as stories that happened to others, long ago and far beyond any help, and he had tossed in frustration at his own helplessness. Now, in the clarity of home, he grasped that in this small instance, at least, he was not helpless. He didn't want to be putting the bridge in its watery bed every night for the next forty years. He would explore the third option Dr. Habemeyer had suggested. Implants.

Mellow Dr. Fisher was on vacation, but Koslowski took a liking to his partner, Dr. Ferrucci, a large, balding man whose muscular build, very like Koslowski's own, suggested an athletic youth. He wore neatly pressed chinos beneath the white smock, and his crooked teeth were reassuring—he hadn't seen fit to have cosmetic dentistry. His matter-of-fact style was comforting too, more that of a plumber or an electrician than a dentist. Koslowski himself, in his capacity of computer doctor, had the same unpretentious manner.

Once the X-rays, taken by a blonde hygienist who resembled Jody, proved Koslowski a fit "candidate" for implants, Dr. Ferrucci announced, "Okay, this is the deal. It involves two major surgeries. First I open up the gums and put the implants in—two metal posts that stay in your head. I might have to go into your sinuses, I can't tell till I'm in there. Then you wait six to twelve months, the longer the better, for the holes to close up and the area to heal. Then I open up those places again and attach screws to the implants. You wait another month or so, and a dentist attaches crowns to the screws. They feel exactly like your own teeth, and they last ten years if not longer."

"Do you do this often?"

He threw back his head and laughed. "All the time. I've done thousands. I have a ninety-three percent success rate."

And the other seven percent? Dead? Surely not. Maybe their mouths rejected the implants, the way some bodies reject a new heart or liver.

Dr. Ferrucci crossed the room and stood with his back to Koslowski, studying his X-rays projected onto the wall. He seemed so sensible that Koslowski ventured to pose the critical question: what was the infernal growing and shrinking sensation, even more mysterious since the feeling had outlived the tooth?

"Oh, that," the dentist said nonchalantly.

A revelatory moment: Dr. Ferrucci's voice traveled across the room as if emanating from his broad white back. "That's because your jaw is in spasm. The upper and lower jaws aren't meeting properly. It can be very uncomfortable. In fact it can drive you nuts. It causes a lot of very weird referred pain. Referred pain is when—"

"I know what it is," said Koslowski.

In spasm. He wished he could invite the whole world to hear this diagnosis: Lisa. His parents. Hal. The human resources director. Cara, the human rights attorney and possible source of his trouble. All the friends who had looked askance till he caught on and stopped complaining. In spasm. That sounded serious enough. He knew when it happened, too. The root canal last winter, when he sat rigid as a corpse for an hour and a half as Dr. Callahan thrust needles into his head. Another season, another life. When he was sane. When he knew, or thought he knew, the difference between real suffering and minor problems.

"So what can I do about it?" he asked faintly.

"Motrin. Hot compresses. It'll ease gradually. Or else not, if it's been going on too long. Don't start with surgery if you can stand it. It's complicated, believe me."

"Why didn't anyone ever tell me this before?"

Still studying the X-rays on the wall, Dr. Ferrucci shrugged.

A few days later Koslowski went to meet Lisa at the airport. He expected that she might look tired, but he wasn't prepared for what he found. Her lush red hair was gone, chopped off in a rough boyish cut: too hard to wash, with no hot water. She'd lost weight, her jeans were ragged, she wore no makeup. It took some effort to match this Lisa with the radiant creature in his memory. He offered to carry her backpack but she shook her head. "There's hardly anything in it. I left most of my clothes there."

"You left your clothes?"

"What else could I do? They had nothing to wear. I have to get my suitcase, though. It's mostly papers and stuff."

"So," he asked in the taxi. "Do you want to tell me?"

"Later." She leaned back and closed her eyes. "What about your dad? How is he?"

Koslowski told her about the move to the hospice.

"Oh, Richie. I'm so sorry. Is he in a lot of pain?"

"Mostly the headaches. I'll tell you later, when you're not so tired."

She went straight to bed. Not the homecoming he had envisioned. He'd been ready to listen sympathetically to the most harrowing details, had vowed not to mention his impending surgery. But there was no opportunity for good behavior. She was sleeping when he left for work the next morning and didn't answer when he phoned. He brought home Chinese food and found her curled on the sofa, pen in hand, leafing through a notebook.

"How does moo-shu duck strike you?"

She smiled wanly and accepted his kiss.

"I bet you haven't eaten anything like this in a long time. So, aren't you going to say anything?"

"It was indescribable."

"Well, try."

"One woman slit her wrists with a pocketknife and I took her to get tetanus shots. We had to go to six places before we found one that had the stuff. A few tried to abort. One almost bled to death. Some of the families wouldn't have anything to do with them anymore."

He put down his chopsticks. It didn't seem right to eat while hearing such things.

"Some wouldn't talk at all. It's bad enough to talk about rape anyway, and especially in their culture they don't, and then in front of the interpreter, and me taking notes, and the social worker and the two lawyers.... Oh; one of the lawyers said she met you at a party last year. That party I didn't go to because I was sick? The night you broke your tooth? She remembered."

"I remember her too. Cara."

"Right. How are your teeth, by the way?"

"Okay. The same."

"Do you want to tell me about your father now?"

He opened his mouth to speak, but no words came. His father's condition was unspeakable. Especially the hallucinations. What froze his tongue, he realized, was shame. Shame that even his father's dying was corroded by the past, inescapable, lodged in him forever. As if he were enslaved all over again, his death not even his own. He shook his head.

"Okay, I understand."

No way could she understand, but he let it go. "My mom's been asking about you, but I couldn't tell her much."

"It wasn't easy to write or call."

"I can imagine."

"No, you can't."

"Okay then, I guess I can't. How could I, when you're totally shutting me out? And why? I don't like that war any more than you do. You think I enjoy hearing about ethnic cleansing?"

"Richie, I did a lot of thinking while I was there."

"I thought you were so busy."

"You can think even when you're busy. When you're far away sometimes things are clearer."

"So?"

"You must know what I'm talking about."

"I don't."

"I think ... things haven't been so good between us lately. I mean, even before the trip."

"Because you were so uptight about it, and I was, I was—you know, my teeth. Well, that's all past. I get it now. Teeth are nothing in the scheme of things. In my personal scheme, maybe, but not in the larger scheme. So, fine. Forget it. I'll never mention teeth again. I want to hear about important things."

"It's not that simple. We're not ... It's just not working for me, that's all."

"This is some kind of, of political difference, you mean? Like I don't have the right scale of values? I should forget my problems and focus more on Bosnia? That's why you want to break up?"

"I didn't say break up. I thought, just for a while, you know? Try living apart? Look, I know this is a hard time for you and I'm sorry. But this is how it feels to me now."

Koslowski stood up and began pacing. "I don't get you. I really don't. You're ready to rush halfway across the world to help people you don't even know, and you don't give a shit about what happens to me."

"That's exactly what I mean. You sound like a child."

"And did you meet some grown-up there? Someone who sees the big picture, who knows what really matters?"

She shoved her plate away. "I didn't meet anyone. That just shows how naïve you are, that you could think I had time for anything like that."

"How do I know what you had time for? You won't tell me."

"Because you don't care. You ask, but you really don't care, I mean in the way I need you to care. I know you're upset about your dad right now, but even before he—"

"Leave my father out of it, okay? So you think *I* don't care!" I met a really nice girl on the plane back, he wanted to say. Really sweet. She wouldn't say I didn't care. She needed help and I gave it. She wasn't a rape victim, but I did what I could. "So, what do you have in mind, exactly?"

"I think I'll move my things out in the next few days. I can stay with Laurie till I find a place. Or with Cara and Jeff. We got really close."

"Just like that. Three years, and it's over in three minutes?"

"I've been thinking about it for a while."

"How long? Since I broke my tooth?"

"Richie! Will you stop with the fucking tooth?"

"But that's how it all started, isn't it?"

"No. I mean, it looks that way, but no. That just brought things to the surface, like profound differences."

"Oh, don't give me that crap. Profound differences! We managed fine before, with profound differences."

"They would have come out sooner or later."

When Lisa left he had fantasies of Jody, fruitless and unsatisfying. He had no desire to see her again. She was simply the most tangible woman his fantasies could cling to. And she was so appreciative. An even more voluptuous indulgence was the thought of his upcoming surgery, an elective procedure that would cost him several thousand dollars. He was deep in the labyrinth again and must journey still deeper to see where it led, how it felt. His parents, the women in Bosnia, the true sufferers all over the world, were the aristocrats of pain. He was a mere peasant. But this pittance had been given to him and he must embrace it. If not for the initial accident, he would have remained an innocent. Anyway, he would have Valium.

As he waited in the surgeon's office, perusing a *Time* magazine article with heart-stopping photos of still more corpses discovered in a ditch near Sarajevo, a lean, middle-aged man with a small goatee stumbled from the warren of inner rooms. Koslowski recognized him as an actor who occasionally appeared in minor television roles, once as an expert witness on *Law and Order*, once as a social worker on *ER*. Actors needed those unnaturally even, generic teeth— God knows what tortures he had submitted to. Obviously drugged, the actor weaved his way toward a chair, using his outstretched hands to guide him. A nurse raced out. "Mr. Becker, wait, you have to lie down in the recovery room."

She steadied him as he was about to trip over the magazine rack.

"I'm okay, I'm going home." His speech was slurred.

"You can't go home yet. Please come with me."

The actor dug in his back pocket and with fumbling fingers extracted a credit card from his wallet. "Here. I'm going home."

The receptionist behind the desk smiled, as did Koslowski. Even in his stupor, the man knew enough to find his credit card.

"You can pay later," the nurse pleaded. "Come on now. You're not ready to leave."

Koslowski rose to assist her, and together they managed to steer the wayward actor to a room no larger than a closet, where they settled him on a cot. An hour from now, that would be his state, Koslowski thought. He would be docile.

"I forgot to mention," Dr. Ferrucci said as he prepared the needle. "I'm doing a bone graft. I hope it takes, because that's what'll hold the implants in place. We won't know till nine months from now."

"Whatever," and Koslowski rolled up his sleeve. As the Valium waltzed through him, he sank into that drowsy, delectable state in which every problem melts away and all is benign, an undulating world of silk and cream.

There seemed to be several nurses or hygienists in attendance, all of them blonde, all resembling Jody, all swimming in a milky haze. Before he could figure out whether there were truly three or whether his blurred vision was multiplying them, Dr. Ferrucci's voice boomed, "That's it. Everything went fine."

Koslowski allowed himself to be led into the recovery room. Was the actor who had lain there before him home yet or staggering through traffic? Would his smile be different the next time he glimpsed him on television?

After a while, one of the nurses—there were indeed three—handed him the familiar post-op instructions along with prescriptions for a painkiller and an antibiotic. Though he assured her he was fine, she accompanied him out and saw him into a taxi. "Remember the stitches come out next week—here's your appointment card. And you can't wear your bridge for six weeks, till the area heals."

Without the support of the bridge, his jaw and cheek sagged into a state of collapse that made eating and talking too great a strain. So he ate and talked as little as possible. The area had sustained so much injury, Dr. Ferrucci explained as he removed the stitches, that the muscles were exhausted and frayed.

Koslowski could barely ask, "When will they recover?"

"In time. Try Motrin. But the procedure went very well. A textbook case, as we say."

Koslowski did not mind so much not talking; he had very little to say.

"What's the matter, Richie? You're so quiet," his mother asked on one of his visits to the hospice—one of the easier visits. His father slept the whole time. It was only when he slept that Koslowski recognized the father he knew and loved. Awake, his face was vacant, except when masks of fury or fear clamped over his features, then, as abruptly and mysteriously, vanished.

"I'm fine. Just a little tired."

"I never thought she was right for you anyway. She was a nice girl, but she didn't appreciate you. You'll find someone else. You're a good-looking boy. Go out, meet new people."

He glanced over at his dying father. "Okay, tell Dad I was here. Give him my love."

Not eating bothered him more than not talking. He lost weight. Skating wore him out. Even his hours at the keyboard were more burden than pleasure. A diet of scrambled eggs, yogurt, and ice cream didn't begin to approach true deprivation—the TV news showed starving children in Somalia and he sent a check to Doctors Without Borders—but it was a hardship nonetheless. Everyone was entitled to eat.

Once the six weeks were up, the bridge no longer fit. "Impossible. It can't not fit," said Dr. Ferrucci. Koslowski didn't argue—his jaw muscles wouldn't permit it. Nor did he obey his first frantic impulse, to return to Rome and Dr. Habemeyer, with his little saw. Instead he called twenty dentists listed in the Yellow Pages until he lit on one who would make a removable bridge. If indeed no reputable dentist in the United States would provide such an object, did that make genial, rotund Dr. Mbuto, recently arrived from South Africa, disreputable? Not at all. His framed diplomas lined the walls. He must know plenty about suffering, too, probably enough to rival Koslowski's parents. And maybe for that reason he was willing to relieve the paltry sufferings that came his way. Not a moment too soon, either. In the bracing autumn air, with the new little bridge securely glued in his mouth, Koslowski wolfed down two empanadas from the Jamaican grocery on Dr. Mbuto's corner.

The next two years were eventful for Koslowski, and not only dentally. He heard from friends that Jeff and Cara, the attorney who had witnessed, and possibly caused, his accident, had divorced. Good. Let her suffer too. His satisfaction soured when he learned a month later that Lisa, once his very own, had moved in with Jeff. Did she by any chance know that Jeff had a bridge? At the fateful party, he recalled, Jeff claimed to have heard the collision of olive pit and tooth and feared for his own bridgework. But however their romance fared, it would not, Koslowski was certain, be undone by teeth.

His father crept slowly and agonizingly toward death. At last he arrived. And in the finality of mourning, as if released or reprieved, Koslowski felt ready to abandon his quest.

But his quest was not ready to abandon him: he had gone so far into the labyrinth that retreat was impossible. The only way out was to trudge onward, through the second implant surgery the following summer, the removal of the infected stitches, the device installed to support his weakened cheek muscles.... All the while, his tongue was repeatedly mangled, since the long-awaited crowns were skewed at a clumsy angle.

Apparently he was among the unlucky seven percent. "You said they'd feel like my own teeth. They don't. They feel like a boulder sitting on my tongue."

Dr. Ferrucci shrugged regretfully. "I had to put them where the bone could support them, Richard. We do the best we can."

Enough. He gave up. He would live with the discomfort, which would earn him a minuscule place in the annals of world pain.

Not long after, he married.

He met Maxine at dusk on a warm fall day, almost a year after his father's death. With his mouth still sore from surgery, he was skating on the boardwalk near his mother's apartment when he noticed a pair of metal crutches propped against a bench. He looked about for their owner but saw no one likely among the sparse strollers. The crutches might get lost or stolen; their owner might be in trouble. He scanned the ocean. Had someone lost hope and walked, or limped, into the sea? Only a handful of people were swimming—it was past the season—and none appeared in distress. A woman with dark flowing hair emerged and headed for shore with a side-to-side hobble. Though she tottered once or twice, she didn't lose her balance, even when she bent to pick up a towel from the sand. She dried her hair and shook it out, fitted a long, sarong-like garment over her black bathing suit, shouldered her tote bag and proceeded up the beach. She was tanned and very pretty, glistening in the amber light, in her exotic costume. Koslowski waited as she made her way up the stairs.

"Are these yours?"

"Yes. Why?" She took them a bit ungraciously, but he understood.

"I'm sorry. I thought someone might need help. Or they might be lost."

"Kind of hard to lose them, wouldn't you think?" She gave him a second glance and softened. "Actually someone stole a pair once while I was swimming. They disappeared, at any rate."

"Really? What kind of weirdo would do that?" He shook his head and offered his crooked smile.

Maxine lived nearby with her widowed father. She did freelance editing at home and wrote children's books that she hoped to publish some day. Her congenital spine ailment might worsen over time. She might end up in a wheelchair. She explained all this once their affair began, but Koslowski was undeterred. On the contrary, he relished the idea of caring for her. She was so beautiful, so valiant.

"A cripple?" his mother exclaimed when he told her.

"She's disabled."

"What's the difference what you call it? Can she have children, at least?" She could and did. Three. She persisted with her children's books and in time was quite successful.

Koslowski gave up dancing. At large parties, Maxine urged him to go on and dance with others—his mother boasted of what a terrific dancer he was, and she wanted to see. But he never did. He gave up the band and his ambitions, though he still played at home and occasionally filled in at the piano bar as a favor to his old boss. He left the music company and took a job supervising computer systems in a brokerage firm that paid well and provided excellent health coverage, so that Maxine had every aid and comfort. When the wheelchair came, he mastered all the necessary routines.

He never mentioned teeth to her or to anyone else as long as he lived: that was part of his discipline. He learned forbearance. He learned to live with the metal posts—titanium, the metal of the future—nestling just below his sinuses, the teeth they supported sitting thick and burdensome on his tongue, a constant reminder of his mishap and his prolonged madness. Now and then, during trying times, his jaw would go into spasm and the teeth would grow by day and shrink overnight—irksome but no longer alarming. He kept Dr. Mbuto's little bridge in a sealed jar of water in the back of a drawer and changed the water from time to time. No rational explanation for this quite sufficed: that it had been so hard to obtain, that it had seen him through, that he might need it again someday. He only knew it felt risky to throw it away; it was part of him.

The madness left its somber residue. He was quieter, as if subdued. He was often plagued by transient but irritating ailments: conjunctivitis, allergies, rashes. He was accident-prone, would bump into chairs and break a toe, hit his head on a protruding shelf, pull a muscle while lifting weights in the gym. He grasped that something coiled in his heart was generating these minor nuisances, but he couldn't make it stop. At least it never generated anything very serious. It was merely trying to teach him something, and would not try him beyond his endurance. Indeed the petty trials it sent mocked his endurance. And maybe, by some superstitious form of bookkeeping, they also kept him safe from the unendurable ones. His mind balked and fogged over when he tried to think through this tangle. Meanwhile he lived as best he could. His growing family absorbed him, and his friends, seeing his patient devotion to Maxine, thought him heroic.

He knew he was no hero. He wouldn't have survived what his parents had endured. He had been given a test—even if it was a mockery—and he had failed. His parents were made of stronger stuff. But he didn't despise himself. There were some things he could do. He wouldn't have been one of the skeletal but resilient bodies that greeted the liberating forces, but he could readily see himself among the stalwart, well-fed soldiers confronting a scene they could never, in their innocence, have imagined. He saw it as clearly as if he had been there to rescue his father and the others. It was spring and the ground was muddy from recent rain. The rancid, smoky smell was choking, like nothing he had ever smelled in his life. The stick figures standing behind the barbed wire might have risen from a tomb. But there was no time to indulge in shock. Things must be done. He must approach them courteously, assure them that their nightmare, or this part of it, was over, see that they were fed and transported to places where they could be cared for. The job might take weeks, months, but he had the stamina. There was no hesitation. He would do what was required, and not only because it was his duty. He would save them, out of decency and out of relief that he did not have to be them. And in this way he would earn his right to live.

The Stone Master

A few of us were exchanging road stories. The conversation inevitably takes this turn when we meet, given that frequent travel, for so many in our profession, has become a way of life. There were the usual tales of effortless seduction and flighty escapades, as well as of the dull dinners in anonymous company, the long, lonely stretches, and the naïveté, if not outright ignorance, to be endured in the provinces. This kind of talk had begun to weary me of late, and if only to allay the tedium by the sound of my own voice, I was about to give an account of my recent visit to the town of M———, which, uncharacteristically, I had never spoken of to anyone.

But I found myself reluctant, and when my guests had left, their mood somewhat dampened by my diffidence, I wondered why. It wouldn't make a good story, for one thing: a mere encounter, it had little drama, certainly nothing in the way of erotic or scenic dazzle. It would do nothing to enhance my reputation; my friends might even judge me to have been hallucinating. For that matter, how could I be sure that my host on that night in M——, the Stone Master, was not delusional, or perhaps having his bit of fun at my expense? I thought not, and yet I had talked to no one else in M——; he had been unwilling, in the nature of things, to let me see any of the gems, which might have served as evidence; and the whole episode so challenged credibility that I too might have dismissed it as my own imagining, except that I have little imagination to speak of.

But beyond all that, to tell of my night in M—— seemed a species of betrayal, and not simply of the Stone Master, who had been extremely kind, and of what he had revealed. This sense of possible betrayal was as unfamiliar as it was compelling. For the first time in a long while, I felt that to broadcast an event that had so shaken the armature of my inner life would be a betrayal of myself.

But habit is compelling too. I find that tell it I must, so I set it down here in private.

It was dark and wet on the drive to M——. My driver, a sullen young man with an opaque stare and a faded rhinestone stud beneath one eyebrow, had rebuffed my attempts at conversation but instead hummed maddeningly to himself. He would switch the radio on and off at intervals to listen to snatches of an interview with a fairly well-known personage, not unlike the interviews I myself would soon be giving in M——, I thought wryly. He drove slowly, because of the rain no doubt, but out of insolence as well, I suspected, as I fidgeted in the back seat; my contacts were awaiting me in the town square, no doubt irked at my lateness.

For about half an hour we had seen no other cars and no signs, indeed nothing at all except an abandoned truck stop. Then there loomed over the highway one of those reassuring large green rectangles. The driver slowed down still more. It wasn't easy to make out the words with the windshield blurred by rain, but sure enough, M—— was listed—ten miles off, it said. A new directional arrow must have been recently painted on the sign without covering up the old one, making it impossible to tell whether we were being pointed right or left. At the fork in the road, the driver veered right. I myself thought the left arrow was the newer, but I was not native to these parts, and besides, I was too disheartened and tired to argue the point. Soon there began to appear along the road the usual diners, motels, and shopping strips that announce the entrance to most cities nowadays.

M——, for I had to assume this was in fact M——, seemed closed up for the night; not a soul was out. I had been led to expect a small sleepy city, but not a comatose one. My driver found his way through the streets with ease and presently pulled to a halt in an old-style square with the requisite church, city hall, post office, and assortment of staid buildings that might have been appealing in bright daylight but offered no cheer on this dank fall night. At least the rain had stopped.

I had been told a car would be waiting at the city hall. Though there was no such car, I had no choice but to alight with my briefcase and traveling bag. The driver accepted his pay in silence, never ceasing his humming. Normally I would have arranged to be picked up after my brief stay, but I found myself unwilling to spend any more time in the company of this person, from whom emanated what I first took as a vast hostility but later revised to a vast indifference, or more precisely, the most disconcerting sense of personal dispersion, a kind of amorphous spill that had left a gaping negativity within. So I said nothing about the return trip. I would make other arrangements.

For a few moments I paced the square, peering up side streets for a waiting car. The two coffee shops where I might have taken refuge—a nostalgia-inducing kind with plastic booths and pastries under transparent domes, and a more chic, awninged one with round marble tables and a conspicuous espresso machine—were lit from within but closed. I used my cell phone to call the two people I'd been in touch with, but a hollow silence suggested the lines were down because of the storm. By now I was angry as well as baffled, and resolved to go directly to the guest house I'd been promised, but when I consulted my papers under the streetlight, I realized I had never been told the name of the place. You'll stay at the guest house, my contact had said; I'm sure you'll be quite comfortable. Even if I'd known the name and address, how would I get there? There were no buses or taxis in sight, nor did I have a street map. From the looks of things, I might have been the only living soul in M——.

The night was warm; the air had the cleansed freshness it often does after rainfall, with an odd sweetness like the scent of honeysuckle or peonies, a relief after the staleness of the taxi. I set off down the broadest of the four streets that converged on the square, planning to check in at the first hotel I found. I must have walked seven or eight blocks down an avenue in all respects ordinary, with shops and restaurants on the ground floors of moderate-sized buildings, except for its being deserted. Suddenly, amidst my exhaustion, irritation, and regret that I had ever agreed to come to M—— in the first place, I spied a man in a white robe walking toward me, some kind of priest or monk, I assumed. I quickened my step to meet him. He would be my salvation, I decided, whether he wished it or not.

He greeted me cordially and knew me at once for a stranger. When I explained my situation, he promptly offered to take me to his house, where I could lodge for the night. I expected that the "house" would be part of some monastery or church, perhaps the church on the main square, and I accepted gratefully. Had I not been close to despair, I probably wouldn't have given myself over so trustingly to a stranger. But I *was* close to despair, and this feeling, along with his monkish robes and affable manner, overcame any instinct of caution. He led me to an ordinary brick townhouse only a few steps away; as he turned the key in the lock I felt enormous relief. Anything, at this point, would be preferable to wandering the vacant streets of M——.

When we stepped inside he removed his white robe to reveal ordinary slacks and a shirt. He was about my height and age, of similar build and coloring, which for some reason I found a comfort. The house, too, was reassuring, with plants, bookshelves, and the kind of pleasant if undistinguished furnishings that might be seen in innumerable towns all over the country. He fixed me a sandwich in the kitchen, and I ate it eagerly.

I know from my travels that people in small cities or towns are highly sensitive to the imputed criticisms of visitors from the metropolises. Though the last thing I wanted was to appear to be deriding the provinces, I couldn't help remarking, in the most mild way, on M——'s deserted streets. Granted, it was late, but still well before midnight.

He wasn't at all bothered by my question. "Yes, it must seem odd. Usually the streets are lively at this hour, but it happens you've come on a special night. It's an annual holiday in the province of M——." He looked at me curiously. "We don't get many visitors."

"You don't? But I have contacts here, and so do many of my colleagues. As I said, I was expected. In fact, may I use your phone? My cell phone didn't work last night."

"You're welcome to try, but I suspect you won't be able to get through. Why don't I show you to your room, and then we can make plans in the morning?"

I hadn't the will to insist. "What's the holiday?" I asked as I followed him up the stairs.

"The Festival of the Stones. You may have heard about M——'s precious gems."

I hadn't heard, but I murmured a vague assent.

"The whole town works all day to get the new gems finished and ready for the coming year, and then we hold our celebration dinner. It ends early, and the town closes up for a night of contemplation. I happened to be out only because I was attending at a birth, the first one after the festival, which is always auspicious."

"Oh, are you a doctor, then?"

"Oh, no. I am the Stone Master of M——."

Whatever this quaint title meant, I was clearly being lodged at the home of an important local functionary. Good. Tomorrow he could help me reach my contacts, who had been so negligent. Had they had the courtesy to let me know it was their holiday, I could easily have come a day later. But I put all that aside for now. The guest room at the top of the stairs was a welcome sight, with its large four-poster bed; all I wanted was to fall into it and forget the travails of the past few hours.

I slept well and went downstairs to the aroma of coffee brewing. From the front windows, I saw cars going by, as well as the occasional pedestrian: so there was ordinary life in M—— after all. Not that I didn't trust my host, the

Stone Master—there was something benignly monkish about him even without his white robe—but I couldn't quite shake the eeriness of last night's taxi ride and lonely walk down the dark, glistening streets. Now a few phone calls to rearrange my scheduled appearances, and all would be well.

My host was in the kitchen preparing breakfast. Not wishing to appear in haste to leave, after his kindness, I was ready to chat for a while before turning to my affairs. As a matter of fact I wasn't in haste to leave: the house and the Stone Master exuded a serenity and self-possession, a gathered solidity and denseness that were seductive and of which I felt badly in need, especially after the taxi driver's nervous fragmentation, which, though I hadn't realized it at the time, had had an alarmingly contagious effect.

"Tell me something about these gems," I said, sitting opposite him at the table. "Do you have any around that I might look at?"

He smiled as if I were a guileless child asking the unthinkable. "I'm afraid I couldn't do that. They're not for casual display. Or they shouldn't be, at any rate."

"Didn't you say M—— was known for its precious gems?"

"For our traditional use of the gems. Not for showing them."

"Ah. I assumed you did a brisk business."

"No. They're not for sale. We sell our products and labor, not ourselves."

I was unprepared for this sort of enigma. Moreover, what were the gems, if not the products of labor? "What do you do with them, if you don't sell them? Wear them?" I had a ludicrous vision of crowds of glittering people studded from head to foot with precious stones, parading through the streets. How different from the bleak scene that had greeted me! What a spectacle I might have missed, arriving on the wrong night.

"I'd gladly tell you, but are you sure you'd rather not be off on your business?"

"My business can wait—if you don't mind, that is. You've made me curious."

He seemed pleased by this. "Very well. Everyone in the province of M—— receives at birth a precious stone that gives off a dazzling, warming light. This is theirs to keep for life. It was these stones we were preparing yesterday, the ones destined for the births of the coming year."

"Are they a kind of individual bank account or trust fund?" This was a more modest vision, and more familiar. I had heard suggestions in my part of the country, too, that each citizen be given some sort of financial credit line on which to draw for life, but to the best of my knowledge these notions were too radical ever to have been taken seriously.

"Not at all." Again he smiled at my ignorance. "Or perhaps yes, though not in the sense you mean. We keep them at home in a private place and look at them whenever we wish, according to temperament. Some are so enamored of their stone that they can gaze for hours, barely able to tear themselves away. It may even keep them from more practical pursuits. Others are much occupied with worldly affairs, but they never forget that it's there." He paused to pour me some more coffee.

"I must say I'm puzzled. You have these splendid costly gems, and all you do is look at them now and then?"

"Ah, but the true value is not in the gems themselves but in the light they emit. The nature of this light is not easy to describe to someone unfamiliar with it. To begin with, the stones are similar, but as time passes their light changes, becoming more distinctive and more subtly nuanced. That is—" and he paused, for dramatic effect, I was sure; as a speaker, I had often used the same ploy myself. "That is, it becomes a faithful reflection, in the shaded language of light, of its owner."

At those words a slight flush came over me. I realized, as I might have done sooner but for my general confusion, that M—— was no ordinary place, and my new friend no ordinary host. Perhaps I should have excused myself right then, but my curiosity was piqued.

"The light of the gems," he said, noting my discomfiture, for he was shrewd, even if possibly mad, "not only warms and nourishes the spirit but continues to modulate as the owners grow in years and experience, in sufferings and in triumphs. The light absorbs everything that happens and reflects everything."

"And will your own gem," I said a trifle frivolously, "soon absorb and reflect your encounter with a curious stranger?"

"By all means," he said, mirroring my grin. "The stones are our chronicles as well as our great sustenance. In their light we see our powers reflected, together with all that has happened to give us our powers. We take pleasure in them, and we take pride. Even in troubled times, the stones are a comfort, for they show that our sorrows have substance, in the elusive manner of light, and that they shape the spirit, in the elusive shapes of light. And so our people are never bereft of themselves even in the darkest hours. They always know who they are."

"Surely you can't all be paragons," I said. "There must be some who seek to profit by their gems—to display them, even trade them?"

"Profit and trade are out of the question," he replied. "The matter cannot arise, since the gems lose their light once they pass from the hands of their original owners. They become worthless, nothing but commonplace stones. As far as self-display, yes, just as everywhere else, we have our share. But this is held in check because the gems have one perilous quality. As you must surely have discovered, anything sustaining and nourishing has a perilous quality."

Was that true? I would have to ponder it later. Meanwhile I asked, "And what is the perilous quality?"

"Their brilliance dims very slightly, almost imperceptibly, each time they are shown to anyone else. And along with their brilliance, their powers of sustenance dim too. Children are warned of this peril as soon as they are able to understand."

So I had stumbled on a cabal of mystical navel-gazers. I was about to suggest something to that effect, naturally in more diplomatic terms, when my host preempted me.

"Don't make the mistake of thinking we do nothing but bask in our light and neglect the world. On the contrary, if we fail to use the powers reflected by the stones, their light grows dull and hollow. No, as in any realm, all are encouraged to do as their talents counsel: to engage in civic affairs, or provide needed goods and services, or make beautiful things, or study the mysteries of the natural world. We neither hide our light nor hesitate to use it. But its visible embodiment, the gems themselves, endures best when contemplated in solitude."

I was speechless.

"Let me assure you," my host said kindly, "that we are no more reclusive, and no less vain, than the rest of the world. Since the gems are beautiful, and each one unique, it's only natural to wish to reveal them on intimate occasions, out of pride or out of love—as all people seek to offer their loved ones the radiant light of their spirit. And with the equally natural desire to show off, few can resist bringing the gems out in public now and then; in fact those few are regarded as a bit selfish, or let us say spiritually arrogant, for their austere refusal. Human nature has its own spectrum like the spectrum of light: some of us show our gems far and wide, while others guard them carefully, reluctant to dim the sustaining power of the light."

"And I suppose those who keep them hidden are rewarded in some way?" I said. "Or perhaps those who show them off."

"No rewards accrue in either case, nor punishments either. It is true that some gain fame for the beauty of their gems—if you consider fame a reward—but this fame is brief: only as long as the fading light lasts. Those who rarely show them gain nothing tangible for their restraint, not even after death, for the gems are extinguished and buried with them. The issue is much debated, as you might imagine. Just yesterday we had the usual discussion of the attendant gains and losses, as always on the eve of our annual holiday. There were even a number of gems on display at the celebration dinner," he said, rather ruefully, I thought.

"And your position?"

"Ah, my position. I am the Stone Master. My position is a difficult one. Ideally, I believe, as have the Stone Masters before me, that the gems should be displayed seldom, if ever, in order for the light to retain the highest degree of subtlety and power. What, after all, can have more ultimate value? But this, as I said, is an ideal, even ascetic, position, attainable by very few. On the other hand, as Stone Master, responsible for the quality and efficacy of the gems, how can I not long for everyone to see the splendor of what we work so hard to perfect? I must confess to fantasies of some great bejeweled display, days on end of glittering festivities, with everyone resplendent. What a riotous indulgence that would be. And after our brief burst of glory, well ..."

I had a sudden urge to cry out a warning. Couldn't he foresee the unhappy results? My passionate impulse left me trembling with shock. What could I know about safeguarding the stones or the fate of these strange people who cherished them? But there was no need to tell him anything. He knew already.

"But these are only passing fancies. The indulgence of a few hours, even a few days, would never compensate for the solitary elixir of the light, its growing brilliance faithfully and dazzlingly giving us our lives. Nothing makes that more clear than the fate of those who spend their light most lavishly: their stones grow dimmer and dimmer until almost nothing is left to show or to see. The light, exposed to light, is used up." We were silent as these melancholy words settled in the air.

My curiosity at this point was urgent. Yet much as I longed to see one of the fabled stones, preferably the Stone Master's, I knew it would be as pointless as it was intrusive to ask. (Not that I didn't entertain the probably sacrilegious and certainly unfeasible notion of prowling through the house for a peek.) Instead I asked if I might meet some residents of M——, so as to judge both extremes for myself. At this my host looked down as if embarrassed.

"Perhaps I expressed myself too crudely," I amended. "I assure you I wouldn't trespass on what you hold sacred. It's simply that I can't help but want to see ..."

He faced me, finally, like someone with the regrettable task of breaking unpleasant news, who would discharge it with fortitude. "Please forgive me, but you are already seeing."

I didn't understand at first, but as the silence deepened, his words bore into me. He, the Stone Master, and I, the stranger, were all I needed to see.

There was no more to say after that. I rose and told him I must be on my way, and asked again if I might use his phone.

"You cannot reach your friends from here. But I can take you to them."

"You can? Why didn't you say so last night?" I thought my asperity was warranted, especially as he had just been so unsparing with me. "Not that I would have troubled you for a ride at that hour, but I might have called for a taxi."

"You looked in need of a night's sleep. And I suppose I indulged my curiosity. It's not often that I get to meet a stranger. Perhaps even a celebrity," he said with a touch of facetiousness. "But I assure you no harm has been done, as you'll soon see."

I gathered my things and followed the Stone Master outside to his car. On the way, he nodded to a few passers-by. M—— looked perfectly ordinary, a modest city on a clear autumn morning; but for my talk with the Stone Master, I wouldn't have found anything the least bit unusual.

We drove through the town square where I was to have met my contacts—in another lifetime, it seemed—then back along the route out of town, past the commercial strips, that my sullen driver had taken some twelve hours earlier. Soon we were at the fork in the road, approaching from the other direction the ambiguous sign that led to M——. My host turned deftly onto the other fork, the one I myself would have chosen the night before but had not had the presence of mind to insist that the driver take.

"So this is the way," I mused aloud.

"You wanted New M——. But you somehow arrived in Old M——," said the Stone Master. "Didn't you see the sign?"

"I didn't notice any 'Old' or 'New,'" I said, a bit petulantly, I'm afraid. "It was hard to see in the rain."

"Your driver must have made an error." He paused. "Or perhaps he was playing tricks on you. A few people, not many, choose to leave M——, notwithstanding its advantages. They find the singular discipline of the stones too constraining."

"Or perhaps they are lured by what is beyond," I couldn't resist saying.

"Very likely."

"The driver had a rhinestone below his eyebrow," I said.

"Not a rhinestone," the Stone Master said sadly. "Never that. Well, you wanted to see an example. His eyebrow!" he muttered, shaking his head.

This road had far more traffic than the one I had traveled the night before. We soon reached the strips of shops and motels, exactly like those leading to Old M——. At the sign announcing the city limits, the Stone Master pulled over. "I'll have to leave you here. You won't have far to walk. Less than a mile." As he pointed the way, I noticed the daylight dimming, as if evening was coming on.

I thanked him for his hospitality and for the ride. There was more I wanted to say, but I hadn't had time to sift through all I was thinking and feeling. For a wild moment, as I got out of the car, I thought of asking him to take me back with him to Old M———. But it was far too late for me to be given a stone like the others. In any case, it would have faded considerably. I would have to make do with what light I had.

He wished me success with my ventures in New M——— and then spun the car around. The sky had grown darker as we said our good-byes and darkened still more as I began my walk into the city. I felt a slight drizzle; the pavement was shining, as if after a heavy rain.

In about fifteen minutes I found myself in the town square, its church, city hall, and post office squat and stolid in the damp darkness. People hurried by, carrying rolled-up umbrellas. Most of the shops were closed for the night, but a few restaurants and a large drugstore were open. At the city hall, two men stood beside a car, gazing around anxiously. As I approached they rushed up to me.

"Mr. B———? We're so glad you've arrived safely. We were getting worried. Did you have trouble along the way? I hope you didn't get caught in the rain?"

I shook hands and apologized for my lateness. "No trouble at all," I said. "The driver was a bit confused, so I walked the last few blocks."

"We'll take you right along to the guest house," the other one said. "I'm sure you're tired out from your trip. Unless you'd like to stop for a bite to eat?" He gestured at the two coffee shops, the old-fashioned one with the plastic booths and the more stylish one with the gleaming espresso machine, both open and lively with customers.

My contacts appeared somewhat tense. Behind their genuine eagerness to please, I could see they had been worried lest I not show up (this has been known to happen with similar guests, though I myself have rarely defected), irritated at having had to wait, and were now anxiously scrutinizing me in the hope that I would live up to my reputation and thus reflect well on them for having invited me—all natural enough in the circumstances, all very familiar. It made me long for the calm impromptu reception of the Stone Master of Old M———.

I declined the offer of refreshment and climbed into the back seat of the car, where we exchanged remarks I had exchanged with dozens of strangers, dozens of times, in this situation—a combination of weather, flattery, name-dropping, and briefings on my scheduled appearances. Besides the allegedly eager audiences awaiting my presence, there would be several media interviews. I took careful note of all they said, as I had done many times on similar trips.

On a street that resembled the Stone Master's, we pulled up at the guest house, a squarish brick building with no special charm, but I knew from experience that it would be comfortable enough. I declined their offer of help with my bags; I carried no heavy suitcase full of samples, only a razor and a change of clothes. I was the product of my own labor, and I was here for the sale.

The Trip to Halawa Valley

The wedding was over, and its residue showed the pleasing signs of success. The guests had been bedecked with leis—now the orchard of mango and lemon trees was strewn with white ginger petals. Coconut shells and half-eaten papayas, wet and succulent, dotted the grass. The table held the leavings of a feast; the air kept the echo of strumming music and afterimages of hula dancing. Tomorrow the bride and groom would be off for an unknown destination.

"Where do you take a brief honeymoon if you already live in Hawaii?" Jim asked Lois. "Besides which, it's twenty-five hundred miles from anywhere." They sat on lawn chairs, exhausted, watching their oldest son, Paul, and his new wife and her cousins cleaning up. At twenty-four, to his parents' amazement, Paul had made an enormous sum of money after just two years in a Wall Street brokerage firm and rewarded himself with a surfing vacation. On impulse, he bought a lush orchard on the island of Molokai, an instructional manual to go with it, and he remained. Paradise, he scrawled on his postcards.

"I imagine they're going to one of the other islands. To be alone for a while."

"Alone?" He gave an amused frown. "They've been living together for eight months."

Lois answered in kind, a wry glance from their old elaborate language of glances, recalled now like a mother tongue. They had married even younger than Paul and Kalani, with a vision of the road broadening before them, unfurling its adventures.

"Well, if it's privacy they want," Jim said, "then they shouldn't have me on the couch in the next room tonight. I ought to sleep in the cottage with you."

"Sleep with me?" She turned to him lazily. "Shouldn't that be illegal or something?"

"For convenience," he said. "A small courtesy."

"To them, you mean? Or to you?"

He laughed out loud, a man with flashes of charm all the more effective because of his usual somberness. Beneath that he was warm-hearted, aggrieved, delicate. The wedding had made him sentimental, thought Lois. He wanted to hold someone, or something, in his arms. A stuffed toy might do as well.

"Ask me later, okay?"

The wedding had softened her too, but differently. She missed having more family present. Above all, she missed their son Eric, who called two days ago to say he couldn't attend. A close friend had died of AIDS. He had to speak at the funeral. When Paul, disappointed, announced the news to the family gathered in the living room, a cousin of Kalani's said, "Too bad. Molokai's a hangout for drag queens. A lot of them work as waiters. In the inn in town, you'll find them."

"Eric is not a drag queen," Jim had said loudly, half rising from his chair, while Lois put a hand on his arm. The cousin's remark barely touched her. How close, she was wondering. How close a friend?

She missed Suzanne, who would have been seventeen. But that feeling was nothing new. She missed Anthony, Eric's twin; that missing was spiked with anger.

At night she relented—sharing the cottage was a small enough courtesy. They sat side by side in its one bed like married people, though they had been divorced for four years. "So, how about reading to me? Is that the guidebook you're holding? Read about that place Paul said we should go to tomorrow. What is it, Halawa Valley?"

"The w is a v," he said, and repeated it correctly.

"You've been studying up." She felt a stab of remembered admiration. An eager traveler, he always arrived ready, knowledgeable, his mind attuned.

"Sure." He riffled through the pages. "The hike is rated Hardy Family."

"As in Hardy Boys?"

"No. Hardy Family as opposed to Experienced Adults or Easy Family." There was a heavy pause. "Okay, first the road. 'It's a good paved road. The only problem is there's not enough of it. In places, including some cliff-hugging curves, it's really only wide enough for one car and you'll need to do some serious horn tooting.' But it's supposed to be an incredibly beautiful drive."

Lois slid lower on the pillows and yawned. This was one of the games they used to play. When she couldn't fall asleep, Jim would read to her from the newspaper, a sure soporific. Next morning he would quiz her, affecting sternness, to see at what point she'd dropped off. "Fill in the blanks, Lo. 'The mayor lashed out at the members of the blank committee. He proposed a blank percent increase in the number of police.'" Or they'd make up excursions for vacations never taken. "Those fjords, weren't they fantastic? The rushing water, the cliffs ...," Jim murmured for weeks after their trip to Scandinavia had to be canceled because he was fired. He did sound effects for films. Nowadays, with horror and violence in fashion, he was in no danger, was even overworked. Back then, the two-year layoff had been harrowing. Plus, the twins were sickly, and Lois's assistant in the dress shop robbed her blind and then disappeared. All very unnerving. Lois acquired the habit of seeing every mishap as part of a series. Could they be jinxed?

"So much for the road. The hike itself is Molokai's most popular trail, they say, though it's a bit difficult to follow. You'll need sturdy walking shoes—did you bring some? 'The one-hour walk up is neither steep nor particularly strenuous, but it is often muddy and slippery.'"

"Oh, muddy and slippery? Sounds great."

"Lush vegetation, fruit for the picking, mangoes, papayas, blah, blah. Keep an eye on the disappearing water pipe. Voracious mosquitoes. Come on," he said as she groaned. "It's an adventure. Let's think positive."

The very words he had used when Suzanne first got the frightening symptoms. A rare degenerative disease, they were soon told. She was eleven. It had taken six months, and toward the end there was no question of thinking positive. Better not to think at all, just do what the nurses taught them to do. Not long after her death, Anthony joined the Hare Krishnas at eighteen, recruited at the airport on his way to college. Seen in the right light, Jim remarked acidly, that might make a great farce. Their living room was not the right light. When Anthony visited with shaved head, peach-colored robe, and dirty laundry, asking for a contribution, Lois became ill and Jim went out to run, tripped, and gashed his knee, requiring nine stitches.

"Go on, read some more." He had new reading glasses with steel rims, more stylish than the old. He still slept naked. His chest hair was grayer.

"You have to ford a stream by stepping across the stones. They can be 'deceptively slippery.' Or you can wade. But if you wade, it says, 'choose your footing carefully. Water depth can go from ankle-deep to knee-high in one step.' After a heavy rain it's almost impossible to cross safely."

Physical challenges held no intrigue for Lois. Jim was the hiker, skier, swimmer. He favored sports where you covered ground. Took flight. Sometimes he'd go out to run in the middle of the night after hours spent sitting up in bed side by side with her, talking until the words became a dull catechism. Maybe if we hadn't moved ...? The power lines? The food? The strain on Anthony ...

How have we sinned? In no way commensurate with the results. How to continue? Acceptance, humility, move forward. But they balked at that next step. They were too alike, they agreed, something stubborn and immutable in their natures. They should have taken turns mourning and soothing, but like cranky children, each one wanted to be It: grief's target.

The litany was enervating; energy seeped away with each predictable word. Sooner or later bile would come up. "It's a good thing we had a lot of children," Lois had said near the end. "Like peasants. So no matter what happens there are some left to work the land and take care of the parents." Jim glanced over, pained at her levity. "On the contrary, maybe we should've stopped while we were ahead." His form of humor was worse. "Why?" she shot back. "Eric? He's okay. I can live with that." "Sure, I can live with it all right too," Jim said. "But can he? He could get sick any minute. He could be HIV-positive right now. Don't tell me you don't think about it all the time." When Eric had called from college to announce that he was gay, they took it well. After all. And gay couldn't hold a candle to the Hare Krishnas—there was no talking to Anthony since his mind had been colonized. Eric was more than eager to talk about his life. Share, as he put it. In return for their civilized acceptance, he gave affection and details. "Be careful," Lois said each time he phoned, and when she hung up, moaned into the pillow, "This is not turning out as I pictured it."

"Once you cross over," Jim went on, "the trail parallels the stream, but you can't always see it. There's that water pipe to follow, but it comes and goes."

"We'll probably get lost and starve in the woods. Remember on the news the other night, they found a hiker in the woods after a week? He looked half-dead. Paul and Kalani won't be back for days, and no one will think of looking for us."

He still found her amusing, apparently. "It takes longer than that to starve, Lois. Besides, there's all that fruit to pick—mangoes, guavas, whatever."

"We could be washed away in a tsunami. Didn't Kalani say it was a tsunami area?"

"Yes, there was a huge one in 1946, it says here, which took all the taro farms and most of the people. Then another in 1957. There are only seven families left in the valley."

"We could visit the leper colony instead. It's not catching. Nobody shuns the lepers anymore."

He didn't laugh this time. Intent, hard-muscled, dark, he was absorbed in the guidebook propped on his raised knees. Friends had found his somberness intimidating, but not Lois. She saw it as a form of concentration, of rooted-ness in his life. No wonder he needed the running, skiing, swimming. When they finally parted, it was not in anger or antipathy but rather in exhaustion and defeat. If it had not turned out as they pictured it, at least they had completed jointly, as best they could, an assigned task, arduous, demanding. With Eric and Paul grown and in college, they could rest. Being together was not a rest. A reminder.

He was inches away. She focused on her body like a scanner but could find no urge to touch him. Right after Suzanne's death she couldn't bear to touch and suspected he felt the same. The touch and the desire it called forth felt toxic. No more, was all she could think. No more. Of course that madness had soon passed. She wouldn't mind, now, when he wrapped his arms around her to cling in the dark, as he surely would. A reflex.

He looked up, smiling belatedly. "Don't worry. We'll have a fine time. When you get to the falls there's a large pool—that must be the swimming Kalani mentioned. 'Partly because the pool is so deep in the center, the water is shockingly cold.'"

"I can hardly wait."

"You'll like it. You'll be hot from the climb." He seemed to grow more eager as he read. In another age he might have rushed off to join the French Foreign Legion. "The water is red. 'Moaula'—that's the falls—'translates as "red chick-en," and fittingly, the water appears red.' Probably iron in the rocks."

"Or the blood of previous tourists."

"Listen to this. 'If you plan on taking a dip here, it's best to first place a ti leaf in the water. Legend has it that a *mo'o*, a giant lizard-like creature, resides in the pool. If the ti leaf floats, she welcomes company and it's okay to swim. If it sinks, it's a warning she wants no visitors.'" Abruptly, he shut the book and curled onto his side, staring at her. He turned to pluck a petal from the vase on the night table and rested it carefully on the sheet covering her. "What about you, Lois?"

"I want no visitors."

১৯

She inched around yet another hairpin turn, peering sideways through the windshield for a broader view, then slowed almost to a halt as a battered pickup clattered by from the opposite direction. She was the steadier driver. Jim was given to fits of rashness or caution that made her close her eyes. Once, driving to the hospital to see Suzanne, he hit a truck. No one was hurt; the police took them the rest of the way.

"Look out there on the right," she said. A sweep of blue sea and surf came into view below the sheer drop of rock, and in the distance, the islands of Maui and Lanai rose green and hazy, low tufty clouds dappling them with shadow. She glanced up to see more clouds amassing in a pale gray sky. It was risky to take her eyes off the road even for an instant, though. She tooted around another absurdly narrow curve. Jim seemed far away, gazing up at outcroppings of jagged black rock like half-finished sculptures.

Pain brought some couples closer and divided others. This was the sort of wisdom purveyed on the back pages of the daily paper, deduced from academic studies. Lois read the articles the way a mutilated veteran might read a text-book account of his battle—sure, tell me about it. A friend who had found Buddhism lectured her on freeing herself of expectations. But how could you live without them? Unless you were a monk or a saint. The world ran on effort and reward, action and results, investment and return. Was it unreasonable to expect your daughter to grow up?

Soon the road headed downhill, ending in a valley walled by bulbous mountains that embraced a jigsaw-puzzle shoreline. Lois parked near the beach and rubbed her tense neck. "Okay. Muddy and slippery rocks, disappearing path, shockingly cold water—here we come."

"You forgot the voracious mosquitoes." He led the way to the tiny green church where the road began. According to the book, they were to proceed for half a mile past several houses, and at the last house to find a footpath.

They found a chain stretched across the road and a mis-spelled hand-lettered sign nailed to a post. "Road Closed. Keep Out. No Acess to Falls." They were slanting block let-ters crudely drawn, crammed close together as they neared the right-hand edge.

"What's this all about?" He stiffened, as though he might stamp his foot in anger. "That can't be an official sign. If they were serious, they'd block the road." He stepped over the chain. "Come on."

"It says it's closed. Maybe there's flooding. It could be dangerous. Anyway..." She looked up at the graying sky.

"We can always turn back. How bad can it be? It's a major tourist spot."

"But there are no other tourists."

A Jeep appeared in the clearing in front of the church, and Jim charged over. The driver, a middle-aged Hawaiian man wearing an aloha shirt and a baseball cap, answered his questions in a lilting pidgin accent. No, there was nothing wrong with the trail and no flooding. But the road was on private property—those seven families awaiting the next tsunami, Lois thought—and the local people weren't happy about visitors going up and back. Specifically, they didn't want to be held liable for injuries that might occur on the trail. They couldn't afford liability insurance.

"But the path and the falls—that's not private property, is it?"

"No, but see? You pass by the houses …"

"I'm sure nothing's going to happen to us. And if it did, we certainly wouldn't sue any of the homeowners." Jim gave a winning smile, a new smile she was not familiar with. He probably used it on new women. Sunny, guileless, quite unlike the sky, which darkened as they spoke.

The man regarded them kindly. "You like go—go. If you see any locals, you tell 'um you understand the situation, 'kay?"

"Thanks very much." Jim took her arm firmly and led her back to the chain.

"Don't you feel it?" She rubbed drops off her bare arms. "Didn't it say crossing the stream is dangerous in the rain?"

"After a heavy rain. This is nothing." And he beckoned from the other side of the chain.

The first house, on the left, was a ramshackle wooden cottage with a refrigerator outside the front door and cut-off jeans hanging on a line. A rusty pickup stood moldering in the front yard. No people in sight. As they neared the second house, it began to pour. They turned and ran, leaping over the chain and making a dash for the car, where they waited briefly until the outburst settled into a dreary patter.

At the car rental window four days ago, a man ahead of them had complained, "With the kind of rain you get here, you need wipers that work. You ought to check them out first." Lois started up the winding road into the mountains, praying that the wipers would work. Her prayers were granted.

∞

"I'll sleep in the cottage. I'm used to it," she said that night when Jim invited her to join him in the empty main house. But she went over for breakfast the next morning. As they ate papayas from the orchard, he urged her into a second attempt at the falls. "Why not, Lo? It's a perfect day." He drove so Lois could enjoy the views. Enduring his last-minute hesitations at each curve and then his heart-stopping dashes forward was almost worth it: the mountains, remains of ancient volcanoes, were deeply scored as if by the tines of a giant fork. A lacework of surf spread out on the shore below, and the neighboring islands appeared untouched, sparkling, mythical. No hints of rain—they'd have to go through with it: muddy, slippery stones, perilous stream crossing, voracious mosquitoes, shockingly cold water.

Again they stepped over the chain. "Ready?" he asked with the new smile.

The shabby houses and yards along the road were brightened by jasmine and plumeria, whose mingled scents rose like a fragrant mist. After a few minutes Lois could see where the dirt road ended and the narrow path began. Good. Anything was better than her anxious anticipation. Suddenly from the yard of the last house came ferocious barking. Three large black dogs leaped about, then bounded toward the open fence.

"Dobermans," she said.

"One of them is lame. Look, he can't run very fast."

"Fast enough. They're heading straight for us. This is too much." She wheeled around. "They can keep their falls."

Jim didn't put up a fight. He'd been bitten by a stray years ago and needed a series of rabies shots. "Okay, but don't run. If we go slow, they'll stop chasing."

They took long strides, trying to cover ground while appearing casual. At first the dogs were close behind, then they must have slackened—the barking grew less intense, but Lois was afraid to look back and check. By the time they stepped over the chain, the barks were intermittent. She turned to see the panting dogs some yards off, standing poised, on guard, then slinking away as if disappointed.

"Do you think we gave up too easily?" she asked from a safe distance. "They might have backed off." Other people, she did not add, might have known how to calm the dogs, even befriend them.

"Dobermans? No! What a nerve. It's one thing to discourage tourists, but this is an outrage."

He was still fuming as Lois drove back. Going round the bends, they met several pickup trucks with young Hawaiian men piled in back, laughing and talking loudly. Perhaps they lived in the ramshackle cottages. One of them might even own the Dobermans.

She headed for the café at the town's single hotel, where they sat facing the sea. Lois studied the horizon. Somewhere out in that vastness were Paul and Kalani. Even farther, Eric. But where, exactly?

"There was a meeting last night about closing the road." Jim was leafing through the island's thin paper. "Exactly what the fellow told us—they claim they're in danger of being sued and can't take the financial risk. Nothing about setting dogs on people, though."

"All right, look, it's over. It's just one sight we didn't see. Like the fjords."

Oh, those magnificent fjords, she wanted to hear him say. Unforgettable. The wind in our faces, the rushing water, the raw fish we ate on the boat. Instead he said, "It's the principle of the thing. It's all political, you know. The liability issue is just a front." He rattled the paper. "They don't come right out and say it, but it's there between the lines. They don't like tourists, they don't like whites traipsing over their land. You can hardly blame them after the atrocious history." He reminded her of how Hawaii came to be a territory—a gruesome account of missionaries turned exploiters and entrepreneurs, of brutal plantation owners, culminating in a sneaky takeover by the Marines a century ago that rankled more, not less, as years passed. "Paradise— hah!" he grumbled. It was a story of trust betrayed, of bitter disillusion, of promise turned to ash. The facts were vaguely familiar to Lois from a few pages in the guidebook, but Jim obviously knew more than could be learned from a guidebook. He had read up about the fjords too.

"With all that," he wound up, "we still have a right to see the falls."

"Right or not, it doesn't look as if we will. Jim, that waitress. Over there." The waitress was navigating between tables, balancing a heavy tray on her upraised arm. "You think she could be a man?"

"Oh, the drag queens." He took off his reading glasses.

"Please. Cross-dressers." They both grinned. Eric, who worked at a left-wing magazine, could be relied upon to teach the latest in proper terminology. He had told them months in advance about Oriental becoming Asian and black becoming African American. Even "queer" was being resuscitated, but he said they needn't go that far.

The waitress was striking, tall and slender, with a strong tanned face and shoulder-length dark hair. She wore a long print dress slit up the center that showed off her legs.

"She has very narrow shoulders, though."

"Lots of men have narrow shoulders." Jim scrutinized with the air of a connoisseur. "And she's kind of flat-chested."

"Lots of women are flat-chested."

Their eyes were following the waitress serving a group of Japanese tourists when just behind her appeared the Hawaiian man of the day before, who had encouraged them to take the path. He spotted them too and headed over.

"You keep following me or what?" he said with a broad smile. "This must be one small island. So how was your trip? You wen hike through the valley and see the falls? One nasty storm, eh? Lucky wen stop fast."

They told him about the Dobermans and he offered to call the dogs' owner and see that they were locked up the next day, if they cared to try again.

They exchanged a private glance in the old language. "Thank you," said Lois, "but we'll be leaving tomorrow. Anyway, twice up and back on that road is enough."

"Okay, then. I hope your stay stay good." He turned away to hail the waitress. "Hey, Tiny. What's up?" They shook hands energetically.

❧

Instead of going out for dinner, they cooked together in Paul and Kalani's kitchen, then watched the local news.

After the weather and surfing reports, Lois heard herself saying, "Listen, what the hell? The giant lizard welcomes visitors."

Jim looked surprised but not baffled. He remembered. His face changed—not mere courtesy, she hoped. No, it modulated to a familiarly dreamy, subtle expression, while his body grew more alert. "That's a terrific idea." He stood over her, extending a hand. "Your place or mine?"

"Yours. Since I'm here already."

But in the morning she was sorry. He was an adroit lover, always had been. After years apart they made love with the excitement of strangers, the tantalizing sense of discovery mellowed by trust. Strangers who knew their way around. Some frozen place in her, shockingly cold, had thawed a bit, and its tenderness was not welcome or comfortable.

ೞ

A twelve-seater plane skimmed low over the sea to bring them to the Honolulu airport. They would fly to Los Angeles, where Lois would change for Seattle. A long time together, she'd thought when she made her plans. Still, it wasn't as if they didn't get along or couldn't bear each other's company.

"The wedding went well, didn't it?" he said, settling in for the long trip. Lois agreed. Here was a new and better litany. How happy the young couple appeared. How beautiful the island was. How lucky Paul was to have found the orchard, to have found Kalani. There was a rich satisfaction in their words, which they felt equally and could feel only with each other. It was as if, in reciting Paul's good fortune, they were congratulating themselves: yes, they had done this part of their task well. And yet they knew—they had been over this ground so often—that pride was as misplaced as guilt. They had labored in the dark, through a mystery, their part in it infinitesimal. Far more potent forces laid claim to their children. To themselves.

They knew, but knowing could not erase—and why should it?—that rich satisfaction, so fine and pure it might even be called love. Why could it not be enough? she wondered. Along with the night before, in bed. Did others, the ones whom pain brought closer, have something more? Know something more? Were she and Jim weak not to hang on? Or strong, seeing the inevitable and yielding with grace?

"A good visit, all in all." His voice, sly and intimate, penetrated her musings. "But I think the most memorable part was the trip to Halawa Valley."

"Halawa Valley? That fiasco?"

"The one-hour walk up wasn't really too strenuous, even though it was muddy. Luckily we had sturdy old sneakers with us."

It was a moment before she could respond. It had been easier to take him into her body. "The path was pretty hard to follow…" She hesitated while his eyes held steady, urging her on. "But we kept alongside the water pipe. You were a good guide."

"Those stones crossing the stream were deceptively slippery too. I'm glad we decided to wade across instead. And we chose our footing carefully."

"It was scary when the water went from ankle-high to knee-high in one step. It was almost impossible to cross safely. But we managed."

"And remember the fruit? Wasn't it delicious?" he asked.

"Yes, though I didn't care much for the voracious mosquitoes." She laughed and scratched her shoulder, even as she felt the tears rising.

"Well, me neither."

"The falls were even more beautiful than we expected."

"Yes," he replied. "Eric would have loved it. A pity he couldn't come."

"But that water! I still shiver when I think of it. Shockingly cold." The mystery of it all did make her shiver, right there in her seat.

"And red," he added. "Don't forget, red. I'm glad the ti leaf floated, though, aren't you? So we could swim."

"The giant lizard welcomed us."

"The *mo'o*. Yes, often she wants no visitors, but I guess she was in a good mood. Or she just liked us."

The plane landed with ease in Los Angeles. They kissed good-bye lightly, then Jim went to find a cab and Lois hurried off to make her connecting flight. The airport was shockingly cold, especially after the warmth of the island that had seeped into her skin. Again she shivered, and again.

Note: Quotations about Halawa Valley are from Glenda Bendure and Ned Friary, *Hawaii, A Travel Survival Kit* (Berkeley: Lonely Planet Publications, 1990), p. 417.

The Word

I've forgotten the word, the word that was so crucial I promised myself I'd jot it down as soon as I got a chance—I was on the street at the time, walking from the bank, where I'd made a deposit, to the drugstore, or maybe it was from the drugstore to the dry cleaner's or the copy shop—anyway, the word was a reminder of the idea for a story that came to me in the bank or drugstore and I vowed to write it down as soon as I got to the library, after I'd picked up my necklace at the jeweler's; it did occur to me to stop right there on the street and get out a pencil and paper—how I wish I had, but I was so sure I'd do it later. There happened to be a scrap of paper in my pocket with a few words on it for another story I was planning, about a writer going blind who hires an assistant to help with his correspondence and then begins to suspect the assistant is lying about what's in his mail, making up fan letters to cheer him up or possibly for some more sinister motive.... (The words for that story were "writer going blind.") That would have been an appropriate scrap of paper for the new word, the two notations

146

forming a little list of ideas for when I got to my desk after my errands, but no, I thought I couldn't possibly forget once I got to the library since the word was so perfect, summing up or representing or by some idiosyncratic connection clear only to me bearing the germ of that excellent, memorable (ha!) idea for a story, maybe even a novel—I can't remember now how far I thought the idea could take me—a word that would suffice to make the idea flower in my mind, or rather re-flower since it had already flowered in the drugstore or wherever, generated by I can't remember what. Certain words can do that, can bear that weight, at least they've done so in the past if I write them down fast enough—but once in the library I did forget, distracted by whatever insignificance took place at the dry cleaner's or the jeweler's or by something I saw on the street or some new thoughts intervening on the way; I don't think it was any kind of self-sabotage since I'm not usually so inclined, and besides, I wholeheartedly liked the idea as well as its word and was eager to take it and run with it.

But now that the word is gone there's no use trying to recall it since, as we all know, that only drives lost words farther away. I've tried to remember what led up to the idea (if anything at all—sometimes ideas appear out of the blue, in which case such efforts are even more fruitless), tried to reconstruct my train of thought in that painstaking, frustrating way one does; I've tried to reconstruct what I might have seen on my various stops that could have triggered it, but no luck, all I come up with are useless details (a man in the dry cleaner's trying on a sports jacket, the tailor with a tape measure around his neck pinning up the sleeves, or the jeweler's long fingers curved around the new and more secure clasp on my necklace), while the word itself and the idea it stood for recede like a tumbleweed in the desert in the wind, and my only hope now is that it might return as unaccountably as it came, some propitious wind blowing it back in my direction so I can write whatever it was I had in mind. But I have no real faith that this will happen. I could try physically retracing my steps of that morning—it's common knowledge that a return to the setting or, figuratively, the context, will often resurrect lost memories—but for one thing, I don't remember the exact sequence of my steps, which might be important, and moreover, if the idea came from something I witnessed on the street or in the bank or wherever, it's unlikely, in fact impossible, that the same events would repeat themselves, and even if by some wild quirk of fate they did, who knows whether they would have the same impact, that is, whether I would be identically receptive; a different state of mind could override the potency of context.

So the story or novel that might have blossomed from the word a few months or years from now will never exist, and maybe it wasn't meant to. But wait, what does that mean, wasn't meant to exist? That's just some rationalizing claptrap. I used to think stories were meant or not meant to exist, and therefore remembering or forgetting their key words was a sign of their preordained destiny—a kind of literary Calvinism—which makes sense in a way: if you forget, then the idea simply wasn't vital enough. But nowadays I think you can forget very vital ideas indeed by being distracted, though of course this can never be proved since the evidence has disappeared. Everything conceived has a potential existence, in theory at least. Its actual existence depends on whether it's feasible and whether one takes steps to make it actual. And while some people are too lazy or passive or otherwise unwilling to take such steps, I'm quite willing, but how can I if I've forgotten the word? Of course the story resulting from the word might not have been any good, but under the circumstances I'll never know, and so that's not much consolation. Anyway, that's not the point, how good it would have been; the point was to take my chances and do it.

And even if the word does come back, days or weeks from now, it might well come without its idea; the idea might have detached from it like something the tumbleweed was dragging along but that fell off and was left behind in the desert, and then the word would be just a word, maybe very ordinary, maybe one I hear and use all the time. But if it comes back announcing itself as the crucial word in the unmistakably portentous tones such words have, it'll be baffling, hollow instead of dense with potential, and while I might recognize it as the word and remember murmuring it in front of the copy shop and planning to write it down, at the same time I'll wonder what on earth was so intriguing or crucial about it. What was that density that evaporated, leaving it so hollow?

Intrusions

It was a warm June day, maybe four o'clock, four-thirty. I was wearing a navy blue and white striped sleeveless mini dress, more like a long tank top actually, and in my right hand I held a slotted spoon, and in a small room off the hall was my eighteen-month-old baby standing up and rattling the bars of her crib the way they do at that age. I was stirring chicken and chunks of pineapple in the electric frying pan—sweet and sour chicken, which I didn't particularly like but it seemed festive—when I heard footsteps. I went to look. Approaching from the end of the long hall was a thin, sallow kid in droopy jeans and a windbreaker and a porkpie hat. My first thought was what a long reach it was from the fire escape to the bedroom window and what a long drop. He'd taken quite a risk. Next I thought he would rape me because of the mini dress, or kill me, or maybe both, and if not for the baby in the crib I would have preferred, at that moment, just to be killed.

I was preparing the sweet and sour chicken for the parents of a Barnard student from Cleveland for whom I was acting as a big sister. They were visiting their daughter in New York City for the first time; I was not much older than the student myself and I wanted to do everything just right. Months earlier, before I met the student who was to be my little sister, a friend in the alumnae office had called to say, I just want to let you know your sister is black, so when she appears at your door you don't look surprised. Her warning was unsettling, even offensive to me as well as to the student. But things were in such turmoil then, thirty-odd years ago, that people of good will often behaved with astounding clumsiness. No doubt my friend was trying to protect the student from my possible surprise. That was unnecessary, I thought; I wouldn't have shown any surprise, or so I hoped. I would never know for sure. Anyway, I was determined to make the evening go smoothly.

I said to the kid, What do you want? and he said, I came to tell you your house is on fire, the hall is full of smoke. I didn't believe him but I had to be sure, so I walked toward him with the slotted spoon raised like a weapon, and past his skinny tense body, to open the door and see. Those two seconds when I passed him, when we were inches apart, I thought, Goodbye, life. He didn't touch me, but now he was closer than I was to the room with the baby. The hall was not full of smoke. I stood at the open door, and if I'd been alone I would have run out, but I couldn't leave the baby. My daily life was full of reminders that everything was different, more fraught with consequence, when you had a baby to think about, but this was the most potent reminder yet.

The boy came toward me, a shuffling, arrogant walk; again we would be inches apart, but I could see he wanted to get out now. Once he was past me and out the door he started to run. Up the stairs to the roof.

I knocked on the doors of two of my neighbors for help. The first was the anthropology professor next door, the flirt, to put it politely; his field was Mayan culture, and he and his wife were always going to Mexico. I knew he owned a machete, something to do with his archeological digs among the ruins, and he had once said to me jokingly, If you ever need help, just bang on the door, and I'll come with my machete. Many of his remarks had a double entendre, but at this moment I literally wanted him with his machete and said so, and he rose to the occasion, wearing his usual plaid bathrobe and carrying the machete as promised.

The other neighbor was an actor who would later appear on *Sesame Street*, the father of four children. My own children—the one now standing up in her crib and the one not yet born—would watch him on *Sesame Street* and be thrilled to see him in the halls and to play in his apartment with his children, who by that time would number five, but the thrill would quickly wear off. He too came with alacrity, and the two men chased the intruder over the roof while I went back to see to the baby in the crib—I was afraid to leave her alone—but they didn't catch him. I thought, well, anyway, my neighbor the professor is more than just a flirt—he made good on his word.

I thanked them and went back and finished cooking the sweet and sour chicken, which seemed the logical thing to do: nothing was really changed except in my mind, and why shouldn't the festive dinner still take place? The parents had come all the way from Cleveland. My husband came home from work and my little sister and her family arrived; the sweet and sour chicken was appreciated, and it was a pleasant evening, all in all. I told my story and my audience was duly shocked: out-of-towners love to hear New York crime stories. They enjoy having their worst fears confirmed, and while that usually irritates me, this time it was gratifying.

After that incident in the hall I couldn't sit still at the front end of the apartment for more than fifteen minutes at a stretch for fear that someone was climbing in the back window. I had to keep walking down the hall to check the window. Every little noise I thought was another intruder. At night, if my husband was working late and I was home alone with the baby, I imagined a boy just like the boy in the porkpie hat walking down the hall. I couldn't concentrate on reading in the living room because my ears were on the alert for his footsteps; sometimes I couldn't stay in the living room at all but had to take my book to the bedroom so I could keep an eye on the window. But out of pride I refused to keep the window closed all that hot summer; I refused to give in to my fear. I wouldn't give the boy—or my fear—the satisfaction of my discomfort in a stuffy apartment. I thought of going to a psychiatrist—it was that bad—but knowing little about therapy at the time, I reasoned that it would do no good since my fear was based on a real incident, not a fantasy or neurotic exaggeration. Things improved slightly when the weather got cold and I had a legitimate reason to close the window, but still that was a dark and terrible year. I thought I would never get over my fright. Then gradually I did.

Later, my little sister married a Columbia Law School student and they had a baby named Chad after the lake in Africa; the name also had some other ethnic significance, which they must have explained but I no longer remember. They invited my husband and me over for an African dinner, a very good stew in which peanuts were a key ingredient. After a while they got divorced.

Many years later, soon after the game professor next door unexpectedly died, there was a fire in the building and the hall truly was full of smoke, but as it happened I wasn't there to see it because I had a temporary job out of town. I was living alone in a large house in a small city and always kept the door unlocked and was never afraid. The children were big then, and I left them with my husband for several months—they had long since stopped watching *Sesame Street* and the actor and his wife were divorced too. She took the five children and moved to the suburbs and he shortly remarried and had two more children. No one was hurt in the fire, but our apartment and the apartment of the actor and of the professor's widow were pretty much ruined. I never made sweet and sour chicken again—I had never made it before that night—and I never wore that dress again either.

ை

That part was easy to write. More or less. Nothing is truly easy to write, but I mean it didn't present any excruciating difficulties or demands. What follows will be harder. In the interests of full disclosure—not my usual mode—I will say that the above is the result of an exercise I assigned to a group of students. I told them to write about an incident from their past, giving as many tangible details as they could manage but omitting all interpretation or subjectivity. Just the facts. It's an exercise that diverts students, at least briefly, from their seductive and endless and often fruitless soul-searching and forces them to concentrate on things and words. They resist, but in the end they're always amazed, as I am, at how much better their writing is when the goal ceases to be self-expression.

I did the exercise with them. That always feels so democratic: look, I'm the same as you; we all have to start from scratch each time. There's not much else to do, anyway, for those fifteen or twenty minutes that they're scribbling. And I thought I might get something useful out of it, the germ of something. When we read the pieces aloud (the students trading papers and reading anonymously to protect their privacy, not that anyone cares much about privacy anymore), I liked the way mine sounded and decided to pursue it. In the process, as is obvious, I broke my own rules here and there, but outside the classroom rules are of no importance.

Maybe it was too easy. When I showed it to someone, she said there was something missing, something maybe I was trying to avoid. She suspected it had to do with race. Was the intruder black, and was there some unexamined connection between that and the student being black? Also, why didn't I close the window? she asked. I thought I had explained that adequately. A reader has to accept a writer's perversities—they are an essential part of the story.

But I thought dutifully about the issue of race. I didn't know what race the intruder was; he had the kind of olive-skinned face that at first glance might have been anything, and I was too terrified to study him closely. His race didn't, and doesn't, seem a crucial matter. I searched my soul the way the students do and found nothing. Only his clothes remained vivid—the droopy jeans, the dark windbreaker, much too hot for the weather, and the ridiculous hat. His race didn't seem to have anything to do with my sister and her family, who viewed the boy as our common enemy; the divisiveness of class can be more powerful than that of race, and my sister's parents were archetypally middle-class and genteel, so genteel and well dressed, I recall, that I was slightly abashed at the artsy-craftsy, eclectic surroundings in which I was entertaining them. I hoped they wouldn't think I was *outré*, a bad influence. Of course the presence of a husband and a clearly well-cared-for baby was a mitigating factor. But at the time none of this felt very important. In fact the more I think about that reader's response the more it sounds like the warning of my friend in the alumnae office: making an issue out of what should be a non-issue. Then again, race is always an issue, which I suppose is why I included it in the first place. The account wouldn't have seemed complete or true to its moment without it, unfortunately.

That warning, though, was definitely an issue. In time I got to be good friends with my little sister, especially after she graduated from college and grew up. But the fact that my friend in the alumnae office had alerted me that she was black always remained as a faint shadow on our friendship, something about its genesis that I could never tell her, and this something was not of my making nor of hers: it too intruded, unwelcome, from outside.

I was fond of that friend in the alumnae office, and yet somehow we lost touch. I'm wondering now if her well-meant remark had anything to do with our losing touch. Hard to say; I've lost touch with many people for no special reason. Only writing this makes me think about it and regret it. I could look her up. I've lost touch with my sister too; she moved back to Cleveland with her child shortly after her divorce and I never heard from her again. I wouldn't know where to begin finding her. Through the alumnae office, I suppose.

But to return: I went back and examined each of the elements of my story to see if and where I might be hedging.

The first thing that struck me was those pineapple chunks I was stirring in the electric frying pan. I would never cook anything involving pineapple chunks today. I noted in the piece that I didn't like pineapple, or to be precise, that I didn't like sweet and sour chicken; today I wouldn't cook anything I didn't like, even to please guests. But beyond that, pineapple chunks are so out of fashion, I wouldn't be caught dead serving them. Also, on the subject of food, I found it curious that I went right on cooking the dinner even though I was so upset. If a similar incident were to occur today—God forbid!—I'd probably drop everything, have a fit, pour a stiff drink, and when the guests came, send out for Chinese or Indian food. I wouldn't worry about proving my stoicism or resilience or culinary skills, which by now have been amply proven. With the passage of time one has so much less to prove. I'm older now than the Cleveland parents were then, and I know they would have understood. (On the other hand, decent take-out food was far less available back then.)

I felt some nostalgia over that mini dress, which I probably wouldn't wear today any more than I would serve pineapple chunks, but for different reasons. Also, on the subject of the mini dress, my phrase "I thought he would rape me because of the mini dress..." is questionable. We all know now, better than we did then, that rape is not caused by short skirts, and thank goodness the "she was asking for it" defense has been discredited, at least publicly if not in some hearts and minds. And yet I might well think the same thing today, even if I know better.

In the end, food and clothing weren't really germane to my quest: even if my attitudes have proved subject to revision, the transcription of them isn't evasive. (It would have been evasive to try to sneak my current revisions into my account, making my younger, naïve self sound more sophisticated, which is always a temptation.)

The hall is full of smoke: those were the words the boy spoke to me. And as I say toward the end, years later the hall indeed was full of smoke since there was a fire in the building. Volumes could be written about that, and as a matter of fact I did write one, so I feel no need to reiterate it here— it wouldn't enhance the story—and I feel safe from the charge of avoiding anything on that score.

I noted the minimal mention of my husband. Was I being cagey there? I think not. He wasn't home for the incident, and I didn't get a chance to discuss it with him in private until late that night when the guests had left and we were cleaning up. We did talk about it at length, and he was suitably concerned and even put bars on the window (though they seemed impregnable, they did little to ease my terror, so I guess a psychiatrist might have been in order). He did all that could be expected, but none of that seemed part of the story.

I thought about the tactic of ramification, which I used, I think, to good effect. Here's where I might be most open to a charge of avoiding something, or rather to being arbitrarily selective, choosing certain details to elaborate rather than others. I chose those instinctively, through a sense of what would be dramatic or piquant or obliquely connected to the subject. (It's lethal to analyze such choices, so I won't go any further.) Other details did occur to me but I passed over them—for instance a couple of items in the lives of my little sister or my neighbors—because however piquant, such items would violate their privacy and to no purpose. The only essentials in this story are the intrusion itself and its aftermath; the details are deliberately arbitrary and reflect the peculiarities of memory and association at moments of crisis. I might have said, with no danger to anyone's privacy, that I once offered my sister a piece of a very hard, sweet Italian confection called *panforte* and quipped, Don't break a tooth on it, and then she did just that, and I felt very bad and arranged an appointment for her with my dentist. Or that my next-door neighbor, the professor, died very suddenly and tragically of toxemia: thereby hangs a tale, as they say. Or that the seventh child of my other neighbor, the actor who later appeared on *Sesame Street* and divorced and remarried, grew up to be a famous rock star. But none of that is necessary. And why, anyway, should I mention his child who became a rock star rather than one of the six others, say, who became an electrical engineer? Because a rock star is the kind of profession one would note if one noted anything at all in that vein; this is not democratic, alas, but true. In any case, that piquant detail didn't figure here.

My conscience is clear now. I have nothing to hide: I wrote the piece in order to write about my fear. To articulate the fear that once gripped me, have it out in the world, shaped and visible, rather than unseen, in me. Even before the actual writing, while I was watching the students scribble away and casting about for a subject of my own, the reason this incident came to mind and not some other is that the fear is always available, always on tap. I don't mean I'm still afraid of intruders; I'm not. I rarely think about intruders. Anyway, since the fire we've lived in another apartment with a different layout; I couldn't feel the same fear without the same long hall and the same window. I mean that the shape and texture of that specific fear—not the momentary fear of the boy but the long fear afterward of someone like the boy climbing in that window, so that for a year I couldn't sit still unless I had my eye on it—has lodged in me for good. Now and then I visit it, say hello. I might even miss it were I to forget it, but there's no danger of that. And I don't marvel at it as a strange thing of the past, the way I marvel that I ever cooked pineapple chunks or calmly prepared and served a whole dinner in a state of suppressed terror; the fear strikes me as entirely natural and comprehensible. It's part of me, like a scar you grow attached to. Precious, if not exactly beloved. I don't wish it gone, though of course I would have preferred the intruder never to have intruded. But since he did, the fear he caused is mine now, preserved in amber, the insect's delicate wing forever caught mid-tremor.

I told my older daughter I had written a few pages about this incident but that something might be missing. My daughter is grown now; she was the eighteen-month-old baby standing in the crib and rattling its bars when the intruder entered, the baby I was afraid to leave alone when my instinct was to flee the scene. Back then I wasn't totally accustomed to her existence but now I cannot conceive of my life without her. She said maybe I should write more, write about my unease with the ambiguities surrounding the piece. She knows me well and I take her advice seriously; this time I felt specially prone to do so, for she was there at the time, exposed to the same peril as I was, and that gives her some rights in the matter. So I've done what she advised, although doing so defies all my writerly instincts, which run opposite to the aesthetic of full disclosure; I prefer concealment, cunning, and artifice. But somehow I felt honor-bound to her suggestion. And why not, I thought, it might be good for me, like the exercises I give students and consider good for them.

I think I didn't do justice, in the telling, to my fear. I didn't do it justice because, for one thing, my own feelings and experiences—recounted in a straightforward way, that is—rarely entice me as raw material. Terrible and frightening things happen every day. They're not enough. What entices is not what happened but the transforming of it. So what I wrote can't satisfy me because it's limited to truth. It's not even cathartic—not that that would justify its existence—since the fear remains, in amber, as vivid and gleaming as the day it was born. I'm mildly glad to have shaped it into words after so long, to have played around with it and made it a thing that stands in the world like a piece of granite rather than a delicate hidden insect in amber. And in some strange way, having shaped it for public disclosure makes it all the more mine. Still, the fear I've described isn't porous or malleable, but rather solid and intransigent. Even when set in its context of class, race, and young urban married life, it doesn't go beyond itself.

It stops short of what's behind the fear. It stops short of the excitement of it, the lure of disaster, the subterranean enticement to let disaster have you, so that after the boy leaves, besides the obvious relief, there's the merest trace of letdown. He came in, he scared you half to death, then he left? That's all? Well, what more do you want? To be raped or killed? No, no. What, then? To know what it's like without having to feel it. To know but not to suffer. (Which is the experience that stories offer us, come to think of it.)

For all those reasons, what I set down isn't enough. It would be enough only if I were to transform all the details—the pineapple chunks, the mini dress, the neighbors, the family from Cleveland—disguise them like guests at a masked ball, making them as unrecognizable and even far-fetched in design as flowers are from their roots, so that only the fear kept its true face, standing out in the masked crowd, its face alone stark and bare, grimacing, potent, leer-ing, and spreading like a stain, consuming everything in its orbit like a hoop of fire. And I'm captivated by it, by the threat of my own destruction.

ಶಿಲ

I would begin with notes, with whatever random images offer themselves, and see where they lead, whether they coa-lesce into anything resembling or remotely equivalent to my fear.

Okay. Someone not me, but scared like me. She's young, let's say twenty-five. She comes to New York right after col-lege, from the boondocks, not too far away, though. She wants excitement. She wants glamour, the kind of life she's read about in slick magazines, where long-haired girls in spaghetti-strap dresses dance all night in discos on a perpetual high from something or other (but let's not get into any drug scene here, not relevant). Or stroll into foreign-sounding restaurants on the arms of rich bronzed men. Yachts. Caribbean vacations. Celebrity parties. All an absurd fantasy, that's clear, concocted to sell magazines to girls exactly like her, from small towns, bored girls with no money who feel they're destined for some-thing better than what they've seen so far. She thinks she's beautiful enough, bold enough for all that. She'll get a job, something in the music business, PR or advertising. Buy the right clothes. Hunt out the right places. No plan, no thought, just fantasy. An incredible naïveté. Sleepwalking through her life. (Thirty years ago, maybe. But can anyone be so naïve today? I think so. Wait and see.)

This is all background. This is not the story proper. Keep going and the story will turn up.

Well, she couldn't swing it. No surprise there. She didn't know where to begin, knew no one, and worst of all she had no money. In desperation she gets a job as a receptionist in a law firm, not what she had in mind. She has to buy suits and silk shirts and pumps instead of slim spaghetti-strap dresses and high-heeled sandals—all on a credit card, naturally. They hire her because she's decorative and has a faintly Latin look—her mother was born in Puerto Rico. She doesn't know that's why they hire her, or if the thought crosses her mind she dismisses it. Not interested. She's never thought much about it, the whole ethnic issue hasn't been part of her suburban life (suburban? Or small-town? Work that out later). She can barely speak Spanish. Her mother came here at the age of two. She likes salsa, but so does everyone else. Whatever. They hire her, that's all she cares about. They say they'll train her to do paralegal work eventually, but meanwhile they need a receptionist. And she needs money, fast. She can't ask her parents. Her father's been sick, out of work, and they're probably hoping she can help them out one of these days. She lives in a tiny, dilapidated but costly apartment on the edge of a newly chic downtown neighborhood. Chic but squalid. A firetrap. The banisters of the hall stairs give her splinters, the bathtub has claws, the sink has orange and green stains, the windows have to be tugged open, the screens are torn, the wood floors are furry with wear, the ceiling fixtures are bare bulbs, and worst of all, there are mice. She's afraid of mice, of small swift creatures in general. (There, that's the ticket! But not mice. A bird? Yes, maybe a bird.)

Still, she tries not to let this, or the drug dealers on the corner, get her down. She'll find the right life, only it might take longer than she expected. If she were an artist, an actor or a dancer, she could hook up with the right people. But she has no special talents. She's not stupid, she knows there are things she can do, she just doesn't know yet what they are and she has no one to help her find out. (How do you find out when you're that kind of girl—sheltered, uninformed, unformed? When what you thought was your boldness shrinks and shrivels in the gust of the city like a cheap shirt in the wash?) She has a couple of friends from school but they can't help; they're pretty much in the same boat. They go to discos together but can't seem to connect with the right people. The guys they meet are creeps from New Jersey.

That's roughly who she is, then, an eager girl who doesn't know yet who she is. Enough for a start. Now for a trial run.

ⱭᎦ

Barely awake in the gray dawn, she heard a hazy fluttering noise, like rustling paper or wind beating on leaves. She concentrated. It might not even be real, might be the last shreds of a dream unraveling. Or the embryo of a new dream.

It persisted. It was real, perhaps from the bird's nest in the maple tree right outside the open bedroom window. There might be a nest of wasps, out here in the country. Sometimes squirrels climbed the branches in the first light and pattered across the roof over her head. Their pattering reminded her of mice, but she knew they couldn't get in.

The clock said ten after six. The mist could lift; the days often started out this way near the sea, then modulated into brilliance. The sound, too, would go away if she ignored it. She pulled the sheet around her, curled her knees to her chest to still any possible rustling from within—yes, there was that, but she wouldn't think about it yet—and sank back to sleep.

When she woke again at nine she had forgotten the sound. She pulled on shorts and a striped shirt and went downstairs. She saw the thing at once and gasped: it lay in the windowed alcove of the dining room, right near a leg of the oak table. Lucky she'd slipped into sandals. She hoped with all her might that it was only a clump of dust, although the house was kept ferociously neat. A wood chip from the fireplace? But it was no use hoping—it stirred. Please, not a mouse—she thought she'd escaped mice forever. Whatever it was, the blob was barely alive, an offensive contrast to the gleaming milky wood floor. She inched closer and tapped her foot gingerly and the blob moved in reply, a slight heave, an intake of breath. She couldn't go any nearer; her heart was pounding.

こめ

So she's pregnant, it appears. Yes, and almost five months gone. Too late for an abortion, almost beginning to show, and yesterday she felt it kick for the first time. It was horrible. It frightened her, like having a stranger, an intruder inside her, trapped and knocking to get out. She'd let it out if she could, but she can't, not now. It's going to be kicking and moving around more and more; she knows that and dreads it. It's like harboring an alien, she's been invaded, no longer owns her body, there's this furtive thing with restless paws, this small creature, trapped inside her. Growing all the time. She knows this isn't how you're supposed to feel. She's read those articles too—she has plenty of time to read magazines at her desk. You're supposed to feel joyous, expectant. But she doesn't, can't even pretend she does. She's terrified.

How did this happen? Let's see. One of the lawyers at work, one of the older ones, say—forty-eight? no, forty-six—takes an interest in her, starts taking her to lunch, then to dinner. Expensive restaurants. She buys the right clothes—she's good at clothes, thinks belatedly she should have tried for a job in fashion, maybe working for a designer—so that strolling in at his side, she can almost imagine she's in the magazine life for a few hours, only he's twenty years older than the companion she pictured. And he's not in music or movies or even real estate, just a lawyer who specializes in contracts. Plus he's married. Technically: his wife's been in the hospital for several years, wasting away, some rare disease she's never heard of.

He's good-looking, he's kind, he's generous, and he likes her. It puzzles her. Call him Roger. She can't bring him to her apartment—she imagines, wrongly, that he's never seen anything remotely like her apartment—and he can't bring her home because of his children—Brian, sixteen, and Nancy, nine, who miss their mother—so they go to hotels. He makes love in a slow, intense, and deliberate way, with a ravenous but controlled hunger, like a gourmet sitting down to a superb dinner, intent on savoring every morsel and making it last as long as possible. This, to her, is an education. Certainly better than the two guys she'd half-heartedly let into her apartment, who fell on her with a stagy, unconvincing, and ineffectual ardor. It has the density of the real. At last.

So, move it along.

ლა

She'd have to deal with the thing, whatever it was, alone. Roger was gone, called back to the city yesterday—a sudden crisis at work—only an hour after they arrived. He promised he'd be back in time for dinner tonight. He'd invited some friends over, an archeologist couple just home from a dig in Mexico, and a lawyer with an actor husband. (Grown-ups, she thought.) He wanted to introduce her to his friends. Not to worry if she couldn't manage dinner, he said. Call the store in town—they'd send over everything she needed, soup to nuts. All he asked was that she keep an eye on Nancy. Brian had stayed in the city. Incredibly, his rock band, a cacophony of raging hormones, had an actual gig in a tiny bar near her old apartment. His absence was a relief. Brian made her edgy: a skinny, surly, slovenly adolescent in baggy pants and a base-ball cap apparently glued to his head, who regarded her men-acingly and played the drums—he had a set in the beach house as well as in the city. The members of his band, three boys cut from the same sullen pattern, would come over and make ghastly music for hours on end. Roger indulged them. The girl, Nancy, she liked better. She was thin and aloof, such an unchildlike air of gravity about her, but at least she spoke; she told Rosa she wanted to be a veterinarian when she grew up.

She stepped backward toward the stairs, keeping her eye on the thing on the floor. "Nancy," she called. "Are you awake? Could you come down, please?"

She heard bare feet on the stairs. Nancy was ready for the day, washed, combed, her sandy hair tied back severely in a pony tail. She was dressed, uncannily, like a miniature, paler Rosa, in tan shorts and a striped shirt. Like a kid sister. "What?" she asked.

"Hi," Rosa said. "There's, uh, something in the house." She mustn't sound alarmed. "A little animal, I think. Remember you told me you want to be a vet, you love animals? Well, maybe you can help get it out."

"Where?" Her face was alert but impenetrable, and her tone, as always with Rosa, one of well-mannered resistance.

"Over there. See? Near the table."

"Oh." Nancy approached it, and Rosa, emboldened, followed.

"Do you think it's a mouse?"

"How could it be a mouse? It has feathers. It's a bird."

As if to confirm Nancy's pronouncement, the bird fluttered its wings and flew several inches off the floor. They both jumped back. The bird came to rest a few feet from where it had started, further in the alcove. An ordinary brown sparrow. Outdoors, where it belonged, it could never cause alarm. Indoors it somehow turned eerie, its movements unpredictable. It's been here for hours, Rosa thought. While she lay carelessly in bed it had been flying around, taking its measure of the house with the beat of its wings, taking possession and injuring itself on the hard surfaces.

∽

Roger's gratitude makes her uneasy: she's restoring him to life, she gives him a reason to get up in the morning. She doesn't know what to say to this, can't say the truth, that for her he's only the beginning. She drifts along because it's so nice, more than nice, such a relief to have someone who cares for her. Only now can she feel what a strain it was, struggling on her own and getting nowhere. He knows the city, knows how to do everything, pays for everything; he even takes her out on a fishing boat one weekend. Since they have nowhere to cook the fish, she finally brings him to her apartment, and when he sees it he looks somber and says this won't do, he must arrange something better right away. She looks at the apartment through his eyes, then looks at him, good-tempered, sexy, generous. What she feels is a generic affection mingled with a temperate desire. More curiosity than desire, actually. That part is an adventure, having her body catered to with such attention, seeing what it's capable of. She looks at the apartment again, and yes, she'll let him help her out. Make things a bit easier. It's too soon to give in, she knows that, she even has twinges of guilt over the sick wife, but it won't be forever. She'll be his distraction for a few months, as long as it lasts, and enjoy some relief herself. That's not giving in, is it? It's a step toward a life. Or is it a step away? She's not sure. But it's something happening, anyway, and she lets the happening pull her in.

Very soon she has a new apartment with all the grace and appurtenances the old one lacked. And no mice.

ფ

"I wonder how it got in. The doors and windows were all closed."

"The fireplace," said Nancy. "They come down the flue." They both glanced over to the living-room fireplace.

There was still a faint smell of smoke in the air; the nights were chilly, and Rosa had lit a fire after dinner, then suggested they play a game. What did Nancy like? Scrabble? Monopoly? But Nancy said she'd rather watch TV in bed. Rosa had sat alone for hours, staring at the flames, willing the thing inside her to be still. Forever. At last she'd gone upstairs, first checking to make sure the fire was out.

"Oh, has this happened before?"

"No, but that's how they get in. Poor thing. It's hurt."

Rosa was losing patience but dared not rush the child. "Do you think you could just, you know, pick it up and take it out?"

"I really don't know how to handle birds. I know about mammals. A bird is not a mammal," said Nancy evenly. "Why don't you do it? You're supposed to be the grown-up."

"You're right. But the thing is … I don't like to hold birds. I don't like the fluttering. I could use some help, is what I'm trying to say." She had a wild vision of the two of them locked in paralyzed intransigence all day, standing in these very positions when the guests arrived for dinner. Roger would be appalled and embarrassed. His wife, when she was well, would probably have swept the thing briskly out the door. Rosa didn't even know where the broom was.

Nancy cast her a look of mild contempt and bent over the bird. She took it in her hands. Her cheeks grew flushed.

"That's it. Good girl," Rosa crooned.

Suddenly Nancy's hands flung open, and the bird fluttered about the dining room in weak, downward spiraling circles. Rosa leaped back and covered her face with her hands. Peering out, she saw the bird plummet to the floor, where it quivered. She despised her fear, yet she couldn't bring herself to touch it.

"Why'd you let go?"

"I don't know. It kept fluttering. I just couldn't hold it anymore. Can't we do it later?"

"I have an idea." Rosa got a small towel from the kitchen. "Here. Pick it up in this, wrap it around, and hand it to me, then open the kitchen door and I'll put it out."

∞

When she tells him she's pregnant he begs her not to have the abortion. Implores. The easygoing manner vanishes; he's a man obsessed. They'll be a family together. She'll meet his children. His wife would never leave the hospital. He stops short of saying she'll soon be dead—that is understood. Rosa would give him a new life, and he would give her everything she wants. (Never mind that she doesn't know yet what she wants. Or that the whole thing doesn't sound right: waiting for his wife to die? What does that say about him? About her? Yet is it so selfish of him to want a life, same as she does? What would she say if one of her friends told her this story? Get out, she'd say. Or maybe not. Go for it, maybe.)

He keeps her busy, as if by occupying all her free time he could prevent her from seeing a doctor. Of course he's busy too—lawyers always are—but he manages. On weekends he takes her to his beach house, a big glass house. Or mostly glass, it seems. A spacious, sleek, airy house, like the kind featured in the magazines she reads. His wife had good taste. She meets the children; they're cold to her. Naturally—they're old enough to get the picture. Dad's girlfriend. She tries to imagine herself as their mother and fails. She's not ready for that. Her own life has barely begun. What had been a relief, a sexual adventure, becomes tangled, strained, fraught. Worse, a cliché. Even she can see that. She owes him. He's bought her, and he's bought the baby that's invading her too. Once she gets rid of it he'll get rid of her. Back to the walk-up with the orange and green sink and the mice: what's known as freedom.

Days pass. Weeks. She can't get herself to the doctor because she dreads confronting Roger afterward with the news. She's never had to face anything so serious. She tries to put it out of her mind. Maybe it'll go away by itself. Some do. With a numb fascination, she watches herself moving into risky territory, like someone who opens a door marked Danger. Except she doesn't have to open any door—the door has been open all along. She has only to stand still and do nothing.

℘

Nancy wrapped the bird in the towel and thrust it disdainfully at Rosa, who accepted the slight package. But instead of moving to the door she stood stiffly, waiting for the light fluttering, as if she wanted to feel what she most dreaded, make the horror tangible. Then she would know it. Along with the desire to flee was the perverse desire to know. It kept her rooted to the spot, clutching the towel.

The bird burst from the folds and zoomed up to Rosa's face. She screeched, staggered back and dropped the towel. "Shit," she moaned, brushing the ghost of wings from her cheek. The bird circled again, flew into the living room and came to rest near the fireplace, as if seeking to leave the way it had come.

Nancy snatched up the towel and swooped down on the bird, but it lifted a few inches off the floor and she jumped back, startled. Determined, she pursued it again and again, stealing up quietly then pouncing, but the bird kept eluding her by inches. Finally, with a last, desperate striving, it soared up, through the dining room, into the kitchen, and disappeared.

Rosa clenched in frustration. If only Brian were here, he would do it. He might even enjoy crushing it between his palms. To think she could ever long for Brian.

"It's organic," said Nancy. "It's going to die and rot and smell, wherever it is."

The rustle began again, but more like faint scraping on a wall now. It seemed to come from the refrigerator. Trapped, nibbling? She looked hopelessly at Nancy.

"Don't worry, it couldn't get in there." As if to show Rosa how foolish her fears were, Nancy opened the refrigerator, took out a bottle of pineapple juice, poured some and drank it. Then she clambered up on a counter and peered behind it. "It's back there," she reported. "Not moving. It must be dead. Give me the broom and I'll sweep it out."

"Where do you keep the broom?" Rosa asked humbly.

"In the broom closet, where else? Over there."

Still perched on the counter, Nancy maneuvered the broom along the back and side of the fridge until the bird was in full view, brown, dusty, inert. She climbed down and knelt to tap it softly with her fingers.

"Better not do that. If you wake it up we'll have to go through this all over again. I'll just sweep it onto the dustpan." Through the length of the broom Rosa could feel the tiny body. Death made it lighter, less substantial. She carried the dustpan out the kitchen door and slid the body to the grass. Nancy followed her out and bent over the bird, while Rosa slumped against the door, breathing in the summer air. The mist had lifted. The air held the scents of grass and sea, the trees were lush with the fullness of July. The tire swing suspended from a low branch swayed slightly. At last she looked at the bird, feeling some pity.

She's dithered so long that it's too late. She could have the baby and leave it with Roger. She'd always be its mother, though. Later on it would ask about her, where is she, who is she? Can she do that to a child? How did this all happen? How could she let it happen?

"It's dead," Nancy said. Her perpetual gravity seemed fitting now.

"Yes, it's too bad." And she'd made a fool of herself in front of the child besides, over a stupid bird.

"We killed it."

"We didn't kill it. It got hurt from bouncing around the house. If it hadn't been dumb enough to fly down in the first place it would still be enjoying its free life." The way Nancy stared at her made Rosa ashamed. "Look, I'm sorry. I just couldn't handle it, okay? It's not like I wanted it to die."

"I'm going to bury it," said Nancy.

"Where?"

"Right here." She chose a place directly under the tire swing, where the grass had been worn away by years of the scuffing of children's feet, and the dirt was soft. She dug fiercely with her fingers.

"Can I help you?"

"No. I can do it myself. I've buried things before. Two turtles. Then I'm going to have a funeral, and you're not invited because you don't really care. Anyway, you're not part of the family."

Rosa was stunned. She went inside and gazed absently in the freezer and cabinets to see what might be around for dinner. She had never hosted a dinner party—the most she'd done was have a few friends over for pizza and beer. She didn't know how to begin, and even as she pretended to peruse the contents of the fridge she knew she'd end up calling the store in town, giving Roger's name and asking for suggestions. The child was right. She had no business here. What stretched ahead made her shudder. Not because she couldn't do it—she wouldn't always be as inept as she'd been with the bird—but because she saw herself learning to do it all: the baby, the dinners for friends, the houses. The life ready-made that had been lurking, waiting to tug her in while she groped at dreams, and the dreams had been ready-made too.

∾

And now she doesn't know what to do. There must be something else, some open space to flee to. But wherever she looks, there is only fear. Fear rings everything in sight like a hoop of fire. And she has set the fire herself.

Sightings of Loretta

Death's intrusion left Bennett a widower in his mid-fifties. An awkward age. Too young for the slow fade, but on the late side to contemplate a fresh start, even had he been one for fresh starts. An age to make your peace with what you have, some would say. Bennett had made his peace early on. He had watched others in his generation wrestling with their lives, locked in the grip of shadowy alternate selves, and felt lucky that he wasn't prone to restlessness. Except with Susan gone his settled life was in rubble, like those sturdy old buildings that implode in a matter of seconds, with one quick astonished shudder.

He attended a meeting of the grief group his friends urged on him. "I buried my husband a month ago," a red-haired woman said. Others referred to losing their mates, as if through carelessness, though they still spoke to them now and then. Bennett listened politely but felt he had had nothing to do with what happened. He had not even buried Susan; she was cremated, by request. She had done it all while he watched, handling her illness in the efficient way she handled everything, until one day her hold loosened and she said, "I'm going," as if announcing a trip, then closed her eyes and spoke no more.

My wife left me, would have been the truthful words to say when his turn came—words he'd been vaguely afraid he might have to speak while she lived. He didn't say them, and he didn't return. Instead he set about going through her things—Susan was a prodigious saver. He used to wince at the mounds of catalogues, magazines, souvenirs, and quaint flea market gleanings cluttering every surface. Over the years he'd nursed fantasies of sweeping away the clutter, and those images gave him a voluptuous pleasure of which he was quickly ashamed. He didn't want her gone. He only longed for clean, bare surfaces. When he saw that his fantasies might soon become a reality, he felt no pleasure at all. Let her live, with all her mess, he murmured, staring up at the ceiling.

Maybe to chastise himself for his thoughts, he didn't attack the most visible piles first but went for the closets and drawers, where the results would yield less satisfaction. Remarkable, what she'd kept: a Campfire Girl manual with cookie recipes and instructions for the proper angle to wear the feathered beret. A forty-year-old certificate for excellence in archery? She'd never mentioned that talent. Susan had been a commercial artist; her oversized files spewed pre-computer detritus. Bennett expected he might brood and weep as he fingered the crackling transparencies and stiff boards with designs for book jackets and brochures. But working his way through her leavings (evenings and weekends—he couldn't neglect his job at the newspaper) did not conjure up thoughts of Susan. Rather, he fell into reveries of his first girlfriend, the one he'd loved when they were six. Loretta.

Ten years ago, he thought he'd lost her. His sister, Helen, had called, as she did every few weeks to "keep in touch"; she considered this fitting for brother and sister, though clearly her heart was no more in it than Bennett's. He knew something was on Helen's mind by the way she curtailed her usual script. Instead of asking about Susan and the boys, she said, "I heard some bad news. I thought you might want to know."

"What?" He thought of their remaining old uncle, then, senselessly, of his two sons. From the next room, as if to reassure him, they let out a whoop for the basketball game on TV. Tomorrow they would all be driving up to New England for Richard's college interviews.

"Loretta. She was in a freak accident." Helen's tone wasn't contemptuous, as it usually was when she mentioned Loretta. It had the piety reserved for tragedy. "A taxi jumped the curb and she just happened to be there. In that exact place, that exact time. Of all the bizarre—"

"Dead?"

"No. But it's pretty bad."

He sank down on the bed, shoving aside the clothes Susan was folding. He could have sworn Helen enjoyed that moment of suspense, letting him think she was dead. It was intolerable, unacceptable, that Loretta might be dead.

"Her parents are in shock. What a thing to happen, I mean at this point in their lives…" Now the words rushed out as if she couldn't bridle her eagerness.

"What about the child?"

"She's fine. She was in school. And she has her father, of course." A pause to let this information register: since Helen had never left their childhood neighborhood, she kept abreast of all developments. "Good thing, too, I'd say."

"You never told me she was married."

"I guess I thought you knew. It was last year. Well, I'm sorry to be the bearer of bad tidings."

He could hardly jot down the name of the hospital, his hands were trembling so. When Susan asked what was the matter, he stared in her direction but saw nothing. "A childhood friend," he muttered. "I should go see her." He went to the closet for his shoes.

"Bennett, it's ten-thirty. You can't visit a hospital now."

"Oh. Tomorrow then."

"We're leaving tomorrow, remember?"

He went into the bathroom and locked the door, and Susan knew enough to let him be.

During the trip north he drove so slowly that Susan persuaded him to let her take the wheel. While the others went to explore the campuses, he lay limp on the motel bed. She might die. He was assailed by waves of missing, in advance, her erratic appearances in his life. They were like those rare moments of grace that descend out of the blue, on a crowded train, or on the beach, or when the mind wanders from a book—unsought, exhilarating, swiftly gone. But in an obscure corner of the soul, you waited for them. They gave meaning to everything else.

☙❧

They grew up on a street of attached two-story row houses, each with a modest brick porch and five steps skirting a narrow strip of grass, where some mothers—not Loretta's and not his—planted rhododendrons. It was a mild New York backwater, in the city but not quite of it, just after the war; the mood was relieved and placid. That would last barely a decade, but everyone lived as if it would last forever. The children on the street were known to all, and the romance of Bennett and Loretta amused the neighbors. They must have looked sweetly absurd, he imagined, walking to school with heads bent in earnest conversation, their mothers taking turns accompanying them. Only his older sister mocked. "Bennett has a girlfriend, Bennett has a girlfriend," Helen sang out, hands on her hips, tossing her head so her long braids twirled. "Are you going to marry her, Ben?"

What on earth they might have talked about he couldn't remember. What do six-year-olds talk about? At that age, his own boys talked about TV heroes and rocket ships; they stood at construction sites transfixed by massive machines rising to claw at the air or kneeling to dump dirt. He couldn't picture them feeling about anyone as he had felt about Loretta. His memories of their time together were more palpable than anything that had happened since, as if carved in high relief against a flat surface. Prowling for treasure in the empty lot on the corner, before they were called in for supper. Squeezing into one swing in the playground. Forbidden forays off their small block. Her changeable face, with its blue-gray eyes and halo of rampant dark hair, was superseded now by the faces she took on later. But he remembered her steady tantalizing gaze: a promise to carry him off somewhere new and exotic, a landscape more glorious than what surrounded them. Come away, it beckoned. Come with me. Together they floated in a bubble of excitement and ease. They weren't imitating their parents; their parents didn't hold hands and whisper in the twilight, or lick the same ice-cream cone. And they had seen few movies. They were inventing romance.

The intensity faded—they were scolded for some escapade, their idyll shattered—and soon they were simply friends. Special friends, with the neural bond of those who grow together into consciousness. And with unquestioned trust, a trust that wrapped Bennett like a shield as they ventured out. The summer before high school, he confided his fears. The school was huge and forbidding; the kids would come from distant neighborhoods. How would they fit in?

"It'll be fine, you'll see," she said. "There are bigger things to worry about. Like what'll we do with our lives."

"What do you mean? What we'll be?"

"No. I mean what to *do*. How to live right. How to be not like our parents and everyone else around here. Dead inside."

"You think they're dead inside?"

"Look at them. They're not aware of anything. They just want to be safe and comfortable and have things never change. That's not a *real* life."

He laughed uneasily. "Okay, maybe. But we're only fourteen years old. First we have to get through high school."

"Everyone does that somehow. It's what comes later that's hard."

She was right. Everyone does it. They found their separate paths. Loretta ran with a crowd of girls who smoked and wore too much makeup and disappeared into spare rooms at parties. Bennett took a more studious route. When they met walking home from school or over math homework, they were like family members from far-flung branches: they might veer apart, but the roots stay entwined. He defended her when other boys told crude stories. "She's not like that. I know, I grew up with her." "Ever get any?" they asked with a smirk. If they only knew the fantasies she spun when they were alone—but he wouldn't dream of telling. She longed to be an anarchist heroine like Rosa Luxembourg—a history teacher had told her story and Loretta became entranced. She wished she'd been born an Amazon. Maybe they could run away to Paris and sit in cafés drinking Pernod. What was Pernod? Bennett inter-rupted over the trigonometry books. She wasn't sure herself, but it was what artists drank in cafés. Bennett didn't know how serious she was, but he liked listening and understood that she needed him to listen. "Cut it out," he told the boys. "I don't believe any of that crap."

At the senior prom she appeared in a navy blue slinky dress—he thought it didn't suit her lanky, big-boned body—while most of the girls wore pastels with wide skirts. Bennett's date, in peach-colored taffeta, was a pert blonde he'd invited almost at random; had she refused, he would have asked another who would do as well. He knew he was good-looking in a conventional, even-featured way, and while he wasn't a star athlete or a fast talker, he was generally liked and could produce enough quips to keep a conversation going.

Loretta danced with one boy after another and let them pull her close and grind their hips against her. While his own date chattered with her friends near the punch bowl, Bennett claimed a dance. "Why are you acting this way?" he whispered. "They're all looking at you."

"Because it's fun." She laughed with her mouth wide open, teeth flashing, the braces she had hated long gone. Her lipstick was a shade close to purple. She looked him straight in the eye—she was nearly as tall as he. "Why, you jealous?"

"Don't be silly," he said automatically. "I just mean, remember who you are." Those were words his mother often spoke in a stern voice. They puzzled him—who was he? And why must he unremittingly remember? But if he wasn't sure what they meant, he knew when they should be used.

"I'm finding out. How else can you find out if you don't try different ways?"

He frowned, and Loretta gave another teasing laugh. "Remember in biology, Mr. Cargill said all the cells in the body replace themselves every seven years? You really become a totally new person. That could happen, I don't know, ten times if you live long enough."

"It doesn't happen all at once," he told her, "like when a bell rings. It's staggered. So you've always got some of the old and some of the new."

"I didn't mean literally. God, Benno, I should really teach you a few things."

Provoked, he wondered if he too should pull her close and grind his hips against hers, but that would feel all wrong. No matter what she said, she was the same Loretta, almost like a sister. No, more than a sister. There was no word for what she was to him. This new gaudy girl was just a pose.

They went to college on different coasts—Bennett stayed close to home, Loretta headed west. He wished her well, hoped she wouldn't get into trouble finding out who she was, and moved on. The tide of life claimed him, and in time Susan, blonde and affable, did too.

෧෨

A year after they were married, Susan lay on the couch with a magazine balanced on her huge stomach and said, "I just can't move. It's too hot, and I feel like this is going to pop any minute. But you go." Some of her old college friends were giving a party, a send-off for volunteers going to Mississippi to work on voter registration. "One of us ought to be there, at least."

"If it's popping any minute, maybe I should stay home."

"I don't mean literally. Anyway, I can always call. Go on, Ben. Please?"

When he reappeared, ready to leave, she said, "Oh, not a tie, sweetie. It makes you look like Clark Kent. It's not that kind of party."

He was glad, when he arrived, that the scorned tie was in his pocket. No one else wore one. Several of the men were in shorts, and the women wore flowered shifts and sandals. The apartment was so crowded that the air-conditioning, if it existed, had no effect. Bennett was drifting around with a can of beer in his hand when he felt a tap on his shoulder.

"Could that be my old Benno?"

Loretta threw her arms around him. It was nearly ten years since he'd seen her, and her gestures seemed larger. She herself seemed larger, occupying space with authority—maybe it was the mass of hair piled on her head, or the gleaming bare shoulders, or the clunky beads and long silver earrings. Her body had density, her face glowed.

She introduced the black man standing beside her as Jim. Bennett hadn't realized they were together. "We're leaving tomorrow morning," she said, and slipped her arm through Jim's. He was very dark, with a bushy Afro, small wire-rimmed glasses, and a mild, inquisitive expression. He wore a green and black dashiki and heavy wooden beads that matched Loretta's.

"You're a reporter? Well, we might need some good coverage." Only half-joking, Jim was very self-possessed. Older than he looked, probably. His obvious possession of Loretta gave Bennett the same uneasy feeling he had had at the prom, although this time he could find no fault with her. She was splendid, grandly confident without the arrogance he disliked in other would-be activists. His mother, maybe even his sister Helen, would have approved of her manners. Except of course for the arm linked through a black man's.

"I wish I could, but I'm just on the city desk. Local stuff."

"Local stuff's been interesting these days," Jim said.

"It has," Bennett agreed. "I wanted to get the Board of Ed. story, but my most exciting piece lately was the subway strike." In their first year of high school, he remembered, still the placid decade though there must have been underground rumblings too faint for common ears, Loretta was the only girl in the class who said yes to the English essay assignment: Would you marry a person outside your race or religion? The teacher had her stand up and read her essay aloud, and afterward she faced a barrage of challenges, some of them insulting. Bennett felt for her, even tried to support her by a few placating comments. At first her voice had the familiar tinge of defiance that always hid her fears, but she quickly mastered herself. In the end, the incident won her friends and a reputation for boldness. He wondered if she and Jim were married.

She started to pull both men off into a corner. "We must have a real talk!" But others kept crowding around— she knew everyone, it seemed, black and white. Bennett was captured too, first by Susan's friends, then by a voluble girl who wanted to know how to get a start in journalism. Loretta caught his eye and gave a hopeless, amused shrug. Toasts, speeches, and the party broke up.

"Good luck," he managed to say. "Let me know how things go." He scrawled his address on a cocktail napkin.

"If I can. Happy new baby." She was off with a flourish, Jim's large hand planted on her shoulder, leaving Bennett unsatisfied. He wanted more. Not to take her in his arms; there were other women at the party he'd prefer for that—paler, less intense, self-contained women like Susan, though he hadn't reached the point in his marriage when he would do more than notice them. He wanted only to be in Loretta's presence. He felt renewed, restored to possibility, energy, adventure. But what was he thinking: he was twenty-nine years old, on the brink of fatherhood.

എൻ

Two months later, her voice on the phone was raked with anguish.

"I need to see you, Ben. Right away. Please."

"Sure. What is it? Do you want to come over now?" Susan was out, he almost added. But why should it matter?

"I don't think so. Can you meet me someplace?"

"I can't get out. I'm sorry. The baby's sleeping." It was a Saturday afternoon, his turn to care for Richard. Susan was struggling to work part-time, and he had pledged to do his fair share. She was in a consciousness-raising group and gave cogent arguments for why he should. Bennett agreed in principle. Beyond principle, he dreaded his failings being aired before a roomful of women.

"Oh, right, your wife was about to have a baby. Congratulations. What kind?"

"A boy. He was born the day after that party." In the flash flood of changes that swept him along, he'd almost forgotten meeting Loretta. "How about tomorrow morning? Coffee? Are you okay?"

"I'll tell you tomorrow."

He expected that she would be late, but she was there waiting for him. It was Helen who called her flighty, he reminded himself, but in fact she had always been prompt and prepared at school. An orderly child. He could still see her homework marching forthrightly across the notebook pages in that firm up-and-down writing. She sat at a table far from the door, drab and wretched in old jeans and a faded tie-dyed shirt. Thinner, sallow, her eyes stained a darker gray.

"What's the matter?"

"Jim's dead."

They'd been seen around town together, she told him, and the locals didn't like it. Jim was driving a pickup truck with three of the other men, late at night, in the rain, and they had an accident. The others, who had minor injuries, swore that a car forced them off the road, but they had no proof, no witnesses, no license plate. There was nothing to be done. She cried as she told the story.

Bennett was horrified. He knew such things happened—his colleagues came home with stories that never made the papers—but they had not touched his life. He leaned across the table to stroke her cheek. That's what happens, he could hear Helen say, when you start putting your nose in other people's business. "I'm so sorry," he said, too loud, to drown Helen out. "But there must be something you can do ..."

"They told me I'd better leave or I might get hurt too. It was two days ago. I just ... I had to leave him there."

"It's awful. Were you married, Loretta?"

She looked startled. "Married? No. What difference does that make?"

"None. None at all. I just wondered ..."

"Bennett." She stared at him as she had as a child, the gaze that had made him feel singled out, transcendent. It was both claim and offer. A promise to transport him to vaster places where unpredictable things happened. But something was expected of him in turn. "I need money for an abortion. Can you lend me some?"

"Oh ... Are you sure ...?"

"I'm sure."

"Well, of course. Do you have someone ... reliable to do it?"

"Yes, yes, it's all set. I just need the money."

"What about your family? I mean, I'm glad to help you out, but don't you want anyone to ..."

"I came to you because I thought you wouldn't ask so many questions. You'd understand. Look, I'm sorry to lay this on you, Ben. But you're the only one."

How could he be the only one, after so long? And what was he supposed to understand?

"So. You're a daddy." She managed a smile. "What's it like?"

"Quite a change," he said, embarrassed by his luck.

She didn't want him to meet her at the doctor's—only give her the cash, which he did the next day on a street corner near his office.

"Will you let me know if everything's okay? Call me at work. Here's the number."

He was out on assignment the next two days—a midtown water main break paralyzed traffic and sent hundreds of people to temporary shelters. When he returned, a message on his desk said, Loretta called, everything's okay. No phone number.

❧

"Guess what your old friend's up to now?"

He moved the phone an inch away from his ear. "Why do you always use that tone for her, Helen? You don't even know her anymore."

"I know what she is. You should too. She started early. She practiced on you."

"That's absurd. We were infants."

"Bennett," Helen said with a sigh. "You're such an innocent, still. You used to let her lead you anywhere."

Wrong, all wrong, he thought, but how foolish even to discuss it at this point.

"Her mother tells me she's going to law school." Helen offered her nugget with sneering relish.

Bennett was relieved to imagine her sitting still, bent over her books. Was she still grieving over Jim's death? Upset by the abortion? He longed to know. Then one autumn day, in brilliant light, he glimpsed her, or someone who looked just like her, from a Fifth Avenue bus window. Her hair flying free, she strode aggressively down the street with four or five people—fellow students?—laughing and gesturing, absorbed in talk. She wore leather boots and a black leather jacket and hauled a large tote bag. He wanted to call to her, but couldn't get the bus window open. He rose to get off, but the bus was crowded; by the time he reached the door she'd vanished around a corner.

❧

Everything was changing so fast. Half the couples Bennett and Susan knew were getting divorced—a rite of passage, it seemed—and it was the wives who led the exodus. Sometimes he feared Susan might join them. Or was she just too busy? He didn't dare ask. She didn't always laugh at his quips lately. She could be acerbic when she was pressured by too many demands. A few times she remarked that he never asked any questions. "I'm glad to hear whatever you want to tell me," he said. "Yes, but you don't ask." He tried to remember to ask more questions but found it a curious effort, not tangible and specific like remembering to stop for groceries or pick up the children's toys.

On a typical Saturday afternoon—Susan spooning puréed carrots into the new baby, Bennett scooting toy trucks along the floor with Richard—the phone rang. Not Helen, he prayed.

"Bennett? Me again. Always calling you to bail me out." He sensed fear behind the throaty, combative tone. Shouting and clattering sputtered through the wires. "As a matter of fact, I am calling you to bail me out. I was arrested."

She'd been in an anti-war demonstration, and the cops had dragged her limp body to the van. "You're my one phone call. Can you do something? Like come down and bring a lawyer? I've got to get out of here. It's a madhouse."

With all her new friends, why me? But he didn't dream of refusing. His job had occasionally brought him inside a police station, but never to post bail. Would he need to sign forms asking for personal data? It might not go over well at the paper.

"I've got to go out," he told Susan, grabbing his jacket. "An old friend's in some trouble."

"Who? Anyone I know?"

"No. I'll tell you later."

Helen's husband was a lawyer, but that was out of the question. Anyway, his specialty was insurance fraud. From a street phone, he called a Legal Aid lawyer he knew through the paper, who owed him a favor and would know how to handle this discreetly.

An hour and a half later, he sat opposite Loretta in a coffee shop, still edgy from the raucous scene at the station. He sympathized with the demonstrators—he sent checks to their cause—but did they have to go to such lengths? They were a rowdy, unkempt bunch, quite different from the earnest group at the party years ago. What had become of her zeal to transform Mississippi? Did she lose heart after Jim's death? Or was it all the same zeal, free-floating, seeking a cause? Still finding herself?

Her patched denim jacket with the peace symbols crookedly sewn on was torn at the sleeve; her skirt trailed on the floor. She was missing an earring, her hair was straggly, her face shiny with sweat and triumph. "Thanks so much," she said. "You're a real friend."

"And you're a mess." Clean up your act, he wanted to say. What do you think you're doing? You used to say we had to figure out how to live right—awareness, choice, responsibility. But the hectoring words stuck on his tongue.

As if she could read his mind, she reached out to put her hand on his. "Listen, I know what I'm doing, Ben. It's important."

"It is important. But there are other ways—"

"They don't work as well. This'll be in the papers, you'll see. You of all people must know that. The bigger the stink, the better the coverage. From now on, that's the way to go."

She was right. The placid time was long over. It had been an anomalous blip in history, a slack loop on the time line; even those who lived through it could hardly believe it had been real. The time of his childhood was discredited, and Bennett was willing to relinquish it. But he felt bereft and unprepared. His adult life was a crash course in reality, and he'd always hated cramming.

"I heard you were in law school."

She jerked her head back in surprise. "I was thinking of applying but I changed my mind. How'd you hear that?"

"Helen."

"Probably my mother told her. Wishful thinking. No, I wouldn't have the patience. Right now we need quicker measures."

"Are you working? Do you need money?"

"Thanks, no. I work on and off. Anyhow, I still owe you. I haven't forgotten. You'll get it back."

He waved that off. "Where are you living?"

"I share a place downtown with a bunch of people. Hey, you're not a spy for my mother, are you?" She tilted her head and smiled, and again the lush eagerness enveloped him like a perfumed mist, restoring him to himself. So what if she wasn't the same girl he had loved? He was the same. It was as if he'd entrusted his soul to her long ago for safekeeping, and repossessed it only when she appeared. Yes, this was what he loved: not the person but the feeling she gave him. But how could they be separated? He turned to see them both in the mirror beside the table. In the glare of artificial light, the outlines of his face looked dim, blurred by confusion.

"Of course not. I'm just concerned. You need to think of the future—"

"I am thinking of the future. That's what I was doing out there. What about your future?"

"I'm so busy with the present, I can't even see it."

"I'd love to meet your family some time. Can I come over?"

"Sure. Today's not a good day, though. Another time."

"Fine, I'll give you a call."

∞

In time an envelope with no return address arrived at his office, containing hundred-dollar bills folded into a sheet of paper: "Thanks again for being such a good friend. Love, L." That lucid, good-natured, upright handwriting: here I am, nothing to hide. Didn't she know how risky it was to mail cash? What kind of people send so much cash through the mail? People without a checking account. People who don't want to put a return address on a money order. And where did she get it? He didn't want to speculate. He'd never expected it back, and was more irked at her carelessness than grateful. The money hardly mattered now. With the boys in school and Susan working full-time, they could afford to hire help. The simmering tension over household tasks had subsided. They'd never really worked it out, they agreed in a melancholy mood. "The problem went away," Bennett said. "No," said Susan, "we evaded it." "Okay, whatever." "I hate that word, you know?" "But you do support freedom of speech?" Bennett joked. "All right, you get the last word, Ben." "I didn't know we were quarreling."

Their rare skirmishes were like that, so attenuated, so offhand, that he hardly recognized them until they were over. All in all, he felt fortunate. They'd managed better than many others. They were getting through, as if these frantic years were an obstacle course on the way to an earned serenity.

"Do you ever dream of the foreign desk?" Susan once asked.

"Not especially. Anyhow, how could I disrupt the kids and all? And your work." She accepted in silence this tribute to the seriousness of her work. He would be faulted for a tactical error, Bennett thought, but he got no credit for right thinking. "Why? You think I need a change?"

"Well, not if you're happy with what you're doing. I just wondered. You never talk about it."

"I'm fine as I am."

"It might be nice to see the world," she said tentatively.

"We could take a trip this summer. The kids are old enough."

"I guess. I meant like try living someplace really different. I don't know, India? Morocco?"

He had no longing for India or Morocco, but now and then he too was puzzled at how he had reached this stasis. Then he would think over his luck: early on, he'd landed a job that was still the envy of his friends from journalism school. It was more than luck by now; he'd kept the job and done it well. By starting high, more or less, he was spared the hassle of rising.

Still, it pleased him that his next assignment was a change from his usual beat of natural or technological disasters that brought predictable, remediable chaos. With local elections coming up, the mayor was paying a visit to a notorious downtown park; no doubt he would vow to clean it up and reclaim it for innocent pleasures. Bennett was among the crowd of reporters trailing after him. The park was a mess, a littered shantytown of refrigerator cartons and corrugated metal held together by duct tape. Marijuana scented the air. Half-naked children played in the stubble or wailed for attention. Men and women in tie-dyed rags or long velveteen dresses sauntered about, some cooking over open fires. At least they weren't handing out flowers, Bennett thought. It was a bit late in the day for flowers. Friendly at first, even hospitable, as if entertaining in their living rooms, the squatters began heckling the mayor as soon as he opened his mouth. Someone lit a joint and offered it teasingly to the reporters. Bennett jotted down notes in haste, excited and repelled by the scene. The police, on good behavior in front of the TV cameras, prodded a few nodding figures draped over benches, lumpy shapes wrapped in shawls though the day was warm. As one of them raised her head, a scarf fell to her shoulders. Her hair hung in clumps, her face was puffy and smudged with dirt. The mayor wagged his finger. "We want to get help for people like this. No way is this liberation. This is a public health hazard." Bennett wrote down the words, planning how he might frame the quote. The woman slumped back down and the cop pulled her up again. She shook him off and opened her eyes wide.

Bennett's every muscle clenched in denial. Transformed, yes, but not beyond recognition.

He should do something, but what? Go over and speak to her? Take her home? Give her a new life? How could he explain her to Susan?

The police began leading the more vocal squatters into a waiting paddy wagon. They tried to drag Loretta off, but the others formed a barricade in front of her. An ugly scene might have erupted—the bigger the stink, the more coverage, as she had said. But one of the mayor's aides gestured at the cops and they retreated. Bennett had almost made up his mind to go to her, but the mayor was rushing off to the next stop on the expedition, mouthing words the other reporters were writing down. He had no choice but to follow.

It gnawed at him that she might have seen him. That he had denied her and she knew it. His dearest friend. No, he protested, she's not your dearest friend anymore. She hasn't been your dearest friend since you were six. Or twelve. Eighteen at the most. The cells had replaced themselves several times over by now; that grotesque crone was no one he knew. Enough rescue work—let someone else take over. One of her hippie friends.

But he couldn't wholly believe this. He didn't know what to believe. He only knew he couldn't crawl out from under the weight of guilt. Had he needed help, she would have rushed to his side. He would stake his life on it. Sure she would, he thought bitterly; it would be a new adventure for her. At least he didn't mention her in his article, which by rights he should have done.

He'd have to go back and do something for her. But the next day Richard fell off his bike and sprained an ankle, and Mark came down with the flu. Schedules had to be rearranged. Even without accidents or illness, there was never enough time. He was forever behind, a lagging, panting runner in a race headed nowhere. Nights, he and Susan fell into bed late and exhausted. His parents and their neighbors had never been so overtaxed. They had time to sit on the porch and read the papers and play cards, swatting lazily at mosquitoes. Yes, it was that placid, dead time when no one did anything. Dead inside, Loretta used to say. Nowadays everyone said it, so it must be true. Such placidity wasn't meant to last. It was insidious. It lulled the privileged, at the expense of others they never saw, or if they saw them, they didn't notice them, which was worse. Bennett knew the ideology inside out. But he was so weary.

By the time he returned to the park she was gone. The squatters were still there, despite the mayor's speech. Moving through the clumps of people playing guitars or stretched on the ground and smoking, Bennett asked for her by name but no one knew any Loretta. He described her as best he could—as she'd looked on that awful day. "Oh, you mean Lulu," said a tattooed man with a harmonica. "Gone, man. Who knows where? She comes and goes."

He should have pressed further, but he was too angry. All right, so now everyone was alive, in perpetual motion. And her perpetual motion had brought her to this—a drugged, collapsed lump on a park bench. Was that better? he wanted to shout at her. Dead inside. He didn't want to find her. Lulu!

ഇൻ

He continued at the newspaper, valued for his competence, even if it was somehow understood he wouldn't be given the major stories. They moved to a larger apartment where Susan used a spare room as a studio—she had more designing work than she could handle. She took to working late in the evenings after the boys had gone to bed. Bennett ambled in.

"How's the new computer working out?"

"It's amazing." She seemed pleased that he asked, and began demonstrating its wonders. It could juggle images and typefaces in a flash, could isolate elements of one image and transfer them to another. Even the human face was fair game. Playing around with magazine photos, she put Gorbachev's bald head above Ronald Reagan's wrinkled brow, then by a series of deft clicks, transformed Woody Allen into Clint Eastwood. "There! A total makeover. It's like dressing up paper dolls. Everything's fluid. You can doctor old photos so in a way you're changing reality. That could be dangerous, you know, politically. But it makes things so much easier. Stuff that used to take me hours, I can do in a minute. Watch what I can do with these headlines." With her fingers dancing avidly over the keys, she was remaking history. The administration was toppled over the Iran Contra scandal. Peace came to Northern Ireland. Famine in Africa was averted by swift UN measures. Bennett stood bemused. Perhaps life was really like that. Written not in stone but in flickering images never meant to be grasped and held firm, relied on, or even remembered.

Watching her, he felt a surge of love. He touched her hair, which showed faint streaks of gray. Her bare arms were taut, the skin smooth; she found time to lift weights and take long runs in the park. "It's fantastic. But maybe you've worked enough for one night."

"Are you listening, Ben, or just lusting?"

"A little of both. I'm not like Gerald Ford. I can do two things at once."

☙

Months, even years, could go by without any thought of Loretta. And then there she'd be: holding up a sign in dripping blood-red letters, "Hands Off Our Bodies," when the abortion clinic two blocks from his apartment was destroyed by arson. He thought he'd tumbled into a time warp: traffic diverted, pedestrians funneled to a narrow path, demonstrators shouting slogans behind police barricades while counter-demonstrators shouted back. He was transfixed by the sign and hadn't even noticed the person carrying it, when she said, "Hey, Ben. Don't tell me you don't remember me!"

He had to stare for a good few seconds, she was so changed: lean and angular in a man's sports jacket and white shirt, her cheekbones jutting, the once-lavish hair lopped off in a severe cut. Then he was levitated by joy. "Hey, Loretta!"

"What're you doing here? Covering the story?"

"No, just passing by." A moment ago, as he glimpsed one of his colleagues, a newly hired young woman, flashing her press pass and elbowing through the crowd, his face had darkened. But on second thought, of course it made better sense to have a woman cover this story.

"Can you believe those lunatics?" Loretta said.

"At least no one was hurt."

"Not this time. Ben, this is Faith." She turned to the woman beside her, similarly dressed, her hair cropped the same way. Chunky and graying, Faith eyed Bennett warily.

"Pleased to meet you." He held out his hand.

"Faith is my partner." A challenge.

"I'm still pleased to meet you," said Bennett, and both women smiled, Faith grudgingly, Loretta with a trace of the old glow. In truth he was not pleased; he was only pleased with himself at having brought off the moment well enough. His Loretta? She should know by now who she was.

"Can you take a few minutes for a cup of coffee?" No, she didn't want to miss the action. "Then let's just get out of the crowd for a second, okay? I need to find out ... I'm so glad to see you looking well. I heard you were in bad shape."

"Strung out. It was so awful, I can't tell you. I met Faith at the rehab center, and she saved my life."

Aha. It wouldn't last long, he thought. He even felt a stab of sympathy for Faith, soon to be jettisoned. "I must tell you something. I've had you on my conscience. I saw you once, when you were ..."

"I know."

"You do?"

"I wasn't totally out of it. I did open my eyes."

"I'm so sorry. I've felt rotten about it ever since."

"It's okay. What could you have done? With the mayor there and all." She gave a mischievous smile. "Anyhow, it wouldn't have helped. No one could've helped me then."

"I should've tried. I don't know why I didn't. I guess I'm—"

"It's over. Let it go, okay? How're you doing? More kids?"

"No, just the two. How about you, I mean when you're not standing here with your sign?"

"Working at a shelter for abused women. Going to business school at night."

"Business school?"

"Why not? I was always good at math, remember?"

That was true. Without her patient coaching, he would have flunked trigonometry.

"I'd better get back," she said.

"Why don't you come over some time? We haven't had a real talk in, I don't know, years?"

"Sure. I'll give you a call."

❧

And last sighted in the lobby of a midtown hotel at a conference for journalists. A total makeover, as Susan might say.

Now she was the business manager for a slick fashion magazine and was dressed accordingly. Rosa Luxembourg was long forgotten. Faith, ancient history for sure. Bennett could tell by the way she moved—he'd looked at women long enough to know.

Impaled by her gaze, he felt an odd rush of pleasure at having kept his good looks. "So what does it all mean?" he teased. "Have you finally found yourself?"

"I was never lost. Well, except that one awful time. Look, it's a new era, we've got to keep up. But seriously, there is a reason." She dug a snapshot from her wallet: a Chinese girl about three years old, holding a stuffed green elephant and beaming at the camera. "My daughter. Tina."

"Congratulations. How did this come about?"

"I adopted her when she was six months old."

"Does she have a father?"

"Not at this point. Maybe she will someday. Why should she have to wait for some notion of the ideal family? I heard about all the babies in orphanages and decided to do something about it."

This is the last straw, came a voice in his head. Helen's or his own? Bennett couldn't tell.

"I see what you're thinking, Ben. But this is different. I've been doing it for three years. Besides the months of arrangements. I can hold a job if I make up my mind to."

"Where is she while you're at work?"

"Day care, where do you think? What is it? You think I'm too old, is that it? I'm not too old. I could even get pregnant if I chose to."

"I know how old you are, Loretta."

"Never mind. Let's get the packets and see what's in store."

She slipped away in the crowd, and he was left stinging with remorse. Two years later, when Helen called about the accident, he stung all over again.

✆

"If you're so upset, then phone the hospital," Susan said, when she and the boys returned from the college tours and found him still lying on the motel bed. But he wouldn't. Not till they got back home. As long as he heard no news, she was not dead yet. Miracles happened. She'd pulled through before. Besides, what right had he to this crushing sense of loss? He'd barely spoken to her in years. Not for the first time, he wondered why he had never desired her, or at least pursued her and waited for desire to catch up. He had an eye for women. He'd been drawn into two brief and secret affairs over the years, attended by such ravaging guilt that they were hardly worth it. Or maybe they just seemed so in retrospect. But Loretta had always felt out of bounds. Now he thought: she would have. I bet she would have. His life might have been vastly different; he had a glimpse of such breadth and iridescence that his eyes teared. Then he shuddered. To live daily in that glow, with that gaze on him? No, he couldn't have stood it. It had been enough as it was. He had even enjoyed missing her between sightings.

Now all her guises were erased, and what he saw with perfect clarity was the real Loretta, his: the small child. The two small children, holding hands, murmuring in the twilight. If she died, they would be dead inside him. Her old phrase, dead inside.

Susan tried to distract him. "Do you think you'll mind the boys leaving? The so-called empty nest?"

"I don't know. It's not for a while yet. Mark'll be around for two more years."

"There might be more time for us," she said.

The motel air between them seemed to stiffen. Time for us? What would they do with the extra time?

∞

The intensive care nurse said he could see her for a moment. She lay swathed in bandages and hooked to paraphernalia. How cruel that all her efforts should come to this, he thought. But he knew those trite words were mired in the grooves of a time dead and gone. Loretta wouldn't think that way—if she were able to think. She hadn't seen her life as a series of guises, nor would she think a life need add up to anything, like compound interest on mouldering capital. A life is whatever it is all along, she would say. He could hear her. He imagined he knew what she would say about everything. He understood—had always understood—that she was responding to what called her moment by moment. That was a way of making a life, a self, as good a way as any other. It was the life she had found, at any rate, and it was distinct from his. Only some fixed perversity in him had pretended not to understand. Some hanging back. Or envy. The Helen part of him.

Her eyes opened, clear and knowing. The steady gaze.

"You!" she whispered.

"Me."

"Talk to me, Ben."

He opened his mouth to speak. He didn't know what he would say, but trusted that words would come. Now, finally, he could be a true friend to her. Now he could do everything he wished he had done. Brought her to meet his family. Gone to see her child. Written something about Jim's death, pressed for an inquiry. Stood beside her at the clinic demonstration. Gone to her side that day in the park. Now he could do it all. And if he could live it again, he would not betray her as he had when they were six. Seeing her powerless under the white sheet, he remembered how their childhood idyll had ended. They had gone too far, far out of the neighborhood, and eaten crushed ice with fruity syrup. They were out on the street on a sweltering August day and Loretta wanted to walk. They ventured around the corner and down a block of row houses identical to their own. They'd done that before, but this time she wanted to go further. They weren't supposed to cross the street, he reminded her, but she didn't care. "Come on," and she tugged at his hand. They were careful to wait for the traffic lights. On and on they walked, while Bennett grew ever more anxious. How would they find their way back? But Loretta said it was easy, she knew the way, and he followed. Soon they were in a neighborhood of shabby apartment buildings with rows of garbage cans at cellar doors set in the pavement. Lots of people were outside. Dark men sat at a table playing a game with tiles. Dominos, Loretta said knowingly—her grandparents played it. Women on plastic chairs fanned themselves with folded newspapers, and children like themselves, but darker, played dodge ball in the street. When a car appeared, the women called out strange words and the children dashed for the curb. Spanish, Loretta said. People smiled at them as they passed. It got so hot that they sat down on a curb, and a fat old woman tried to talk to them in a friendly way, but they couldn't under- stand her. Loretta talked anyway. She counted up to five in

Spanish—the weekly cleaning woman had taught her—and the fat woman and her friends clapped. After a while they got up and walked some more, to a stand where a thin young woman in shorts and a red halter was selling ices. "Let's get some," Loretta said. "We have no money." "Maybe she'll give us some anyway." They watched as the woman scooped crushed ice into white paper cones, then squirted colored syrup on top from an array of huge upside-down jars. The colors were dazzling—red, green, purple, yellow, and blue. They stood staring until at last the woman did offer them some. Loretta nodded eagerly. The woman pointed to the jars of syrup to ask which color they wanted. Loretta chose blue, Bennett red. Thank you, they said, and everyone standing around laughed. *Gracias,* the woman said, and they repeated it after her. The ices were delicious, cold and sweet, the syrup thick and gooey. They sat on the curb sucking at the cones until there was nothing left, then they turned and headed for home. But they couldn't find the way. Soon they were crossing streets at random. The streets were broad, with hurtling trucks and buses. Nothing looked familiar. Loretta tripped and cut her knee, and they wiped her blood with their shirts. She didn't cry but Bennett was nearly in tears—he thought they'd never find their way home. At last he spied something he recognized, the huge plate-glass windows with bright new cars inside, and then he was able to guide them back. A block from home they met his mother, leading Helen by the hand. "Where've you been?" she shouted. "We've been looking everywhere for you." Bennett thought she'd slap him, but she didn't. "What's that stuff all over your faces?" They told her about the free ices, and she said, "You ate that garbage! You'll be sick from it, wait and see!" Loretta's mother was hunting in the other direction, she told them. They were very bad to make everyone worry. "Whose idea was this?" She glared at Loretta as if she knew already. Bennett pointed. "She wanted to go for a walk." His mother shook her head at Loretta, but all she said was, "Look at you, you cut your knee." "It doesn't hurt," Loretta said.

Loretta was kept in the house for three days as punishment. Bennett's mother told him not to play with her. "She's too wild. There're plenty of other children. And you don't have to go wherever people tell you. You could've gotten into trouble. You could've gotten really lost." But we were really lost, he thought. Of course he still played with her—he knew his mother said things in anger that she didn't really mean. But it was never the same. "Were you punished?" Loretta asked when she was back on the street. "No, she just yelled." "You're lucky. But it was fun getting lost." "It wasn't. I didn't like it." "You liked the ices. And we got them for free."

He wished he had been a bolder boy. He wished he could have told his mother that he wanted to go too, that he loved Loretta because she urged him on. That without her he would lack the courage or the will to move out into the world. But the past was irreparable. Now he could do it all. At least he could talk, if that was what she wanted. Just at that moment, though, a heavy-set man with a bald spot walked up to the bed. Loretta strained to smile, and gazed at him the way she used to gaze at Bennett. The man shoved aside the tubes and bent down to kiss her. The husband. He had forgotten about him.

"The doctor says you're going to be all right," he said, stroking her hand. "You'll walk, you'll talk, everything. It'll just take some time."

Bennett stepped back to leave them alone. "Tina?" he heard her breathe. "She's okay," the husband whispered back.

At dinner that evening, Susan asked how his friend was. "Who is this anyway? Some great love of yours I don't know about?"

"When I was six, I was in love with her. I've hardly seen her since high school."

"Six? I wouldn't have thought you were such a romantic boy."

Had she questioned him further, now he might have told her. But Susan didn't ask anything more. Way back, she'd complained that he didn't ask many questions, was not curious, and in time she had become that way herself. He'd heard that long-married couples often take on each other's traits.

⚮

Now, with the task of clearing out her things, he wished she had taken on his orderliness instead. He emptied shelves and mused about his meetings with Loretta, and the more he mused, the more indistinct they became, as if each scene, once sharply reconstructed, degenerated into blurring fragments. After a while she was hardly more than a cloud that changed shape as it meandered across the sky. A shadow, a breath, a trace of something essential but indefinable. A name to which he attached feeling and longing, a memory diminished to a color or a vapor, a muted phrase of music in the mind. But without it there was no life to speak of.

Finally the shelves in the closets were nearly empty, and what little that remained was stacked in neat piles. Near the door were four black plastic bags of trash. He was about to take them down in the elevator, pondering whether to do it in one trip or in two. Or maybe leave it for morning—it was past midnight. Surprising himself, he sat down on the floor and opened a bag stuffed with lists and notes in Susan's loopy artist's hand. He studied them. Her handwriting. She had used black thick-tipped pens, and her writing was bold and arresting, quite legible, except when the idiosyncratic "r's" ran into the next letters. The capital "T's" had a peculiar flourish at the upper right tip. The capital "S's" were slim and snaky. He brought a page to his face and sniffed it. Nothing—the ink was too old. There was an ancient Chinese silk robe, almost in tatters, that she liked to wear, with a red and turquoise dragon on the back. He had joked that she could treat herself to a new one, had even bought her one in Chinatown while he was doing a story on immigration, but she was devoted to the old robe and wore his gift only once in a while, no doubt for his benefit. He brought the robe to his face and the scent hit him with force. Susan. There was a tiny makeup brush, stained beige from use. Those tiny hairs had swept her face. A pencil, for her eyelids, he supposed, worn down to a stub. This had grazed the liquid of her eyes. There was a half-used box of Tampax he had unearthed in the depths of a closet. It was some time since she had needed those. He took one out and stared at it. Strange to think of putting that unlovely, utilitarian thing where he had been.

He began walking around the house touching surfaces she had touched: the kitchen counters, her drawing table, the computer keys, the handles of the dresser. Since her death they'd been dusted several times—it was an illusion to think he would find any trace of her fingertips, but he touched them anyway. From the bedroom, he dialed her studio number to hear her voice message, then remembered he had erased it after she died. Maybe even before, in those last weeks when she couldn't possibly use the phone. He went into the bathroom, but nothing of her was left—for an instant he'd thought of using her toothbrush. Back in the bedroom he stared into her mirror and tried to envision her face there, but he saw only his own. His pleasant, squarish, aging face. Women would look at it and want him, and someday, later on, he might go with whoever made the most effort. He recalled Susan's concentrated expression as she brushed her hair at the mirror. So intensely serious—she might have been puzzling out a mathematical problem. Maybe all women at the mirror had that look. He couldn't recall whether the two women he had loved in secret did; he hadn't often watched them dress, and in any case he had not paid much attention. Not to Susan either.

He sat on the bed with horror seeping through him. He was ready to pay attention now. There were questions he needed to ask. Many questions, all the ones she said he never asked. What do you think? What do you feel? What is it about string beans that makes you hate them? How did you get so good at archery? Did you ever fire a gun? What was it like giving birth? Why do you never wear green or use it in your work? Did you really go around selling those Campfire Girl cookies? Did you ever love anyone else, after me? Did your mother ever hit you? Your father? What age did you learn to swim? He knew these things, or things like them, about Loretta. He had lived as if knowing them about her was enough. It wasn't. A vast curiosity, dormant for years, rose to choke him.

Why had Susan stayed, to be dragged through this wasteland? Love? Convenience? Could she have loved him that much, to subsist on the next to nothing he gave? It didn't seem possible. Did you live this pallid life because you loved me, he longed to ask, because it was a shadow of what you wanted? Or did you give up? Maybe you were the same as me. He would never know. The people in the grief group were right; he had lost her. He had given himself to a vaporous dream, to nothing. He stretched out on her side of the bed and studied the blankness of the ceiling. He understood now why people talked to the dead. But he didn't know how to begin. Susan, he whispered. Tell me.

By a Dimming Light

There was no worse fate for a writer.

The eye drops made the dim room more blurred than usual, and everything in it seemed to drift about on waves of air. Unable to write, unable to read. Nothing but drab life, unmitigated. The raw materials with no means of refining them.

There wouldn't be total darkness, the doctor told him, as if that were cheering. Instead the world would suffer a relentless meltdown. He would lose the details and edges; borders would merge, fixed objects would come loose and shimmer, suspended in mist. It was snowing outside when Eric finally left. It was snowing in the cab as well. It snowed everywhere. He kept forgetting that the snow was falling on his retina. It would snow forever, he thought with a savage self-pity.

It had happened so gradually that the doctor's sentence couldn't be called a shock. Yet he'd trusted in stronger glasses and stronger lights, until the messages his fingers sent to the computer screen, destined for his revising eyes, ended up as dead letters. In the weeks after the prognosis Eric came grudgingly to admire not just the doctor's accuracy but also his language. He couldn't have put it better himself. The world's fine seams, hidden but ready to spring into sharpness with the aid of a magnifying glass, were gone, glass or no; shades oozed into windows, food merged with the plate; squinting at the mirror, he couldn't find the line between his sand-colored hair and his skin, and all was shaggy, atremble.

Once he knew for sure that no light would ever be strong enough, he fell into despair, always an easy tumble. But for the sake of his new book he hauled himself out of the pit, summoning his resolution to call the nearby university where he had often been invited to lecture. It was the start of the term and students would be scrounging for part-time work. Send someone, he said, a perfect student. He would pay well. Male—and never mind whether such a preference was legal. He was in no mood for the distraction of a pretty girl—he thought he could still make out prettiness—nor for simpering adulation or kindly feminine concern. A literate boy, meaning not just literary, but one who could spell and punctuate—the two talents didn't always go hand in hand. Unobtrusive, obedient, diligent, trustworthy, a regular Boy Scout. If such a student existed. All Eric's hope and dread hung on the new book. His agent, Bill Benson, congenitally optimistic—well, that was his job— assured him that the publishers, however crass they'd grown, would be glad to hear from him again: Of course you'll pull it off, it's like riding a bicycle. But Eric doubted. The image of his rough phrases abrading the screen like flecks of grit tormented him far more than other losses—paintings or the slant of light on a tree or a woman swinging down the street, all sifted into dust.

He was spared the worst indignities. He could dress and, with effort, prepare simple meals. He knew the phone digits by their location; his fingers kept the memory of locks and keys; and he could manage the elevator buttons in his building (but shuddered at the prospect of someday learning the pimpled Braille codes beside them—maybe he'd die before he needed to). Shopping was out of the question—he couldn't read the labels. The bills in his wallet, even with their new kindergarten numerals, all looked alike. Fortunately his cleaning woman, Lucinda Perkins, was willing to take that on. She must feel sorry for him, he thought. Always a peaceful presence, now Lucinda glided silently through the apartment, as if his failing eyes made his ears and nerves more sensitive. Over the years, especially the ten years since Ada had left him, Eric and Lucinda had grown mutually indulgent, tacitly comprehending. If only she were computer-friendly, he could ask her to help with the novel.

Tad Hopwell, the graduate student, turned up at his door, earnest benevolence and competence written all over him, apparent even to Eric's faltering sight. He stood stamping his heavy boots on the mat, glistening eyes and hair giving him a cherubic glow, until Eric realized the effect came from melting snow. The boy stepped in and with easy shrugs slid a bulging pack from his shoulders, then shed his down jacket. Tall, fair-haired, lithe and lean, he felt familiar, like some old college friend. His indistinct face was smiling tentatively; Eric couldn't make out the color of his eyes or their expression. His voice was light, almost silky. Reassuring. An acceptable balance of confidence and deference, and thank goodness he didn't claim to have devoured every one of Eric's books, as did Grace, the girl his agent had been sending over twice a week to go through the mail.

Tad came from Oklahoma, he told Eric. He grew up with horses, working on his uncle's ranch. Also books: his mother was the town librarian. He had sung in the church choir all through high school. A graduate of Brown University, he was taking an advanced degree in comparative literature. Excellent. Not an aspiring writer who might seek guidance or, God forbid, make suggestions. Tad read *The New York Review of Books* and the *TLS*, or so he said. He liked reggae. He liked skiing. His dissertation in progress had something to do with the influence of his favorite author, Borges. He was fluent in Spanish. Eric could have hired him on the spot, but his natural wariness prevailed. Later, with Lucinda's help, he called Tad's references and reached all three immediately, a miracle these days. A good omen. The boy was a paragon, they raved, and could be trusted with anything. Even Lucinda liked him—she'd made sure to bring them coffee during the interview, to have a look. And she didn't suffer fools gladly.

Four mornings a week Tad arrived at eight-thirty, while Eric was getting dressed, a process much slowed down. As he passed the study, he liked seeing Tad bent over the big mahogany desk, deftly slitting open envelopes. Light glinted from the silver letter-opener, an ancient gift from Ada and sharp enough to slice a finger. The first morning, as Tad tilted his head to ask about sorting the mail, the serene reticence was again familiar. It might have been himself in younger days, that was it, Eric realized. The smooth good looks, bright hair and easy comfort in the body, the steady, reliable intelligence, the assurance held in check. The sense of more than met the eye. There was plenty of time for the assurance to become high-handed, the arrogance to show itself.

Before he left that first day, Tad printed the forty-odd pages of the new novel, about an idealistic young lawyer named Brenner investigating the illegal trade in organ transplants. As Brenner moved through what Eric had in store, he would find his convictions gradually undermined until he ended up in the quicksand of moral ambivalence. "You'll find it a far cry from Borges," Eric said. And Tad smiled, or Eric thought he did. After a pause, as if weighing his words, the boy murmured, "Borges was blind, you know."

Eric had forgotten that. Of course, and Borges hadn't been daunted. He had turned out reams, and he relied on assistants too. Well, fine. Tad would have a stake in his success. If the book revived his name, years from now Tad could contribute to the genre of self-effacing, self-serving essays recounting his aid to the famous author, complete with pithy quotes.

The next day Tad began reading the pages aloud, with Eric interrupting to make changes. He read with ease, in a relaxed voice—the choir training served him well. As soon as he got the drift of the plot and characters he began injecting a touch of drama into the dialogue, until Eric stopped him: "No expression. Read deadpan, so I can hear the words. I know the story."

The days fell into a comforting pattern, beginning with the mail. If it was one of Lucinda's days, she brought them coffee with croissants. Lucinda was built on a large and splendid scale, with big breasts and green eyes and an auburn-colored Afro cut close to her head. She padded around the apartment on bare feet, even in winter, and he used to like observing the changing hues of her toenails. He'd even used them in a novel, along with her distinctively broad cheekbones and tapering ankles. But he could no longer make out any of this. He wouldn't hear her enter, but as she came near, he felt her vibrating presence; she had a delectable odor of oranges that mingled with the buttery croissant smell. His little family, he thought, watching her set down the cream and sugar. Mom and Dad with their successful grown son, passing through town on a business trip. Or, with a stretch of the imagination, since Lucinda was nearly forty-five, he might be the proud father of the handsome pair—Lucinda from an adolescent first marriage to a black woman (a daring act at the time), Tad from a more recent one. The wives had disappeared, either died or, like Ada, found true love elsewhere. With an even further stretch, he could become their near-helpless child, Lucinda taking care of his physical needs and Tad keeping his affairs in order.

Without them, the evenings were long. He had never been a television watcher and was even less inclined now that his eyes shed clusters of graininess on already grainy blobs. Nor could he sit still listening to music. It was through sight that the world reached him. In the old days— not really so old, no more than six months back, but another epoch—he used to wander through museums and galleries. That was his reward, especially after hours of patiently working out plots and time lines. He took pride in the intricate plots, mapped on sheets of squared paper like webs, as cunning as if he were writing spy novels, but the plots were only the material reflection of the psyche. He'd used that phrase once with a radio interviewer: the material reflection of the psyche. He would never say anything so pompous today. Loss, he thought, makes you humble. It wasn't age that bred pomposity, but the robust entitlements of youth.

And not of youth alone. Of tangible success. He'd held it in his hands, but not firmly enough; it slipped from his grasp like a frantic fish. Despite some excellent reviews of his last two novels, one about corruption and racism in the South during Reconstruction, the other set in the political turmoil of Jamaica in the '80s, with a character based loosely on Bob Marley, sales had been disappointing. He didn't mourn the money: in better days he had invested wisely. What ate at him was the sense of sliding into eclipse. Always painful, now the term made him wince. That was also the time when Ada left. For her announcement, she chose a benign moment when they were unpacking after a ski trip. She was so, so sorry—clutching a folded sweater to her chest like a shield—but she had found out belatedly, at forty-two, what real love was. Eric sank down on the cluttered bed and stared. And ours wasn't real? Isn't? It was, of course it was, darling, but this is different. He felt a fool for not noticing. You were busy, I guess, said Ada, not even with the resentment of a neglected wife, which made it worse. So it wouldn't have made any difference had he not been busy. He'd thought she was busy too—she grumbled about the many evening receptions her foundation job demanded. They had no children by choice, and now Eric regretted that more than he regretted Ada. Fifteen years of her had granulated—rock crushed to sand. His own heroines were more solid.

The address book he could no longer read was crammed with names, the harvest of decades, yet there was no one he wished to see. A few friends still asked him to dinner, but it was like visiting a foreign country where he only half-grasped the passing scene. He missed the visual nuances, the small stitches that wove the social fabric of the evening.

And he hated his hesitancy at the table; he hated being helped to food and not recognizing the food, waiting for taste to do the work of sight. Taste wasn't all that reliable. Taste, he discovered, worked on the instructions of sight: if you couldn't see the dish, often you couldn't identify what you were eating, and he wouldn't insult his hostess by asking. He couldn't trust himself to pour anything—the rim of the glass wouldn't stay still. Practicing at home, he found the best solution was to fill everything half-full, taking no chances, and since he couldn't help seeing metaphors everywhere, his half-filled glasses and bowls became an emblem of his future.

As if Tad could sense his acrid resignation, he arrived the morning after one of those dinners with two thick catalogues listing books read on tape. Eric bristled. Occupational therapy? He wouldn't be patronized.

"Hold on a minute," said Tad. "Let me read you what they've got. They're good books. And they're not just for the blind. I listen at the gym all the time." In the end, he acquiesced. Tad was right. The evenings were no longer an agony of exile; the tapes gave back a world he belonged in and had all but renounced.

∽

Tad was a paragon, as heralded. A good researcher, he returned from library missions aglow with success, bearing tidbits of data like a happy dog fetching the ball for his master. He could trawl the Net, compose letters, field phone calls and e-mail, pay bills, and handle tedious dealings with Eric's accountant and stockbroker. Sorting the mail, he had an uncanny sense of which appeals Eric would respond to: yes to Habitat for Humanity and earthquake relief in India, no to Alzheimer's, yes, definitely yes, to Recordings for the Blind. Most of all, he willingly read long passages again and again so Eric could feel their shape. And his sentences in Tad's genial young voice and unaffected Western diction sent hope through his blood. The study was electrically charged again, the air humming with words. Vigorous, compelling, precise words. Contemporary, as if kin to Tad's sky-blue jeans and battered pack and what might be a stud in his right ear—Eric thought he glimpsed a golden flash each time the boy turned his head.

After Tad left, Eric scrawled notes for revisions on legal pads; he couldn't read them and feared they might resemble hieroglyphics, but Tad had no trouble. The method was laborious, but the thought of Borges consoled him. Also of the aged Henry James dictating to a secretary what turned out to be his best work.

One day he heard a word that wasn't his. "Deny." Brenner, the gullible attorney in the novel, "couldn't deny" the facts of the case, which involved dubious statements on grant applications for organ transplant research.

Not "deny," he told Tad. Anyone could write "deny"; it had none of the punch and ambiguity that was needed. "It should be 'defy.' Maybe I mumbled." He never mumbled. But it was almost a relief to find the boy was fallible.

"I'm awfully sorry. I'll fix it right away."

A few days later he thought he saw the gold flash again as Tad looked up and said, "Hey, here's something nice. A fan letter."

"No kidding. Who from?"

Eric had told him to watch for clippings about the reprint of his first novel, a Korean war story that was a near best-seller thirty years earlier. One reviewer had even alluded to *The Charterhouse of Parma*. "Combines the drama and action of the battlefield with the psychological subtlety of the great masters" was the quote Eric had wanted on the new edition, but the sales force didn't think psychological subtlety would fly nowadays. They opted for "A dynamic tale of men at war and political intrigue." The reprint was an oasis—if not a mirage—in the desert of recent years; it might even revive interest in a movie, twice optioned but never made. He hadn't expected fan letters.

"His name's Jim Ward, from Little Falls, Nebraska. Listen to this. 'Dear Mr. Malverson, I just came across your terrific book, *The Way to Dusty Death*, and wanted to let you know how much it meant to me. My father was a pilot shot down in Korea—I was a kid so I barely remember him—so while I enjoyed the story there was a certain amount of pain in reading it. Nothing ever showed me so vividly what it must have been like for him, so I want to thank you." He was a high-school shop teacher and would recommend the novel to his students. "Aside from the personal angle, it was a real page-turner."

Eric's face flushed. The first such letter in months. He silently cursed his blindness, which stole the delight of studying the handwriting, picturing the address and the writer, maybe a loner in a shabby apartment heaped with yellowing magazines, but more likely a family man in a tract house, aluminum siding, pale curtains, skateboard on the lawn.... Reading fan mail was an intensely private pleasure, a kind of unwilled, effortless masturbation, and it embarrassed him to hear the words aloud in Tad's presence, in Tad's voice. He wouldn't let the boy see how much he relished them. "Okay, let's get on with it." Yet afterward they seemed to share an intimate complicity, as if Tad had seen him admiring himself in the mirror or making love to a woman. Almost as if Tad had procured the woman for him and insisted on watching, as payment.

There was also a letter from a woman in Beverly Hills who described herself as head of a small production company, asking whether the movie rights to *The Way to Dusty Death* were available. Tad was excited but Eric blew it off; there'd been too many dead-end inquiries in the past. "Send it along to Bill Benson and forget it," he muttered.

He wasn't sure when the suspicions began. Maybe the week in late February, during another snowstorm, when Tad reported several online reviews of *The Way to Dusty Death.* "Really? How'd you find them?" "Just checking Web sites here and there." "So what do they say?" he asked casually. "I'll have to find them again and print. Is it okay if I do it tomorrow? It's almost two and I've got a class." The next morning Eric heard the printer chugging while he shaved; when he entered the study Tad waved some pages, then read aloud three short favorable notices. Eric was ready to dismiss them—who were these self-styled critics, anyhow?—but Tad said they were widely read. "If you want reader response I could set up a Web site. You'd have stuff pouring in." "How about getting through the novel first," he answered dryly. Then, and he didn't know where the impulse came from, he added, "Jot down the Web sites and pop them in an envelope so Bill can have a look." "I can e-mail them. It's quicker." "No," he said, suddenly alarmed by the sleight-of-hand possibilities of cyberspace. He blinked and squinted to bring Tad into focus, to study his face, but to no avail. It seemed the boy was deliberately eluding him. And from that moment his faith was shaken. "Do it by mail. I'll speak to him once he gets it."

ളൗ

When the snow stopped he tried going uptown to the galleries. He could navigate on the street if he kept alert; the traffic lights' green and red were distant jagged blotches, so the best strategy was to move when others moved. There was some satisfaction in arriving safely, but what had once been a joy turned into a penance. Filtered through his haze, blotches of color shivered over the canvases, lines blurred, brush strokes vanished, patterns bent. The representational paintings turned abstract, and the abstract ones morphed into crazy quilts. It was worse than not seeing them at all, a kind of sacrilege, as bad as someone jumbling the sentences in one of his books. He felt he ought to beg the artists' pardon. On the way home he paused before the windows of a huge new bookstore but couldn't make out the titles on display. Each week Tad would read Eric the first two paragraphs, and the last, of the reviews in the Sunday *Times,* and had suggested that he go to bookstore readings to meet the new authors. Tad didn't know bookstores were an unspeakable torture, with Eric's own books mostly out of print and the gleaming jackets as meaningless as the splotches on the museum walls. He kept walking. Better to let it all go. Stay home and stick to the tapes. They were the only reliable thing left.

The stories ripening in his ear each night gave him an idea. Why not have Tad tape the revised passages in the new book? He could do it first thing in the morning, while Eric dressed and fumbled in the kitchen, then they could spend their time moving ahead with the new sections. At night he could listen and make notes as best he could. The work would go so much faster. Now that he was well into the books, Eric practically lusted to reach the end. Its shape was clear in his mind, clearer than anything the material world could offer. It would be short, swift, and emotionally violent, the kind of book that left the reader stunned by inexorability, all soothing distinctions between good and evil blurred. He could already see the ending, with poor Brenner, his hero, plunged into bitter and lasting disillusion. It was just a matter of finding the routes to get there, a kind of Harrison Ford-ish hacking through the underbrush.

So after Tad left each day, his voice lingered in the study, measured and confident, the distilled essence without the physical presence. His reading, under Eric's guidance, was neither dramatic nor monotonous but colloquial, disinterested. He inflected the sentences according to their syntax, not their emotional valence. The book was good; Eric could feel it. It seethed with energy and conviction. It had the penumbra of thought. It alluded to more than itself. And it was just the right temperature. He imagined the sections as moving back and forth from cold to hot, calibrated to precise degrees like seasons in an ideal climate, storms and frosts and heat waves distributed in perfect rhythm, divided by temperate spells that never lasted long enough to grow dull. His words, Tad's voice. He played the tapes over and over, murmuring along with Tad to feel the shapes of the sentences in his mouth, the words skittering on his tongue.

Two more letters arrived, one from an English professor who praised his novel in an arcane language which Tad, fresh from his seminars, had to translate, and another from an ex-corporal who'd served in Korea and had a few small corrections, one geographical, the other about the kinds of food served in Seoul bars.

Eric shrugged. "Better than nothing, but basically second-rate."

That made Tad laugh. "What kind do you like?"

"Earnest. Heartfelt. Like that shop teacher. Or else cranks, for the entertainment value."

"I'll keep that in mind," said Tad, "if I ever write to an author."

"Everyone has different tastes, though. Keep that in mind too." He told Tad to answer them in two polite sentences and put them in the folder called Reader Mail. When he began that file years ago, Eric was tempted to call it Fans but was restrained by a kind of modesty that seemed prescient now, with his intimacies on exhibit.

⁂

Bill Benson's assistant called, the girl who used to come to sort his mail. "Mr. Malverson?" Everyone else had dispensed with last names, but Grace was meticulous. Maybe that was why Bill kept her on. It surely wasn't for her looks or her brains, Eric thought. "Mr. Benson asked me to tell you he checked the Web sites you wrote him about, I mean Tad wrote about, and actually it was me who checked them, but I didn't find any reviews."

"But Tad showed me ... He read them to me."

"Well, sure, they were there, but these online sites only keep the stuff up a few days. Next time if you e-mail we can do it the same day."

"And where do the reviews go after they, uh, take them down?"

She hesitated. "Nowhere, I guess. They're just sort of ... over."

"I see. Why didn't Bill call me himself?" Because you're old and blind and obsolete and from now on you're relegated to the underlings, a voice in his head supplied.

"He's out of town. The booksellers' convention in Phoenix."

"Lucky Bill. Oh, another thing, Grace. Ever hear from, what was it, Garden of Eden Productions, something like that? The movie interest?"

"Children of Paradise," she corrected. "Not yet. But it's only a couple of weeks. You know those movie people, they can take forever."

A woman from Texas wrote saying her book group had had a stimulating discussion of his novel. They didn't usually go in for war books, but the husband of one member reported that it wasn't primarily about war but about fear and mortality and the illusions people construct to ward them off.

Tad looked up after reading it aloud, as if for approval. "So, you like this one better?"

"Nice," he granted. "Very nice. I told you I have a weakness for corny and explicit. Go figure."

And a few days later came a classic nut case, full of rage about geopolitical ethics beginning with the Opium Wars. Tad held the letter up close so that, with the aid of the magnifying glass, Eric could make out the italic typeface with every tenth word in boldface capitals. They both chuckled. "Excellent crank," said Eric, and Tad seemed very pleased.

After Tad left that day, Eric called Lucinda into the study. "Lucinda, my love, light of my life, could I possibly trouble you for something not in your job description?"

"I told you before, I don't do ironing and I don't do sex and I don't move furniture. Want me to look up a number for you?"

"No thanks. And I never asked for sex, Lucinda. If it didn't work out I'd lose you. Take a look in the first folder, bottom drawer on the right. Reader Mail. Got it? Read me what's on top."

She sat down opposite him and put on the large glasses she wore on a chain around her neck, which gave her a studious air. She was wearing an orange sweatshirt, tight black jeans, and huge gold hoops in her ears. Like everything else in the room, Lucinda shimmered in a halo of dots lit by a bright March sun streaming in the west window. The air was warmer than usual, a premature touch of spring. Eric blinked. He couldn't seem to stop blinking, as if that could dissipate the haze. Lucinda cleared her throat and adjusted the glasses. She would have made a good schoolteacher, he thought. She could have been many things. She didn't have the fighting spirit. He, on the contrary, saw life as an armed struggle where strategy was decisive; it was why he wrote so often about war, the best ready-made metaphor. Lucinda had had a brief career singing in cabarets, then came the children—she never mentioned any father—then she worked for two years as a dental hygienist. But she preferred cleaning apartments to cleaning teeth. "I don't like standing in one place all day," she told Ada when she first came. "I'd rather move around." Too easygoing, his Lucinda. She liked to count her blessings and had on several occasions suggested that Eric do the same. If she were a character, he'd toughen her up and write her a grander destiny. Shrewd campaign manager for a politician. Or why not the candidate herself? A crusader. Battered women, human rights abuse, something that took guts and endurance.

"Okay. 'Dear Mr. Malverson, Your novel, *The Way to Dusty Death*, reminded me yet again, not that it's ever far from my mind, of the American, or I should say WEST-ERN, or let's just be frank about it and say CAU-CASIAN'—I'm saying it that way," Lucinda put in, "because that's how he writes, in big letters, 'CAUCASIAN intervention in places we have no BUSINESS—'"

"Fine, enough," he interrupted. "What's the one before that?"

"'Dear Mr. Malverson'—this one has a nice handwriting—'Our book group in Dallas had a truly enlightening discussion of—'"

"What else?"

"Let's see. Someone who served in Korea. Then we're back to last year." She started to get up. "Is that it?"

"No. What about the envelopes?"

"There's no envelopes. That Tad, he is one neat boy. I'm making a lentil soup you can heat up for dinner, so if that's all, I better—"

"Wait a second. When did you last take down the trash?"

"From this room? A couple of days ago, I guess. I'll do it on my way down. Sorry about that."

"It's all right, I'm glad you didn't. Lucinda, please, would you mind ...?" He pointed at the wastebasket under the desk.

"Go through the trash? Oh, come on now, Eric."

"It's just papers, dear, not fish bones or apple cores. Help a blind old man. Make believe I'm trying to cross the street. See if you can match up the envelopes with the letters."

She shuffled for a moment. "Bingo. Joseph Borowski, the one about the CAUCASIAN intervention. The guy's got a point, if you ask me."

"Sure, put him in charge and he'd be worse, I guarantee. The same address on the letter and the envelope?"

"Yeah. Two-seventeen Salmon Run Road, Hoboken. That's where Gerard's from, Hoboken." Gerard was her boyfriend, who drove a bakery truck and was in town only intermittently.

"Postmark?"

She held the envelope up to the light. "Hoboken. Just like I said." She shuffled through more papers. "That's all. The others must have gone down last week." She stood and faced him, hands on her hips. "What's with you? Don't you trust that boy?"

"I'm not sure. Do you?"

"Can't you tell a good thing when you see it? It's possible you lucked out, you know. It does happen."

"Anything's possible. Is that a stud in his right ear?"

"It's real tiny. If you saw that, maybe you're taking a turn for the better."

"No, I just saw the light flashing from it. What does it mean? Anything? Does it mean he's gay?"

"I don't think so. It used to mean something, but now they've all got them. Anyway, he told me he has a girlfriend. Angela. A law student."

"Oh, he tells you things?"

"He liked my scarf and wanted to know where he could find one for her."

"Very chummy, aren't we? You wouldn't happen to know anything about Web sites, Lucinda?"

"Are you kidding? I told you before I don't like those machines. I don't even like dusting yours. My kids got them, but I think they're the devil's work." She turned and ambled toward the door, then stopped. "And you did ask for sex."

"I did? I swear I don't remember."

She nodded, one hand propped on the door jamb, the other fiddling with an earring. A fine pose. The hush of Vermeer, but not delicate enough. Manet, maybe. Waiting, unreadable. It was like one of those critical moments in a story, when a word or gesture sends things irrevocably down one path and all other paths close over. But he couldn't tell if her face was teasing or disgruntled. That was the worst of being near-blind. How could you know how to proceed if you couldn't read the signals?

"I would remember if you'd said yes." He paused, but no clues came. She didn't stir toward him or away. I can tell a good thing when I see it, he wanted to say but didn't dare. "When? Before Ada left or after?"

"Right after."

"Well, then. I wasn't myself."

"Really. Who were you, then?" She turned to walk out.

"Lucinda? I hope I wasn't, you know, rude. I wouldn't like to think I was rude to you."

"Well, I'm still here, right? You know what, Eric? You need to get out more. You're not a cripple. You're not even all that blind. Hop in a taxi and go someplace. Meet people."

Women, she meant. Someone whose face he'd never really know. Some soft, amorphous body to sink darkly into. But seeing them was what stirred him most. Keep the lights on, was the only detail he'd ever insisted on in bed. Someday, maybe. Not yet.

"Should I count my blessings too?" But he said it with a smile.

"Took the words right out of my mouth."

When he settled in with the tapes that evening he caught another wrong word. "Dissect." This was no case of mumbling.

"My word was 'analyze,'" he said offhandedly the next morning. "How'd you ever come up with 'dissect'?"

"Oh, I remember that line. It was a great moment." Tad was grinning so broadly that even Eric could see it. "When the woman, Laura, is trying to figure out what her husband's weird behavior meant, the day before he vanished. She goes over it step by step."

"I'm glad the story interests you, but I'm sure I didn't say 'dissect'. What's going on, Tad? Want to be an editor?"

"I'm sorry if I made a mistake. I wouldn't dream of editing you. I'll fix it."

"Do you see any difference between 'analyze' and 'dissect'?"

"Well, sure. 'Analyze,' used in this context, is more abstract. I mean, you can analyze anything, but in novels mostly it's ideas, or maybe behavior or motivation. 'Dissect' has a more physical feel. Like dissecting frogs in high school. Sort of an autopsy." He paused then grinned again, a kid hitting on the right answer in a test. "Like, anatomize."

Eric stared at the golden blur of Tad, haloed in morning light. Anatomize. "Not bad," he allowed. Fair was fair. The kid was developing.

"Yes," Tad agreed eagerly, with relief. "You're dealing with the black market in organ transplants, you've got body parts being flown back and forth ..."

Eric's mind raced. Yes, Tad was right. And as for the character who was doing the analyzing, or anatomizing—

"And in a way," Tad broke in excitedly, "what Laura's going over is a dead issue, it's the past. Her husband could be dead too for all she knows. I mean, I don't know what you have in mind, what you plan to have happen to him, but for her, well—"

"Okay. 'Anatomize' it is. But Tad."

"Yes?"

"Be more careful in the future."

And he was. At least Eric couldn't be absolutely sure he hadn't uttered the next two dubious words. They were good words in any case, so he said nothing and let them stand.

⁎

He followed Lucinda's advice and went to a couple of book parties, with her choosing his ties and inspecting him like a mother with an adolescent bound for his first dance. He wondered, as she plucked a speck off his lapel, if he could really have come on to her. Not that he hadn't thought of it on and off, mostly in between brief and half-hearted erotic forays, post-Ada. Unlike the women he had pursued or was pursued by, Lucinda was so luscious, sympathetic, so near at hand. The sheer convenience. Still, a move like that wasn't his style, nor the sort of thing a man would forget. Why would she lie? He'd studied deception all his life, written time and again about the exploitation of the innocent by the canny, the shortsighted by the far-seeing, the shrewd chess players, and Lucinda wasn't one of the chess players. They were more like Tad, biding their time, proceeding cautiously but inexorably.

She made sure he had enough twenties in his wallet for taxis and an impromptu dinner (Tad had become his personal ATM banker; no worries on that score—he was scrupulously honest) and sent him off. Once there, he had to watch out for high floating trays of canapés and swift jostlings by the young and presumably talented. Presumably, for he would never know, never read their books, yet he wasn't so blind that he couldn't see their newness, the women's short skirts and clunky shoes, the men's longish hair and collarless shirts.

The trouble, he thought, was not being blind enough for the warning emblems of stick or dog. Trying to pass, so to speak. People greeted him, but, unable to read the name tags, he was reduced to squinting blankly. Even when they declared themselves he didn't quite trust them: in the dim haze of faces, anyone could claim to be a long-lost editor or reviewer. With sickening clarity, he saw himself as prey to every farcical or sinister deception that cunning minds might devise.

He drifted home through the dark April streets in slow motion. Sparse traffic, luckily, for he couldn't make out anything solid more than thirty feet off, only the pulsing glare of headlights, huge and explosive as fireworks. He walked the mile and a half downtown to prove he could do it, then resolved once more to stay home. Maybe, he thought wildly, he could have Tad tape all his other books. Then whatever dark time was left to him, he could spend listening to the record of his passage. It was all that remained. In the old days, the press of images everywhere had fooled him into thinking he had a life. Now the mist he inhabited was yielding up the truth. It was so fitting, so novelistic, he almost laughed.

In the morning, one of Tad's days off, on impulse he called Bill Benson. Grace answered with all the perkiness of ambition. "How are you, Mr. Malverson?"

"Grace, you can call me Eric, and I'm fine. Would you put Bill on, please?"

"I can't, Eric. He's not in."

"He always used to be in when I called. I haven't spoken to him in weeks. I need him. Where is he this time?"

"Actually, he had to attend a funeral."

"Whose?"

"His mother-in-law." Grace paused, a nanosecond of respect for the dead. "She had a stroke on Monday."

"Oh. Well, give him my condolences. Grace. Have you had any fan letters for *The Way to Dusty Death*?"

"Not that I recall. I would have forwarded them. But some might still—"

"I got a few letters at home, mostly back in February."

"That's nice. I'll tell Bill."

"Doesn't it seem odd to you, half a dozen letters the first month the book is reprinted, without any reviews?"

"But why not? You have a very loyal readership out there, Eric, and *The Way to Dusty Death* is probably your best known book. I don't see anything odd. Why not just enjoy it?"

"I didn't get any fan letters when you were going through the mail."

She gave a wry chuckle he wouldn't have thought her capable of. "Well, I wish I could have done better. I certainly wasn't sequestering any. Maybe Tad is your good luck charm."

"Okay, don't get the wrong idea, Grace. I'm not losing it. Just a little bit on edge. Maybe a tiny bit paranoid."

"No problem. Aren't we all. Have a nice day."

☙❧

"That new character I introduced yesterday," Eric began as he opened the door to Tad. "The cardiologist. I heard the tape last night. His name isn't Bergen. It's Burton."

"I'm sorry," Tad said. "Did I say Bergen?"

"You did. Several times."

"I'm really sorry. I'll fix it."

"It's hard to mistake Burton for Bergen. I think it is. How'd that happen?"

"I don't know, Eric. I guess either I misheard or I jotted it down fast and then couldn't read my writing. Anyway, I'll change it right away."

"Maybe you just like the name Bergen better than Burton. Or maybe you thought Bergen was a better name for that character."

Tad was staring. Maybe even glaring. Eric blinked and squinted to read his face but couldn't. "No," Tad said. "Nothing like that. Just a simple mistake."

"Maybe you think it makes no difference what a character is called. It might seem unimportant. But believe me, to a writer it makes a very big difference."

"I believe you and I'm sorry. I'm in the middle of two papers and haven't been getting enough sleep. I must've been careless."

This time the imperturbable Tad was perturbed, but whether out of guilt or innocence, Eric couldn't see. Either way, he was gratified. And five minutes later, ashamed of himself. Was cheap sarcasm the only weapon he had left? He muttered a half-hearted apology, and Tad said it was no problem.

But he couldn't get over his vexation. He'd said the name half a dozen times. Could it be a simple mistake? He felt shaken like a rag doll and stayed up half the night, fretfully pulling apart the roast chicken Lucinda left. Dissecting it, he thought, as he stood nibbling in the kitchen. Anatomizing it. Definitely not analyzing it. How could he be sure the manuscript would be his words? For all he knew, Tad might be constructing an entirely different story. A happy trusting story, the kind of story a fortunate boy who grew up with horses and books might write, all the ambiguity and deceptions sanded away, from the common lies of self-interest to more elaborate machinations or self-delusions. His own intricate web shrunk to a simplistic tale of good and evil.

He would need someone else to read him the final version. Grace might do. But could he stand her slick humility for that long? What if she and Tad were joined in some unholy alliance? Maybe Grace was the girlfriend, postmarking the letters from far-off locations. But the girlfriend was Angela. Or so Tad said. No, Lucinda said. He had to trust Lucinda. And yet, there was that Hoboken postmark. Her boyfriend Gerard could have done that. Gerard drove all over the country, dammit. He could be mailing letters from anywhere.

He couldn't let himself doubt Lucinda. It was all Tad's doing. He'd have to get rid of him. Banish him as soon as the book was done. Never mind if he was a good luck charm, devil or angel (Lucinda had reported scornfully that angels were in vogue—she'd heard idiots testifying on talk shows). Or a fantasy he'd conjured up? Could you banish your own fantasies once they got the upper hand? Wasn't that precisely what madness was? No, Tad couldn't be a fantasy. Lucinda was no fantasy, and she'd seen him come and go for months, even fed him croissants. He could eat two or three at a sitting. Fantasies wouldn't eat so heartily. What if, real as he was, he refused to go? What if the book had become his personal mission?

What have you got for me today, Eric thought when they next went through the mail. A note from the Nobel committee? How about the White House? Medal for the arts? Nothing. It was almost disappointing. He enjoyed the odd bits of good news, real or not. He was the perfect mark, a co-conspirator. Pitiful.

Nothing unusual happened all week, in fact the work went so smoothly that Eric almost forgot his pre-dawn frenzies. Until one evening he heard the sentence about the barking dog. The novel's principled attorney, Brenner, no longer quite as gullible as at the start, had hunted down a witness in Prague. Eric had spent some time there years ago at a conference and found to his dismay that dogs were welcomed in his local café. A yapping terrier at a nearby table almost drove him wild, though no one else seemed to mind; they stroked him and gave him scraps. It was the kind of droll detail that stuck and was bound to turn up in a novel. The dialogue between Brenner and his prospective witness, the doomed victim of a botched illegal kidney transplant, took place in that very café. The mood was tense, even threatening, and made more so by the frantic yelps of a dog at the next table. Brenner was adamant—in the name of truth, naturally—and the cowed witness skulked away, knowing he'd have to testify; there was no hiding out from the law or the managed-care establishment. Brenner watched him leave with satisfaction (that would be shattered soon enough), and the scene ended with a sentence about the dog. "Sometime in the last few moments the dog had stopped yelping, but Brenner was too exultant to notice."

Eric clicked off the tape. He'd never uttered those words. A moment later, as they echoed in his ear, he wasn't so sure. They sounded right. Necessary. They were words he might well have said, should have said. If he hadn't said them this time, he would surely have added them later.

He decided to take a new tack. "That closing sentence about the dog was pretty good, Tad. Pretty sharp. I should thank you."

"I don't know what you mean. Let me find it." He leafed through pages, then glanced up with the familiar elegant tilt of the head. "That's exactly what you said, Eric. It's right here."

Eric wanted to hear more. A more forceful denial. Protest, impatience, even anger at his badgering. But Tad held his peace. Tad had learned to handle him. There were no words to confront that bland innocence. Let it go. Let Tad go ahead and write the fucking book, for Chrissake.

Later, alone, he tried to be reasonable. The work was going better than he had dared to hope. There was no firm proof of fabrication. A word here and there? Even Borges's assistants, even James's, might have made a mistake or indulged themselves now and then to relieve the tedium. The book was inseparable from Tad's voice; he couldn't send him away now. Once they'd finished, not long off, they would have a day of reckoning. He would be understanding and fatherly, he knew young people could get carried away by well-meaning enthusiasm, and Tad would own up—he was a good boy, basically—and Eric would forgive him. He just needed to know. He needed to be told the truth because he couldn't see it for himself.

ಐಶ

"Eric," Tad began as they sat down the next morning. "The term is almost over, only three more weeks, and at that point I'll have to leave. I'm going to Oklahoma for the summer to help my uncle on his ranch. I hope that's not too inconvenient." He waited but Eric said nothing. "It feels like we're coming to the end anyway, aren't we? I mean, I can see you're tying things up ..."

Eric didn't speak for a long time. "What about next fall?"

"I don't think so. I'm sorry. I've been offered two freshman comp classes to teach, and with that and the dissertation, well, it's about all I can handle." He paused, waiting. "But it's been terrific working with you. I've learned so much, and I'm really looking forward to reading the book when it comes out." He gave an awkward laugh. "I mean really reading it." Again he waited. "If you like, I'll ask around. I might be able to find someone else for you."

"I've gotten used to you, Tad," Eric said at last. "With your help the work's gone very smoothly."

"Thanks. I'm glad I could be useful. But I'm sure someone else could do as well."

"By the way, there haven't been any fan letters lately."

"I noticed. I guess after the first few weeks ... Is that how it's usually been in the past?" Tad asked.

"It varies. Still, one or two more before you leave would be nice."

But of course none arrived. Tad wasn't stupid, after all.

He came day after uneventful day until the term was over and the book was done, a neatly stacked pile of pages with the requisite disks placed dead center above it like a paperweight. A firm handshake for Eric, a hug for Lucinda. Eric wouldn't have been surprised at this point if Tad had dissolved and vanished before his eyes or flown out the hall window or sunk through the floor. But he merely hoisted the pack onto his back, tucked his T-shirt in his shorts, opened the door and shut it firmly behind him.

Something had been visited upon him, Eric thought. Whether it was very good or very bad almost didn't matter. What mattered was that he hadn't the vision to recognize what it was. He could only stand beside Lucinda, both of them gazing at the closed door as if something more might happen.

"Did he ever ask you to mail any letters for him?"

"No. Why would he?" said Lucinda. "He was out all the time. He did ask me to pick up a silk scarf like mine, though, at that shop in my neighborhood. For Angela."

"And did you?"

"I tried. But they were sold out." She sighed. "I'll miss that boy. He had such a sweet way about him."

It was just what Ada had said about him, soon after they were married, when he asked what made her fall in love with him. He suspected it might be the glamour of the early success and the money, and he wondered if she'd be frank enough to say so. What she said instead was startling, for he'd never imagined himself the least bit sweet. She must have come to see the truth.

Deadly Nightshade

No question that she was brave. But it had to be something more than bravery. Nothing so stark as hunger—there were easier ways to satisfy hunger. Curiosity, surely. How could she help but be tantalized by something both beautiful and forbidden? Beyond curiosity: youthful defiance, that acute lust to court danger. It might even have been despair, not giving a damn anymore what happened—let it kill me or cure me of this misery. Love misery, it must have been. Why else would she choose the love apple, smooth and luscious-looking, red as the heart's blood? It's safe to say "she" rather than "he," although like everything else about the matter, that too is unknown. But a woman is more likely to seek adventure or death by something as humble as a fruit.

No one in living memory had eaten it, and there must be a good reason, the elders warned. Never mind the old sailors who returned from voyages over the horizon with stories of natives who ate the fruit and thrived. Everyone knew sailors made up tall tales. They brought home seeds too, and though the vines those seeds bore were good to look at, danger often lurked behind beckoning surfaces. The fruit would kill.

She went alone to the edge of the village where the woods began, grabbed one off the vine before she could stop herself, bit in swiftly, expecting bitterness and startled by sweetness, then ate all the way through the soft wet pulp, the juice dripping down her palm. And waited for the griping pains, the vertigo, the dimming in the eyes, the convulsions and hallucinations.

The first hour of anticipation was the worst. What would it be like when night came and pain clenched her in the dark? Would she fall into a swoon, never to wake, or die screaming in remorse? She thought of what she would leave behind, family, friends, most of all the one who tormented her by his restless leaving and returning. The pain and dizziness didn't come, but that hardly eased the terror. It might be a slow poison, more excruciating than the quick kind. She waited alone in the woods so no one would witness her suffering. As night fell she drifted toward sleep, first fighting it then yielding, her last slippery thought being, This might be my last thought.

Light surprised her awake, light and hunger. She leaped to her feet in triumph and relief, then shrank back. Too soon to rejoice. It might be an extremely slow poison.

She gave it almost a whole day to do its work. As the uneventful hours passed she grew more confident and more reckless. She ate a second one, and waited, until at last eagerness sent her racing back to the village. By the time she reached the square her cheeks were flushed with excitement, nearly as red as the fruits that filled her basket. Breathlessly, she told what she had done. Look! she cried. Here! Eat! But people being what they are, they didn't rush to take what she offered. Some didn't believe her, suspected her of a malevolent urge to poison the lot of them. She'd always been eccentric, they muttered, always needed to go her own way. They didn't even trust when she ate one in full view. She didn't really want another just then. She was worn out. The strain of teasing death had wearied her, and all she wanted was to eat something familiar, something like bread, and lie down. But she couldn't show any reluctance or weariness; they would think the fruit had sapped her strength. She knew it wasn't the fruit. It was the historic moment, and historic moments are exhausting. But she ate it anyway, just to show the stodgy cowards. And it was good, the best so far.

Finally a loyal friend ate one in solidarity, then another stepped forward, and another, a small plucky group. For the next few days the talk was of nothing else; the village was tense, waiting for the dire results that never came. And so before long, as might be expected, a good number of people began sampling the fruits, some cautiously, a mere morsel or a few drops of the juice added to a stew, others exuberantly eating them raw and whole. They were a great success. How could they not be? We all know, thanks to the forgotten woman, what a fresh tomato tastes like. Even now, it's the rare person who doesn't like tomatoes. There were a few holdouts, naturally, the sort who would never eat what their grandparents had warned them not to eat: woe to those who turn their back on the old wisdom. Sooner or later you'll be sick, they warned the tomato eaters. The poison will do its work in its own good time. In fact for years to come, whenever the tomato eaters fell ill with some ordinary transient illness or exhibited any peculiar behavior, those die-hards would shake their heads with satisfaction and blame it on eating tomatoes.

But for the most part people welcomed the succulent fruit and felt lucky to be alive in the dawn of the tomato-eating age. Think of the numberless maligned tomatoes left to rot on the vine, they marveled. And innocent all the while. What pleasures untasted, what hungers unappeased. People were grateful, and for a time the woman was known and revered far and wide for her brave deed. But since the drama of her deed was so quickly over and its results so benign, unlike the drama of the invention of gunpowder or the colonizing of a new land, her fame soon declined. Tomatoes were sliced, chopped, crushed, stewed, fried, turned into sauce, and in no time at all incredulous children would laugh to hear that the versatile, ubiquitous tomato had once inspired dread, and that the ordinary woman whom they saw every day had shown unprecedented courage in eating one. Thus her name and origins and circumstances are lost to us. We can only imagine them.

What was it like for her, this Prometheus of the vegetable world? At first the excitement attending her act distracted her from her misery, if it was misery. No doubt she was courted by many. Even the one who had caused her misery was all too willing now to have her, heroine that she was. But she no longer needed him. The first bloom of excitement bedazed all other feelings, and when that passed, she found her despair had passed as well, the not caring what became of herself that had driven her to begin with. Had she been shrewd she might have used her fame, at the most propitious moment of its brief arc, to attract a wealthy and powerful husband. But she was not shrewd, only daring and passionate. She remained in the village where she was born, and the only significant change was her knowledge that life could come up with something new even when it seems most depleted.

And yet she suffered ever after from a vague disappointment. It had nothing to do with her faded renown nor with tomatoes themselves ceasing to tantalize her. She had known all along it was the act, not the fruit or the fame, that mattered. She had known, even as she sank her teeth into it, that no tomato would ever again taste as good as the one she ate in the village square, in front of all the people, after her night alone in the woods. The disappointment rose from something less tangible. Life could bring the vastly unexpected, and yet it did not. Nothing she did in later years came close to the elation of that single act of abandon. She was a daring woman who found no more opportunities for daring, or for the kind of daring peculiar to her, which was biting into the perilous unknown and letting it travel through her. She wished there were other fruits to be braved, but there were none.

It was a different sort of person who ate the first artichoke, a spirit not so much daring and impulsive as patient and ingenious. But that is another story.

Francesca

I thought I knew what my life was. Through most of it I have been sober and single-minded, for the last twenty-odd years studying the curious eruptions of wayward cells, cancer cells. Most of them cause turbulence and ruin, while a few, especially in older bodies, nestle harmlessly in a corner where they can be virtually ignored, though we forget them at our peril. But then something happened. It seems my passage through the world has been generating trails I could never have imagined, and which might be better ignored as well. After all, so much of human history, private history, goes unacknowledged. Yet I find myself unwilling to let this particle rest. It refuses to, in any case. It has reappeared through a turn of fate and in a troubling, even terrifying, form.

I should note, by way of preface, that I have never been a man who had difficulties with women or who had hurting ways. Now two women are hurt on my account and they will never know why.

Twenty-four years ago I spent a semester of my senior year of college in Rome, on one of those programs abroad that have become so common. At the time, it was, if not a rarity, at least more of a special privilege than it is today. And so the dozen of us who were chosen set foot in Italy with a giddiness, an almost unreal elation, sharpened and sustained by our knowing—the men, that is—we might well be drafted and sent to Vietnam soon after graduation. Now or never: we had to cram all our youth into those five months. And what better place? Our group made some side trips, to Florence, Siena, Ravenna, a few other cities. But mostly we stayed in Rome, which even without any threat of imminent danger provides giddiness and elation enough. With all that, I have to say I was on the stodgy side for a young man in those unstodgy years. Not by choice but through shyness and inhibition.

The program was in art history. I was doing a double major—art history and biochemistry. I had trouble making up my mind, though I was leaning toward biochemistry. It was more practical, and I thought my bent for the meticulous and measurable would serve me better there. Still, I kept up the art history major, partly because I wanted the trip. I wanted something to shake me out of my stodginess—I knew it would take shaking from outside. And since my family was poor and I spent my summers working, there was little chance I would get abroad any other way.

An Italian professor of art history at the University of Rome was attached to our group. He had a long, difficult name we had trouble pronouncing; it sounded to me more Greek or Romanian than Italian. He would walk around the city with us, expounding on its architecture, its churches, its history, as well as amble through the museums, murmuring with nonchalant erudition about the paintings, and finally, he conducted a weekly seminar in his large, ornately cluttered apartment on a small street just off the Piazza Navona, where, he explained, gladiatorial contests, chariot races, and all sorts of rowdy festivities were held in ancient days.

This Roman professor, tall, stout, and rather imposing, with thick strong features, an unruly black mustache, thinning hair, and a genial bemused manner—as if he found us lovable, benign aliens—must have been forty or so, though we naturally saw him as advanced in age. He had an American wife eight or ten years younger than himself, a rangy, firm-boned woman with hair the color of honey and an imperturbably ironic manner, and on seminar nights she would serve us elaborate, rum-drenched pastries with wonderfully muddy coffee in thimble-like cups—translucent white with a rim of gold at the top—and later, dense, sweet, tart anisette liqueur. She had two small daughters, fair-haired like herself, maybe three and five, who would cavort among us babbling in incomprehensible Italian, so that very soon we realized the seminars would not be excessively scholarly or purposeful: we should regard them instead as a way to get an inside look at a real Roman family. Though as one of the girls in our group pointed out, it was hardly a typical Roman family since the wife and mother was American, like us.

She—Janet was the wife's name—did not seem American. So far as I could tell, her clothes, her mannerisms, and gestures were all Roman: decisive, dramatic, mellow. She appeared to have taken on the coloration of her chosen environment, and when she spoke Italian to the children, which at first we understood only in bits and pieces, she sounded to us like a native, but of course we were not the best judges.

She was only ten or so years older than we were, yet it was enough of a gap to make us treat her deferentially, as the professor's wife, the role in which she was presented. One evening one of the more outspoken girls asked how she and the professor had happened to meet and marry.

"I was a student here in a program like yours," she said. Her English had a very faint tinge of otherness, not an accent exactly, for she was a native speaker, but a hint that the words and inflections were seldom used, taken out on special occasions like fine linen—crisp and slightly self-conscious. "The professor was doing the seminars, the tours, the whole bit. At the end I ... just stayed. We got married. That's the story." She smiled ironically and shrugged, the way the girls in our group sometimes smiled and shrugged, as if to imply they possessed more information and wisdom than we men could dream of, and withheld it out of a teasing, challenging perversity. At that instant I saw her as having been one of us, the young and unsettled, rather than as a grown-up, established, foreign sophisticate. She became a person who had taken a risky turn, surprised and perhaps even dismayed her family. Tricked fate, as it were. A palpable illustration that we might do the same.

Often at the end of the seminar the professor would disappear for lengthy telephone calls, or to say goodnight to the children, or on unknown errands, and Janet would sit with us. I thought she was simply fulfilling her duty, till after a while I saw she was genuinely interested. More than interested—on the lookout for something. I don't know how I sensed it: she didn't seem bored with her own life— there was a shimmering animation about her, a sense of being richly present—but she was restless too; she enjoyed stirring things up and inducing revelation. She would ask questions that coaxed our awkward self-doubts to the surface, and she managed to do this without being rude or overbearing but by being charming. Once she had made us speak of our uncertainties they no longer felt awkward but brimming with possibility.

Gradually I became the one she spoke to most often. Looking back, I think perhaps I seemed most in need of being shaken loose, released from the clutches of naïveté. We would sit in the glow of the dim lights as she interrogated me like a curious, unconventional aunt from far away. What did I think about my past, did I like my parents, what were my ambitions, what did I want to find out about the world?

"How things work," I said hesitantly.

"What things, for instance?"

"Well, cells."

"Cells," she repeated. She got me to talk about a fairly commonplace project I had undertaken in the lab, involving crossbreeding in fruit flies, and though she was attentive there was a playful note to her attention, as if, while these were important matters, we must not take them too seriously. I found her easy to talk to, but confusing.

One late afternoon I came upon her in the Borghese Gardens, where I often wandered on my own, semi-intoxicated by the mere idea of being where I was. After chatting for a moment I was about to continue on my way, but she suggested a coffee. I was impressed with the way she ordered the waiter about in typically imperious Roman fashion and tossed back the dark brew in one gulp. I expected we would talk in our usual manner; I was still acting the boy prepared to be questioned, to indulge my fantasies in her adult attentiveness. But after a few moments of this she said, "Don't you have any curiosity about what's around you? Do you ever feel the need to ask questions?" I was puzzled. Mired in deference, I had little experience in talking to adults on equal terms.

"Well, sure. How come you went so far from home?" I asked.

She laughed. "I came here to get away from people like you." She spoke in a friendly way, a way that invited further questions, but in my puzzlement I said nothing. "From innocence," she added, as if I had urged her on. "American innocence."

I had an inkling, then, of what she had in mind, for even the most untried young man can sense a sexual challenge. But I simply couldn't believe it. She went on to tell me she had grown up on a farm in Nebraska—not all that far from my own small Minnesota town, yet I doubted that I could ever grow so comfortably urbane. Even after three years I was not quite at ease in my Ivy League college, which I attended thanks to a scholarship. As a matter of fact I am not quite at ease even now.

As she talked that afternoon, she would occasionally touch my arm or wrist. Just before we got up to leave, she let her fingers rest on my arm for an unsettling time. I knew, but was still afraid to trust my instinct. Or my luck, as a college boy would doubtless have put it then.

"Why don't we walk for a while?" she said. "Or are you dashing off to pursue your studies?"

Of course I agreed to walk. By now I was desperate to touch her, my hands were drawing into fists, the blood was rushing through me—all of which she surely knew. But I was afraid. Italians were famously demonstrative, affectionate;

if she were simply doing as the Romans do I might be making a shameful mistake. I could end up in trouble, be sent home in disgrace. What would my parents say? It sounds absurd now, I know. Young Americans are no longer so ignorant or inept.

"Do you have a girlfriend here yet?" she asked. "An Italian? Or is that all happening within the group?"

"No," I said. "There's very little of that going on, unfortunately. We haven't had a chance to meet too many Italians so far. And we're mostly just friends."

"Just friends," she mocked. "What wholesome young people."

We were walking up toward the Pincio—for the view, she suggested. It was about five o'clock on a March afternoon, still fairly cold. At the top of the hill we stopped to look down at the traffic and hubbub circling the great column in the Piazza del Popolo, and in the distance, in the fading light, the ruins. Hugging her shoulders against the wind, she turned to me in such a teasing way that even a dolt such as I knew I was supposed to kiss her. If before I had feared it might be a disgrace to kiss her, now I knew I would be disgraced if I didn't. And I wanted to very badly anyway.

What followed is easily imagined—how I was initiated into the intrigue of secret meetings and deceptions, how I felt this to be the great adventure of my life (as indeed it was). She was not only a restless woman, I discovered, but a beautiful and rare one. I had hardly noticed her beauty and rarity—I was so predisposed to see her as the professor's wife. Naturally I felt guilty throughout, above all when the professor spent time helping me with a term paper, or when, after the seminars, he said, "Janet, would you bring us the coffee, please?" I would watch her, deft and gracious, the very picture of an elegant faculty wife, serving the coffee without taking any particular notice of me.

Guilty, but also boundlessly thrilled and excited: it was at those moments, in the presence of the group, in the presence of her husband, that I craved her the most. One night I couldn't bear it, and followed her into the kitchen on the pretext of carrying some cups and saucers, to run my hand along her back and hips. She looked over her shoulder as if I were a mad vulgarian, as if our intimate hours were a boy's dream.

"What on earth do you think you're doing?" Like a boy, I quickly drew my hand back. I almost apologized, but I was not that much of a boy anymore. The next day, when we were alone, she said, "That simply isn't how you go about things. You're ruined if you start taking those chances."

"Oh, do you do this often? You sound like you have the routine down pat," I said, seized with jealousy.

"No," she said. "Just once, a few years ago."

"Also a student? Do you specialize?"

"Not a student," she said, and wouldn't say more except, "Don't be nasty, don't spoil everything."

"And will you do it again?"

She laughed. "How can I tell?"

"Why with me?"

"Do you really need to ask?"

"I guess I do."

"I liked you. You seemed the right sort."

"What sort is that?"

"Oh," and she pretended to think it over, or perhaps really did think it over. "Decent. Clever." I was flattered then, but later dismayed. Decent and clever? Not exactly stirring declarations to an ardent lover.

I assumed she must be miserable with the professor: why else would she have sought me out? But she laughed this off as another sign of my conventional ignorance. She said nothing disparaging about him, never talked of him at all, except to answer, when I inevitably asked, that they made love infrequently. I realize by this time how many women say that to their lovers, yet I believe it was true. I believed everything she said—there was such an air of conviction about her—though while she told the truth, it could not have been the whole truth. Possibly she thought I was not ready to hear the whole truth, or possibly as in my own research, truth can never be told in its entirety.

I asked if she minded being called on to serve coffee to students week after week and she said not at all, there was no indignity in serving coffee. Besides, it was part of the bargain. What bargain, I wanted to ask, but was too uneasy, and I suspected she wouldn't answer anyway. Explanation was hardly her style. She liked talking to the students, was all she volunteered; it gave her a chance to speak English.

"But this person who made the bargain, the person you are with him—is that really you?"

"It's no more false than this. I can be any number of people. Don't you find that?" Not a new notion by any means, but the first time I had seen it enacted. "Do you think," she said tauntingly, "that the person you see is the only 'real' me? Do you think there are real and unreal selves?" I had in fact thought so, but from her ironic tone it would have been mortifying to confess it.

I found her a riddle. Later, of course, I would see her as a complex, self-willed woman, and such types tend to be inscrutable to men. But back then she was older than anyone I had ever known, far older than her age—a thirty-one-year-old woman with the mind of an eighty-year-old. It was she who described herself that way, and I came to feel she was right. She lived as though she had seen and assessed everything and had had the time to put it into perspective, and now had very little time left and need answer only to herself.

When the semester ended I scrambled to find a way to stay for the summer. For her. She urged me to stay, but I didn't need much urging. The professor was going to Holland and Germany for several months to do research. I managed to get a job as a waiter in a café. I knew enough Italian, by then, to take the imperiously snapped orders. We made love whenever we could, when the children were napping, or late at night, or on weekends when Janet could leave them with her in-laws. However unique and indescribable it felt to me, our love clearly belonged to a well-documented genre: brief, heedless, intense, and transforming. But my story is not about the loss of innocence or the discovery— it felt like the invention—of passion, or about loving in an unidealistic, futureless, encapsulated, carnal way, which may be what loss of innocence is. The real story takes place two decades later.

ॐ

After I returned home and finished college I was drafted, as expected. I spent two months in Vietnam surviving in a way I could not in a million years recount. In truth I have done all I can to forget it. I was wounded early on, in the shoulder, and luckily spent the rest of my time at a desk. I seldom watched the news reports or read the papers about it afterward. I was no soldier and no activist. I am not interested in politics but in science. I know how irresponsible that sounds—I have often been lectured about it. And when I am, I say nothing, simply remind myself that I work, however marginally, on a cure for cancer. That should be enough.

Graduate studies in science are among the most laborious and demanding: you can get to be thirty or more before you assume a real position, draw a respectable paycheck, and feel like an adult. Most of the students came from more comfortable backgrounds than mine. My family had a hard time figuring out why, in my late twenties and after so many years in school, I was still writing a dissertation and earning a workman's wage. They said that with the same efforts I might have gone to medical school and become a prosperous doctor. It wasn't their fault that they couldn't see how specific my interests were. When I was finally done I wanted some ease. I wanted not to have to account for myself all the time. I married a woman with whom that would be possible. A nurse—I met her in the emergency room when my bicycle swerved in a pothole and sent me flying. She was, and is, a stocky, pretty, able woman with pale brown boyishly cut hair. I loved her and still do, even if it is not the kind of love pictured in books or films, or that I knew with Janet. It is love all the same, and arguably stronger than what I knew with Janet, possessing a structure and endurance. This sounds unfair to my wife, perhaps, now that I see it set down so baldly, and yet she enjoys a good life. We have our children and our house and our work and our friends, and we sleep close together at night still.

Several months ago, in an Italian scientific journal, I came across a series of articles on migratory cells. With my dregs of Italian I could see they might be crucial to my research, but returning to a long-lost language is not, alas, like riding a bicycle, where no matter how long ago, they say, you remember how. A colleague suggested I call the Romance languages department; they could send over a graduate student to translate, who would be glad to earn some extra money. The secretary called back promptly to say she had just the person, a very bright Italian student who was bilingual—her mother was British or American or something—besides being punctual, reliable, and so forth. I was rushing to class and didn't ask her name, just said to send her over the next morning during my office hours. I didn't really think of her as a person at all, then. I was excited about what I might learn and couldn't wait to see the translation. The student was merely a step on the way to satisfying my curiosity.

She arrived promptly at ten: tall, slim, pale, and auburn-haired, wearing a soft gray wool skirt, a green sweater and leather boots, not the usual jeans and sweatshirt uniform. She wanted to appear professional, I thought. Her manner was un-student-like as well. Students are usually shy and fumbling or else excessively candid and enthusiastic, which comes to the same thing. This one seemed reserved, not shy. She presented herself in an economical way, just as much as necessary for the purpose. All in all, she was extremely self-possessed.

"I've come about the translation work," she said, and announced her name. Francesca. The last name—well of course that is obvious by this time. Life, like science, is full of the coincidences that unleash discovery.

I was glad to be seated, because I might have toppled over. I had the oddest sense that my face was escaping me, I was losing control over it. I felt a jumble of wonderment, panic, curiosity—I had no idea what might be happening on the surface. I tried to smile and be polite, but for all I knew I looked stunned.

How could I be sure so quickly? The name, as I've said, was unusual even for Mediterranean names with their syllabic frills and furbelows. There couldn't be many with that name. Still, I needed to be absolutely certain.

"I spent some time in Rome when I was a student." I tried to seem casual though my mind teemed with memories and frantic calculations. I hoped my worst suspicion wasn't so, and yet I hoped it was. "On an art history program."

"Really," she said mildly.

What did I expect? Thousands must have done the same. I made myself stumble on. "One of my professors had your name. His first name was Federico."

She showed no great surprise. "That's my father. He's a professor of art history."

"Is that so?" Now it was legitimate to sound a bit excited, so my feelings had some release. "Isn't that a coincidence! I knew both your parents. They used to have the students over all the time. That little street near the Piazza Navona. Did you grow up there?"

"Yes, I remember the students. They were coming over until quite recently." She smiled indulgently, as if hosting American students was a lovable eccentricity of her quaint parents.

"What a coincidence!" I said again.

"Well, really not that strange. They must have entertained hundreds of American students. What did you think of them, my parents, that is?"

That sort of abrupt slashing through pleasantries was exactly her mother's style and unsettled me for an instant, like hearing the rustlings of a ghost. But I was not a boy now; I had had the beneficent experience of her mother. "I found them wonderful people. They made us feel so at home, especially your mother. How is your mother?"

"Mother died last fall." She looked down, to get away from my gaze. This was private, delicate territory. She was still grieving. And I, I could not even tell what I was feeling, apart from grim surprise and a pressing warmth behind my eyes. I fended it off, for I needed all my forces just to speak casually to the girl. I was not permitted to express anything out of the ordinary. I would take the news home with me, for later. "I'm so sorry. She must have been still relatively young, as I remember. What—what was it?"

"It's all right, you can ask. She had cancer. Lymphoma."

"Ah."

"It was pretty quick. She wasn't sick very long."

"And you—" I felt slightly dizzy and gripped the edge of the desk to anchor myself. "I wonder if you were one of the little girls I used to see playing? I don't think there was a Francesca, though. One was Elsa, I remember. Rosa?"

"Very good." She smiled as though I were a clever child. "There's Elsa and Rosalia, then me, then Pietro—he's two years younger."

"I see. Well, I was there in sixty-six …"

"A year too soon for me. I was twenty-three just last week, in fact."

"April."

"April, yes." She frowned ironically, then laughed. The eyes, green and witty, were her mother's. "Why, do you follow astrology, like your former president? Americans are so amusing sometimes. The cruelest month, as one of your poets says."

If they know nothing else, I have found, the students all know that line; in that respect, she was generic. Then I realized her knowledge would be more than superficial: my daughter was a student of literature. For as I feared and hoped, I was looking at my own daughter. I wanted to leap up and embrace her. I wanted to do all sorts of things at once, laugh, weep, mourn her mother, find out about the family, even reveal myself. For a moment I thought I might do this—not right away, but some day in the future. But only for a moment.

How could I know for sure? one may ask. Oh, I was sure. Even if the dates hadn't worked out, even if it weren't true that Janet rarely made love with the professor, this girl was mine. I could see it. She had my coloring. My hair, before it faded and started going gray. My family's body, tall and narrow and energetic, though her movements had an un-American mellowness. She reminded me of my mother and my older sister. I wondered if they would notice, were they to see her. Could I ever manage to introduce her? How could I explain her? Yet all the while I knew this would never come to pass. I wouldn't mind shocking my family at this point, but I could not shock her, Francesca. She had her father—she didn't need another.

"No," I laughed. "I don't follow astrology. In your mother's case, April was a lucky month, I'd say. And how is your father?"

She passed over my compliment. "He's fine. He just retired from the university, but he still writes papers. Of course it was terrible for him, my mother … They were so devoted. So close. You must have noticed. But he has lots of friends. And my sisters live nearby and keep an eye on him.

My brother is in school at Berkeley. We both flew back when Mother was sick. Well, you don't need to hear all this. Would you like to tell me about the translation?"

"No, no, I really do want to hear. I remember them so vividly."

She smiled. "There's nothing more to tell."

"When you write will you give him my regards?"

"Sure. But there were so many.... The house was like a—a port of call. My mother was constantly serving them coffee and listening to their problems. I guess you know."

"Yes." I couldn't stop staring at her, trying to find traces of my children, my other children. She was beautiful in a way it took a while to appreciate, even more so than her mother, whom she did not resemble except for the eyes and the cool, self-possessed manner. Like Janet's, her statements were assertions, with a tinge of irony.

She was also, like Janet, decisively, provocatively polite. "About the translation ...," she prompted.

"It's only natural," I mused, "that this should be an amazing coincidence for me, while for you ... I mean, to come upon an old acquaintance of your parents, all the way across the ocean—no big deal, right?"

"On the contrary, it's a pleasure to meet you."

What I felt at that moment was pride, I must admit. Paternal pride. Few Americans of twenty-three would speak with such aplomb. And her speech was not diluted with the nervous, meaningless tics, the "like's" or "you know's" that disjointed the talk of even the brightest students. Well, God knows I had nothing to do with it. Credit her mother. "But it can't be quite the same pleasure."

"Nothing is quite the same as anything else, is it?"

"How true." I laughed faintly. "Well, let me tell you what I need to have done." I showed her the articles. "Do you think you'll have trouble with the technical terms?"

She didn't answer right away but leafed through the pages. "I don't think so. It's the technical terms that are similar in both languages. Besides, that's what dictionaries are for, aren't they?" She gave me a rather impish grin, and suddenly I felt something new stirring in the room. I was grown now—it no longer took me weeks to identify it. The girl, I was almost sure, was flirting with me. She had sensed my interest and was responding. I would have to be more careful.

"It's about cancer cells."

"So I see."

"I hope that's not—I mean, will it upset you?"

She gazed at me as her mother used to, as if I were ludicrously inept. "I've already had the reality. There's not much the words can add."

"Yes, I see. I'm sorry. So, when do you think you can have this ready? Is three weeks too soon?"

"No, that's all right."

I arranged to pay her fifteen dollars an hour, which she seemed to find generous. "Then we're all set, uh—do you mind if I call you Francesca?"

Again she smiled coolly. "What else?"

"Well, I might call you Signorina." I didn't mean to encourage her but couldn't help myself. I was at a loss. I only wanted to get closer to her, befriend her.

"I don't think we have to be quite that formal. Professor." This time there was no doubt. She flung her tweed coat over her shoulders and was gone.

I locked the door, then sat down, bent my head to the desk, and allowed myself my grief. It could not wait to be taken home. And nothing about Janet belonged at home.

When at last I looked up I thought of her, Francesca, again. My daughter. I had three fine, healthy sons: nine, twelve, and fourteen. I had renounced—my wife and I had, I should say—the prospect of a daughter long ago, without any great pangs. Yet how luscious the idea seemed, now that I'd seen her. Had she been in my department I might have invited her over, taken an interest and helped her with her work. Even so, mightn't I befriend her through the translation, ask her over as a kind gesture to a foreign student, make her part of the family? I was aware that faculty wives didn't appreciate their husbands' befriending beautiful students, and in the couple of cases I had observed closely, their lack of enthusiasm was borne out by the facts. My wife was not particularly suspicious or jealous; I had never given her reason to be. How would she react to Francesca? I might tell her the truth (though not the whole truth): she was the daughter of people who had been hospitable to me in Rome years ago and I wanted to return the favor. But I knew myself. I could not live comfortably with the pretense.

Besides, my wife knows me too, in that unnerving way that wives do. She knows, for instance, that I am less interested in finding a cure for cancer than in charting the erratic paths of the cells or unraveling the logic that makes them travel and hide, erupt and masquerade. At the university hospital—she is head nurse of the intensive care unit—she sees dying patients every day. She respects my research, yet I have a feeling she finds it somewhat abstract and irrelevant. She finds me abstracted too—though I hope not irrelevant. Maybe, in her plainspoken way, she sees the same ingenuousness Janet found so amusing. Maybe it has never fallen away with age, only transmuted into what Americans dignify with the term "absentmindedness." I suppose I am absent, in a sense, from my life. I was present with Janet— as who could not be?—and I am present in the laboratory, and often with my sons. Otherwise I suppose I hold myself in abeyance, I don't know why, or for what. I don't mean any harm that I know of. I only feel vague. I'm not disappointed with my life; sometimes it feels better than I expected. There was a period, after we had been married a few years and had our first child, when my wife accused me of being disappointed and having cooled, but I denied that, and soon she stopped mentioning it. She finds great satisfaction in her work as well as in the boys, and we get on companionably. I am grateful we never had the turbulence of divorce that I have seen disrupt and sometimes destroy the lives of friends and colleagues.

❧

Though the Romance languages department is in the building across the lawn from mine, I had never noticed Francesca before. Now I saw her everywhere—lounging on the front steps; in the gym, where I played racquetball and she swam; in the local drugstore; in the faculty club, where she was eating with, apparently, some boisterously entertaining young instructors from her department. Each time, she came up to greet me with her mother's provocative, ambiguous tone. And I responded. She was my daughter: how could I be aloof? I was inexpressibly touched to see she liked me, was even drawn to me. I am a pleasant-mannered, nice-looking man, but I don't flatter myself that I cut a dashing or romantic figure. Something more obscure drew her. I felt as I do in the lab when I approach the heart of the mystery—troubled and excited, and though it is where I want to be, I want also to step back.

I tried to keep a proper distance; I would ask how the translation was going, and she would say fine. Once, coming out of the library, she said she was stopping for coffee, did I want to join her? Naturally I did—I wanted any chance to be near her.

She ordered an espresso and tossed it back in one gulp. She was in her first year of graduate work, she told me. She had gotten her undergraduate degree from Harvard. Harvard! She was studying comparative literature; she had learned French in school and, with her Italian, found Spanish a breeze. German was more difficult. She wasn't sure what she would write her dissertation on—at the moment she was fascinated by the Latin American novelists, but she had a new enthusiasm every month, she said with a self-mocking smile. "Intellectually fickle is what I am, I guess," and she waved regally for another coffee.

I said very little, just basked in her presence. In retrospect, I see I must have appeared entranced, as I truly was. I kept thinking how delightful she was, and how she would never know the truth about herself. Unless Janet had told her, and she, Francesca, was playing some sly game of privileged information. No, knowing Janet, that was most unlikely.

"And what about you, Professor?" she said with a droll glance. "I can see from the articles what you're interested in, but what else? Are you married?"

"Yes." I told her about my wife and children. I even pulled pictures from my wallet to show her, and while she said all the proper things—What adorable boys!—she seemed a trifle daunted. I wanted so badly to tell her she was looking at her brothers. Half-brothers. "Are you sure your mother never mentioned me? I know there were lots of students, but I— well, I must confess I had a bit of a crush on her."

"Is that so?" Francesca gave her ironic smile. "You were hardly the only one. She was Queen of the Students. She loved it. She was going strong well into her fifties, until the end. She must have broken quite a few hearts."

"Oh, but not really— You're not saying that—"

"Of course not!" With all her sophistication, she seemed shocked, as children are invariably shocked at their parents' adventures. "They were kids to her. She and my father used to joke about them after they left. He would guess which ones liked her and she would correct him. I remember them laughing over their coffee. They could never agree on which ones."

"I see."

"What do you mean, you see? What on earth does that mean?"

"I don't know, it's just something to say when you don't know what else to say."

"Don't worry, it wasn't malicious laughter. They loved being around the students. They said it kept them young."

I was newly disturbed when we parted. So close, she had said the very first day. So devoted. But I couldn't lose myself in brooding all over again, at this late date. I would understand no better, only feel more pain. What did it matter now? She was dead. The boy I had been was as good as dead. Except for Francesca, that is.

A few days later she turned up in my office, very businesslike, with the translation. I thanked her and made a note to have the secretary send her a check. She said to contact her if there were any problems with the text and wrote her phone number on a slip of paper.

"Do you live in the dorms?"

"No, I'm a grad student, remember? I'm too old for the dorms. I have an apartment across campus."

"I see."

"Ah," she laughed, "there you go again. Seventy-four Crabtree Street, if that's what 'I see' meant this time."

"No, it didn't, actually."

"I see," she said, still smiling, taunting. There are countless rules, nowadays, regarding the most tenuous innuendos chanced by professors. One has to be wary, even someone like me who has never chanced anything of the kind. No rules for the opposite, I thought.

"Do you have a boyfriend?" It was fatherly interest—I hoped she would say yes. I could invite them over together. It would be easier for me, as well as for my wife.

To my surprise, her face turned sober. Younger. "There's someone back in Rome I've known a long time, and I always thought ... but now I'm not sure anymore."

"You mean someone from before college? But you were so young."

"Well, yes. We both knew there might be other people. We're far apart and I'm not ... shy that way—" She paused and gave me the oddest look, half-earnest, half-coy, utterly young, yet I had seen enough of her, not to mention her mother, to know it was also maddeningly canny. Economical as ever, she was accomplishing a great deal at once. "Still, there was some understanding.... When I went back last fall, when Mother died, we spent a lot of time together. And at a time like that, when someone is close to you and acts kind, you tend to accept what they do for you, and then they think … Do you know what I mean?"

"I think so."

"But now I wonder. I feel it would be retreating, in a way. From I don't know what. From life. I see people around and I'm, well, interested, what's wrong with saying it? Everybody is. Why should I have to hold back because I promised things when I was almost a child and didn't know any better? And yet he's a dear friend of the family, he's— Oh, look, I'm sorry. Why on earth would you want to listen to all this? I've got to be going."

"No, really, I am interested."

"You are? Why?"

"I just am. I guess because I knew your parents, and, well, you're such a lovely young woman."

She mistook my words again, willfully, it seemed, and as easily as slipping out of a dress, she slipped out of her earnest, girlish mode. I was sorry, for I loved hearing it, loved her talking to me as if I might be a father. A father figure, anyway.

"Indeed," was all she said. She sounded like her mother. I could see how she might be irresistible.

"'Indeed.' That's hardly better than 'I see,'" I teased.

"You're right. What else can I say to a mixed message?"

"Mixed message? Not at all. I meant just what I said. Look, you really must come over for dinner one night, meet my family."

"Meet your family?" She looked dubious. "Well, thank you. That's very kind. Do you want to check it out with your wife first, maybe?"

"I'll see what night is convenient and let you know. She works some nights. And thanks again for getting this to me so promptly, Francesca."

❧

I told my wife about the translation. I told her the almost unbelievable coincidence of the translator being the daughter of a couple who had been generous to me in Rome when I was a student. I told her I needed to go over some small points in the articles with the girl and would like to invite her for dinner one night, partly out of gratitude to her parents and partly to be kind: her mother had died recently. I had never been duplicitous with my wife in this way, but found it remarkably easy. It was what Janet and I had had to do, with her husband, her babysitter, my fellow students. Like riding a bicycle, it all came back. I even remembered it was not necessary or propitious to add lies, such as that Francesca seemed lonely and found it hard to make friends, and so on. My wife was struck by the coincidence. Okay, she said, how about Friday night?

Ah, she had many guises, my old-world young daughter did. She performed graciously the role of foreign student enjoying the hospitality of kind Americans. She praised the food, bantered easily with the boys, helped clear the table, and answered with tact and patience all the usual questions asked of foreigners, comparing life abroad and in the States. After dinner, in my study, we went over a few small points in the translation. I saw I could relax: she was quite professional, as of course was I. I remembered how her mother had chilled my caresses when the professor and the students were in the next room.

When we returned to the living room the boys had gone upstairs and my wife was curled up in the easy chair, reading the paper. I said I would drive Francesca home. She and my wife exchanged the customary thank-you's and hopes to meet again. They didn't kiss as some women do even on first meeting—neither was expansive enough for that—but the warmth between them seemed genuine.

"Crabtree, was it?" I said in the car.

"You remembered."

"It's nothing special. I have a good memory for details."

"Oh. Well, you have a very nice family. I enjoyed meeting them. You must be quite pleased with yourself." The lower part of her face was buried in her scarf; she was peering out at me sideways.

"I'm pleased, yes, I suppose so."

"Your wife is a good cook, too."

"Yes."

"Did you accomplish what you hoped from the evening, then?"

"I had no specific hopes. I thought it went nicely. Why, were you disturbed about anything?"

"Not at all, it was fine." She was silent for the rest of the short ride, except, near the end, to point out the house, an old-fashioned three-story frame house divided into apartments, with an ample porch.

"I'd invite you to sit on the porch for a while, but it's too cold."

"Freezing for this time of year," I said. "Anyway, I should get back."

"Yes, you should. Definitely."

"I'm very sorry you're irritated. I can't explain."

"There's nothing to explain. It's not too complex to understand."

"Please don't be angry, Francesca."

"Oh, all right." She gave a bit of a laugh and again seemed to shake off the mood as easily as a dress. "I'll see you around." And she laid her hand on my arm, just the barest touch.

"Yes. Good night. Thanks again for the translation. You did a terrific job."

"Good night." She leaned over and kissed me very lightly and swiftly on the lips. It was nothing really, no more than a fleeting feathery brush, but then she waited. I was supposed to kiss her back. And maybe it would have been better if I had—just once, and properly, with ardor; then she could have kept her illusion that, like many a timid professor, I wanted her but didn't dare risk my domestic peace. A benign, bittersweet illusion, not one of the noxious kinds. Better than my sitting there unmoving and righteous. Yes, I suppose I did the wrong thing. I suppose it was a disgrace not to kiss her, but I feared the disgrace, in my own eyes, of kissing her even once. Besides, I didn't want to kiss her. I wanted to kiss her mother.

Back home, my wife was still reading the paper in the easy chair. "That was quick," she said.

"She doesn't live far."

"Still, I thought you might take longer."

I threw my coat on a chair and headed for the stairs. I was utterly exhausted.

"There's something between you and that girl, isn't there?"

I stopped on the third stair and faced her. "Nothing of the kind. How could you think that?"

"I'm not wrong. Maybe nothing yet. Maybe you don't even know it yourself yet, but there's something."

"You don't know how wrong you are. It's out of the question. I'm surprised you should even suggest it."

"You should be surprised by me once in a while."

"That may be. That may be. But this is inconceivable."

"All right, never mind then," she said, and turned back to her paper.

She didn't speak of it anymore, but she thinks it.

I have never invited Francesca home again. I see her on campus all the time. I watch her from afar and try to avoid coming face to face, for when I do she is cool. To talk to her, to ask her to lunch, which is what I long to do—simply to sit across from her and look at her—would be unfair. In a couple of years, when she finishes her studies, she'll go away, and I'll be relieved and bereft, never knowing whether she goes home to marry her childhood sweetheart (doubtful, I think) or falls in love with someone new, maybe an American. It's not inconceivable that I could run into her somewhere in twenty years, and then will she smilingly, ironically recall how she once had a slight crush on me, very slight, just a vague sense there might be something between us—but I wouldn't give it half a chance? Would it be possible to tell her then? Or even worse than now?

All this might happen, unless something changes erratically in me and I do what she wishes and my wife suspects. I believe I am incapable of that, but I know some organisms are capable of the most unpredictable, riotous, malign behavior. I hope I am not.